THE HERO'S COMPANION

TALLENT & LOWERY: BOOK THREE

BY AMY LIGNOR

SUSPENSE PUBLISHING

The Hero's Companion
Tallent & Lowery Book Three

By
Amy Lignor

PAPERBACK EDITION

* * * * *

PUBLISHED BY:
Suspense Publishing

The Hero's Companion: Tallent & Lowery Book Three
Copyright 2013 Amy Lignor

Cover Design: Shannon Raab
Cover Photographer: iStockphoto.com/amwu
Cover Photographer: iStockphoto.com/duncan1890

ISBN-13: 978-0615907161 (Suspense Publishing)
ISBN-10: 0615907164

To my 'sister from another mother,' Shannon Raab;
Thank you for always being so supportive!

ACKNOWLEDGEMENTS

As always, I begin with the fans. Your excitement, letters and reviews continue to give me inspiration. I am humbled that Leah & Gareth have provided the adventures you've asked for; and I hope "The Hero's Companion" continues to give you a thrill!

This book is dedicated to Shannon Raab for some extremely good reasons. I thank her for her support, the pats on the head when I act five, and most especially for the fact that without her vision *Tallent & Lowery* would not be a 'cut above'.

To Diane Lunsford; you are a debut author with talent, but even better—you are a friend with a great heart and great big hugs that allow 'Austen' to find her way again. Thank you for that.

To Mark Adduci (AKA: The masterful writer, J.M. LeDuc)—thank you for the words. Your encouragement means a lot to me, especially since you are the best at what you do.

To Ellen at The Feathered Quill and Tammie King—your reviews, friendship, and Top Picks are always such a thrill. You've made *Tallent and Lowery* 'meet the masses.'

To Joy . . . what can I say? Life keeps on moving. Hopefully one day in the right direction.

Always, to Nicole; it's because you allowed *The Angel Chronicles* to soar that *Tallent & Lowery* were allowed to breathe. I owe you a tremendous debt for being the first to show faith in me.

Uncle Ron, Kathy, Keith, Maia, Ryan—"Best Family Ever!"

To Mom . . . you are the best of the best. You are the inspiration for Leah and my inspiration every day to attempt to be better than I was the day before.

Shelby . . . You made this. Your creation made a dream come true, and continues to do so each and every day.

"While we live; let us live!" A character in this book taught me that. I'm making sure that I live by those immortal words, and I hope everyone out there does the same!

Until Next Time, Everybody,

Amy

PRAISE FOR "THE HERO'S COMPANION"

"I have to say that Ms. Lignor has done it again in providing her fans with a heart-stopping third installment of the *Tallent & Lowery* series. Right from the start, my heart was pounding in my chest from all the intrigue and adventure that awaited me."
— Tammie King, Night Owl Reviews

"When we think of historical thrillers with a biblical, epic twist; the names of Dan Brown and James Rollins come to mind. Move over boys, there is a new name on the top of the list and HER name is Amy Lignor!"
— J.M. LeDuc, Author of "Cornerstone"

"Abduction and strange maps, mysterious locations and intriguing players, Tallent and Lowery…Amy Lignor has, once again, put together a story that will turn up your anxiety level and have you wringing your hands until the very end. Lignor has hit literary paydirt with "The Hero's Companion" and her *Tallent & Lowery* series."
— DJ Weaver, co-author of "Collecting Innocents"

PRAISE FOR "THE SAPPHIRE STORM"

"A flat-out, slam-dunk, no-questions-asked-terrific-adventure. Try not to turn the pages too fast because the wonderfully complex characters deserve your time! This is truly a magical story that had me in its thrall from the very first page. It's so exciting to discover a new talent like Lignor and have more books to look forward to."
— International Bestseller, M.J. Rose

"Full of mystery, wrapped up in just enough historical fact to make

it all seem so real, and with plenty of sizzle between the two main characters, "The Sapphire Storm" is a definite winner!"
—Ellen Feld, The Feathered Quill

"Outstanding! In book two of her *Tallent & Lowery Adventures* Amy Lignor has combined science and religion to create an unforgettable journey to the center of the earth. Brilliantly written with a riveting plotline and engaging characters who had me laughing and crying, "The Sapphire Storm" has found a spot on my keeper shelf.

"This masterfully told page turner is fresh, innovative, descriptive, and intense but I must warn you, prepare to stay up late because it's not a story you can easily put down. I was blown away by Ms. Lignor's knowledge and imagination and can't wait to see what she comes up with next. I want more!!!!"
—Cat Kalen, author of the RT's 'Top Pick' *Pride Series*

PRAISE FOR "13"

"Snappy dialogue, fast pacing and attention to detail complete the formula for this successful novel!!"
—Romantic Times (4 ½ Stars)

"Get ready for a thrill ride with Amy Lignor's "13" in the Tallent & Lowery adventure series! Sharp writing, witty dialogue and a quest that rivals "The Da Vinci Code."
—Susan Fleet, author of "Natalie's Revenge"

THE HERO'S COMPANION

TALLENT & LOWERY: BOOK THREE

AMY LIGNOR

PROLOGUE

Screaming wouldn't do any good.

Just like the teenage babysitter in a 'slasher' movie running away from the masked, knife-wielding killer, David Tallent knew that death was inevitable. But, in contrast to the grotesque Hollywood flicks, he was also entirely certain that his death would take far longer than ninety minutes to achieve.

In fact, they'd told him he was looking at seven days. Seven days of worry . . . seven days of regret, and seven days of sitting in this luxurious room waiting for something to happen that would unveil the truth that'd been hidden for centuries under the mound of dirt sitting right outside his window.

Walking over to the double doors of the penthouse porch David closed his eyes, attempting to find a prayer for forgiveness, but none would appear. Considering all the hours, days, weeks—*years* that he'd spent immersing himself in various religious cultures; it seemed almost like a punishment that he had no words to say in order to escape a final judgment that he knew was going to be beyond painful . . . even if it was completely deserved.

Sighing, he opened his eyes once again and stared down at the smaller building attached to the mighty hotel that rose from the desert sands like a stalagmite of glass and steel that some futuristic god had created—bringing the new and old world together.

Night was approaching and the neon lights below grew brighter, casting David in an unearthly pink glow. He could almost hear the clanging of silver coins falling through the slots down below and the jubilant shouts of excited gamblers who'd finally scored their lucky break.

Stifling his bitter snort, he watched people flow through the big glass doors to pray at the altar of the almighty dollar. The American capitalism that so many here condemned had made its way across the ocean quite easily. This was no Vegas, but it was certainly a bevy of greed and sin located smack dab in the middle of the locale that was once home to the heroic deeds of mankind.

The hand-carved oak doors suddenly flew open behind him, slamming so hard into the newly painted walls that a chunk of plaster fell to the plush Oriental carpet. David stifled his cry of fear as he watched the two large men who'd been guarding his door carry a package into the room. He stayed back when they heaved the burlap sack on top of the glass table, shattering the fragile piece of furniture into a million pieces.

David's throat grew dry as the lump hit the floor with an audible moan. He glanced at the polished guns that sat in the belts of the two giants, warning him against any ill-fated attempts to escape.

One of the greasy, black haired men stepped forward; an evil grin beamed from his pockmarked face. "We thought you could use a little company."

His grimy cohort grunted, "Yeah . . . a little family reunion."

With those words, David immediately shifted his gaze to the lumpy sack sitting on top of the mound of twisted metal and glass, and his heart stopped. Sucking in his breath, he noticed the deep, red stains appearing on the coarse fabric; like patches of rust that were found on the permanent residents of a salvage yard.

"Family?" he whispered. A wave of nausea hit him hard when the picture of his beautiful wife and daughters appeared in his mind. He rushed toward the figure and dropped to his knees, trying with all his might to loosen the ties at the top. Attempting to block out the laughter of the guards as they walked from the room and slammed the door behind them, David did recognize the haunting echo of the deadbolt falling into place. Knowing his accusers were gone for now, he pulled with all his might on the twine that held

THE HERO'S COMPANION: TALLENT & LOWERY BOOK THREE

the sack together.

When he spotted a tuft of brown hair through the opening, his breath released. Thankfully the figure enclosed in the sour-smelling bag wasn't a match for his blonde-headed beauties back home; nor did it mimic the brilliant auburn hair of his beloved firstborn.

He jumped back as a pair of large hands suddenly reached out and tore through the fabric, like Dr. David Banner ripping off his shirt when he announced to the world that the Hulk had arrived. The head of a man emerged; his skin was red from a combination of adrenaline and fear as he burst through the tough cloth. Taking a deep breath of the clean, cool oxygen inside the air-conditioned room, he then whipped his head around to face his predator.

David Tallent exhaled when he recognized the wide, panicked eyes that glared at him.

Recognition immediately lit the stranger's face. "David? What in the hell are you doing here?"

David Tallent stood up and tried to back away from the intense rage that suddenly radiated from the man's pupils. "Aaron, I . . ."

Aaron Cain stood up quickly and discarded the burlap; glass dangled from his torn clothing and threads of blood ran down his skin like dark veins that'd chosen to take up residence on the outside of his skin. "I should have *known* this was about you," he growled. "You promised you'd never come back here! You wanted a new life, remember? You chose to leave . . . to protect the girls. Why the hell are you back here now?!"

David swallowed the instant tears of regret, remembering the last time he'd laid eyes on the man before him—that awful, heartbreaking night when they'd made a pact that would forever seal the other's fate. David had tried for years to forget that awful moment, the moment he'd struck the deal that'd ripped his soul in half. But he never could. The moment when he'd left the warm Egyptian sun far behind and made his way to America's shores had remained in the forefront of his mind for all these decades, and now the past was literally coming back to haunt him.

"They took her," Aaron stated. "Did you know that, you scum? They took my daughter!"

David flinched at his choice of words, and a spark ignited in

Aaron's black eyes. "They sent her to America to pay Leah a visit."

Finally David found his voice, "What are you talking about? If they hurt my family, I'll—"

"What do you know about *family*?"

"Aaron . . . please," David sighed.

The man rushed forward and grabbed him around the neck. "If anything happens to *my* family, I will kill you. Make no mistake about that, David. Whatever this is—whatever you have done—*my* family will not pay the price!"

The oxygen was quickly disappearing from his lungs as Aaron's grip grew stronger. Reaching behind him, David grabbed the silver candlestick off the table and brought it down on his attacker's skull.

Aaron yelled in pain and tumbled to the floor, but David kept the polished weapon in his hand, feeling the rush of air finally invade his chest. Sadness immediately overtook him as he stared down at the bloodied man who was holding his head in his hands.

Sighing heavily, David walked over to Aaron and helped the larger man to his feet. He supported him as they stumbled across the once lovely carpet that was now covered with bloodstains and shards of glass. Sitting him down on the leather couch, David backed away as he took in the sight of the one and only person on Earth who he'd trusted with the biggest secrets of his entire life. A crushing weight descended on his shoulders when he witnessed Aaron's quiet tears race down his cheeks.

David struggled, wondering if he should attempt to offer a familiar hug. "Look . . . Aaron—"

The voice that interrupted him was cold and lifeless. "You had your life . . . your money . . . everything. You gave this part of it up and promised me . . . you *promised* me you would never return! Now, she's in danger." Aaron raised his gaze. "They both are."

Looking down at the rug, David Tallent felt as if he was nothing but an angel that had fallen from the sky—kicked out of the peaceful afterlife and ordered to walk the world for eternity. He no longer cared what the henchman would choose to do—what torture they would conceive—because nothing their vile minds could come up with would possibly make him feel more humiliated, alone and pained than his own brother's words.

Walking to the double doors in silence, he stared out into the glowing pink night. Slowly, he moved his gaze up to the dark mound in the near distance and felt the terror build in his chest. He knew Aaron was right. Leah was in danger . . . she would come after him. No matter what they told her, she would find the clues that he'd left behind and piece the puzzle together. After what his firstborn had told him before Christmas, David already knew that she was not afraid to follow dangerous trails in order to unveil secrets and legends that were long buried—if the reason for the unveiling was to save a person she loved.

Closing his eyes, David let the tears fall. He knew that even if Leah solved this mess and survived, she would never be able to forgive him for what he'd done. His beloved daughter was the epitome of loyalty, and she would never understand the deception and lies and utter betrayal that came from the choices he'd made so long ago.

It had been such a foolish quest; a journey that'd ended with a discovery that may just seal everyone's fate for a second time.

Feeling the large man come up behind him, David could sense the tension and fear crackling in the room, mimicking the bolts of heat lightning that could be seen striking the sands miles and miles away from their location.

Aaron's words felt like a final verdict being issued from the bench, dooming him to seven days of agony as he waited for his brilliant child to walk directly into a trap—a trap that he put into place a long time ago by being an overeager soul with too much ego to take the warnings seriously.

"Some secrets *were* better off staying buried," Aaron spoke beside him.

"It's too late," David whispered.

As he stared out at the shadow, he could only imagine the treasures that lay beneath the huge mound of dirt and sand. He wondered how the rich patrons below would feel if they knew there was one million times more wealth out there in that nondescript location than in all of the casinos around the globe.

The icy tone of Aaron's words scared him to his very core, "David . . . I think this is the beginning of the end."

CHAPTER 1

"We are about to begin our descent."

Even though she'd escaped the confines of the plane over an hour ago, the voice of the annoyingly perky flight attendant seemed to be ingrained in Leah Tallent's mind. She was still saturated with sweat from the claustrophobic cabin; the rancid odor of the re-circulated air that smelled like the regurgitated breath of a minion from Hell still clung to her clothes.

Leah tried to shake the thoughts from her mind as she stared out the window at the new layer of snow on the fields. The blanket of ice was smothering the dark green New England countryside.

Leah was so filled with anxiety and fear that she could barely feel Gareth Lowery's cold, clammy hand clenched in hers. Exhaustion wracked her body as pictures flashed through her mind like snapshots from an unbelievable nightmare . . .

It seemed like only yesterday that Leah had rushed from her parent's holiday table to arrive at the side of Gareth's sister in Los Angeles, after they'd received a frantic phone call from his sister begging him and Leah to hurry up and come quickly in order to find Kathryn's missing fiancé, Emmanuel. From there, they uncovered a secret that was buried in the words of the 'Bard of Avon,' leading the trio to a forgotten cave where two extremely famous brothers were buried, a well-known family that shared a truly unbreakable bond. Leah could still feel the power of the brilliant blue light that'd come from the famous Sapphire Staff as she'd held the artifact in her trembling hands. The news, the secrets uncovered, the legends proven, the battle they faced . . . and won—all of this was a mess inside Leah's usually well-organized librarian mind.

Dropping her head back against the limousine's pristine leather seat, Leah sighed, knowing that the frightening adventure was now far behind them. Kathryn and Emmanuel had married after the harrowing trip had ended. Their wedding at the historic monastery had been beautiful; millions of doves had soared into the sky announcing the start of a life filled with peace and love.

Leah and Gareth had held hands when the newlyweds embarked on their honeymoon to the warm sands of a private island, reveling in the fact that they were together and, thankfully, very much alive.

Soon, Leah knew they would be heading to France in order to get back to work. For the next few months, Emmanuel and Kathryn would be helping UNESCO repair and preserve Chartres Cathedral—the place that'd served as the location for Leah's showdown between good and evil.

Keeping her eyes closed, Leah tried her best to ignore the cold that was infiltrating her veins. She thought back to the luxurious hotel where Gareth had taken her to rest after everything had been solved and 'good' had actually been victorious once again. She so missed that brief pause—that brief moment of peace she'd felt while lying by Gareth's amazing form in a room that looked like a scene taken directly from the *Arabian Nights*. Leah also tried to fill her mind with the face of Mary, the ten-year-old little girl who'd sworn her eternal allegiance and friendship to Leah for saving her life. But neither of those two fantastic memories would stay in Leah's mind for long. They were no match for the fear that she knew was coming . . .

All she could remember was the harsh voice coming through the telephone interrupting her serenity, informing her that Leah's father had been taken. All she could hear playing over and over again in her head was, *Merry Christmas, Princess. You'd better come home soon or the only thing you'll find at the bottom of the sea is your father's dead body.*

Leah dropped her head in her hands as tears of frustration

and fear ran down her cold cheeks. She had no idea what she and Gareth would be walking into when they pulled up in front of her childhood home. Her father was everything to her, and Leah could not even fathom what happened to him. He was so kind and had so many friends—who on Earth would possibly want to hurt a man like that?

She tried to calm her ragged breathing and turned to stare at the love of her life. Except for a jaw that was clamped tight, Gareth's face was expressionless. Leah knew he was feeling the pain and agony that was washing through her soul. After all, they were a part of each other. They'd stood before both Heaven and Hell together and then, Leah laughed to herself; the relationship had really gotten interesting.

She felt the smile creep across her face when she focused on his handsome profile. She thanked Jesus for everything that Gareth Lowery was; the soft, blond hair; the brilliant green eyes that seemed to stare into her soul knowing what she needed before she could put her wishes into words; the strong hands that held her in his grip, no matter what monster may be running directly at him to claim his soul; his charm, humor—there was just so much to love that Leah had a hard time cataloging all the qualities that Gareth possessed.

As if he could feel her intense study, Gareth turned his face and smiled at her. Leaning over, he kissed Leah on the lips; his cold hand squeezed her own trying his best to warm her with his love. "Everything's going to be okay, you know."

"Always the optimist," she said with a smile. "I'm sorry . . . I'm sorry you got into this."

Sitting back against the seat, Gareth's eyes filled with confusion. "There is no place I'd rather be. Besides, if you remember correctly, you saved my sister. You saved her . . . friend." Stuttering over the final word, he stared out the window.

Leah snorted, "They're married now, Gareth. I think you finally have to accept the fact that Emmanuel is your sister's *husband*."

When the large, 'manly-man' winced at the dreaded 'H' word, Leah almost burst into laughter.

He shook his head, erasing the idea that his baby sister, who would always be a preteen at the most in her big brother's eyes, was actually a woman now. "What I was I saying?" Closing his eyes, he muttered, "Oh, yeah . . . you also saved *me*, Leah Tallent . . . years ago. And, together, we will most certainly figure all of this out and save your father."

Leah threw her head back against the seat and let loose a frustrated sigh, "But, save him from what? I don't get any of this, Gareth. My father is just a boring businessman."

He shrugged. "To be successful in business you usually make enemies over time."

Leah shook her head at the idea. "At the worst, he's just a hard boss. But he's always been fair. Everyone loves the guy. I swear to you. Every person who I've ever met since childhood praises him up and down. This just doesn't make any sense!"

Gareth remained silent.

"I'm sorry," she said, reaching out for him.

"Don't ever be sorry," Gareth replied, taking her into his arms. "We'll figure all this out when we get to your parent's house, I promise you. I'm sure this is nothing more than a case of . . . mistaken identity, or something just as silly."

"Exactly," Leah said. "That's what it is. Someone's just got the wrong guy."

Gareth leaned forward and tapped the window between him and the driver. "Can you go any faster?"

Leah barely registered the almost imperceptible nod, but the large car immediately accelerating down the two-lane blacktop was definitely a sign that she was speeding toward the answers she desperately needed.

It was so dark in the Litchfield Hills of Connecticut. There were no stars, no moon—only the all-consuming blackness met her gaze. Leah took a deep breath, fighting the fear that was raging inside her soul. "It'll be just fine. We'll figure everything out once we get there," she whispered to any entity that was listening and then allowed her normal calm, controlled persona to take over.

The Head Librarian of Research at the New York Public Library took her rightful place, basically shoving the scared little girl out of the way. The card catalogue in Leah's brain sprang to life, as she searched for any information buried in there that could better help her to understand.

Frustration weighed like an anvil on her chest when she came up with nothing. There were no images from the past that would lead her to believe someone she'd once met was now holding the power to end her father's life.

As her brain continued to swirl like a tornado causing havoc, all Leah could hear was that perky stewardess announcing the fact that Tallent and Lowery were, indeed, beginning their descent.

Although what they were descending into was anyone's guess.

CHAPTER 2

Curse words streamed from Leah's lips like a river of lava as she stood in front of the huge, hand-carved door and punched the doorbell again and again. "I don't believe this! I called from the airport and Mom knew we were coming! Who locks their door in this out of the way town anyway?"

Gareth pulled her away from the door and into his arms. Reaching out, he picked up the heavy brass cross and knocked it soundly against the wood. "The doorbell's obviously broken, love. By the way," he continued, staring up at the grand stone mansion before them. "*Anyone* who owned this house is going to lock it."

Leah turned on him. "Where are the police? Huh? Answer me that. Why isn't this driveway filled with red and blue lights flashing like crazy? What the hell is wrong with my mother?"

Gareth squeezed her shoulders and sighed. "Relax, okay. We don't know what's going on yet, remember?"

The veins in her forehead throbbed as Leah slammed the brass against the door over and over again, offering a solid 'thunk' that was synchronized with her demand, "Open. This. Damn. Door!"

Finally, the large, heavy frame slowly opened at her request. Creaking inward, a frail white hand appeared from behind the door.

Leah wrenched her arms from Gareth's grip and flew across the threshold like an angry detective who wanted answers. She barely recognized her mother standing in the dimly-lit foyer, as she marched to the slew of switches on the wall and brought the lights to life. Immediately, she took a step back. "Jesus, Mom! I told you we were coming. Why aren't there any police here? What—?"

As the large area became bathed in the bright golden light from the huge chandelier above, Leah focused on a face that looked almost nothing like the mother she remembered. Her mouth fell open in shock as she took note of the stranger dressed in a soiled bathrobe that clung to her pasty flesh. The always beautiful woman now looked like a cross between a vampire and a poverty-stricken child. The golden-blonde hair that was usually coiffed by a million-dollar hairdresser—full and rich with soft, luxurious curls—now hung limp and unwashed around her mother's face. Her face was make-up free, allowing all the lines of age and worry to be exposed to the world, which is something Leah knew her mother would never allow.

She gasped, "Mom? Is that you?"

Gareth put out a hand to steady the silent, trembling woman and Mary Tallent's fingernails suddenly pierced his flesh as she grabbed on to his muscular form like a life raft in a raging storm. She stared up at him like an orphan who'd lost her way. "Mary? It's all right. We're here," Gareth said softly.

A blanket of guilt fell over Leah as she watched the scene play out before her. In fact, she suddenly had the intense urge to kick herself in the ass. She had no right to be loud and mean and harass her obviously desperate mother. Stepping forward, Leah tried to calm her voice. "I'm so sorry, Mom."

The words that flowed from Mary Tallent's lips seemed to echo from an empty cave where her heart used to be. The sound was cold, dull, yet filled with an undeniable anger that was bubbling just below the defeated surface that she was showing to the world. "You should be sorry. All of this is *your* fault!"

The bitter words knocked the wind from Leah's chest.

Gareth placed his hand on Mary's cheek and stared into the red, weary eyes. "You don't really mean that, Mary."

Pushing against his chest with all her strength, Mary threw herself backwards. Her tattered slippers slid across the polished floor toward Leah, and she raised a finger in the air, thrusting it

22

into her daughter's face like a knight jabbing his lance into the flesh of his enemy. "They came in the middle of the night. New Year's Eve. Your father and I were celebrating," Mary choked on the sobs that were accompanying her words. "We were happy. The girls were out and your father was so thrilled at how well they were doing in college, at the Club, meeting the right people—and YOU!" She turned back to Gareth. "He was so happy that Leah had found the right man. He went on and on about what a wonderful man you are and what a good match you were for his oh-so-*perfect* daughter."

Leah remained silent; her head was reeling at the possessed look on her mother's face. Her eyes, the snakelike hiss in her voice—every inch of her appeared like that of a serial killer who was about to destroy the only real prey she'd ever wanted.

Mary's finely-manicured fingernails sliced through the air like sharp swords of death, and she screamed at Leah, "He was so proud of whatever it was you accomplished that you two talked about while you were here. What the *two* of you talked about . . . leaving *me* out, again!" Her voice began to fade, as she dropped her gaze to the floor. "He loves you so much. He even started talking about going on an adventure of his very own. He wanted to take me overseas . . . experience legends and see ancient cities. He talked about his books and things he'd discovered."

Her head snapped back up and she thrust her body forward, so close that Leah could smell the brandy coating her throat.

Mary hissed, "It was YOU who made him think about all that ridiculousness again. He'd left it behind! He'd left all that nonsense behind when I finally convinced him not to be an *Indiana Jones* wannabe. He became a man and protected his family. And then *you* came . . . full of your wild tales, and turned him back into an idiot!"

Leah stood straight and tall against the violent onslaught.

"I hate you," Mary said, spitting her disgust in Leah's face.

Gareth shouted, "Wait just a minute! I will not allow you to hurt the woman I love."

Leah immediately raised her hand in the air. "It's okay. Let her speak." She addressed the now snarling beast. "You can hate me, Mom, it doesn't matter. Maybe you always have. I don't know really."

Mary remained silent at her comment.

Leah took a deep breath, "But you love Dad."

The tears overtook her mother's violent eyes and erased the rage, like a deluge of water extinguishing a blazing fire.

Leah continued, "So you need to tell me what happened. Whatever this is, if it's my fault, then I have to fix it. I have to get him back. In order to do that, you have to tell me everything you know."

For a brief moment Leah wondered if her mother was going to raise her hand and slap her across the face. Instead, Mary took a step back, turned on her heel, and marched across the marble floor.

Following, Leah watched as her mother stopped at the door to her father's den, opened the door and flipped on the soft, amber lights. The green and teal hues of the room were soft and comforting, offering Leah a moment of joy when she stepped over the threshold into the only room of the mansion that'd ever held any warmth. As a child she would sit for hours by her father's side in this room as he taught her the words of ancient philosophers, educated her in the ways of mythology, and promoted the healthy practice of learning.

Swallowing the lump that immediately welled up in her throat, Leah stared at the familiar sight. The old books that lined each and every wall seemed to cry out for their owner to pick them up once again and journey through the adventures they offered. The large, comfortable desk chair sat vacant, as if waiting for David Tallent to reappear so that all could be right in the world. Leah could almost feel the somber feeling that was left behind after her father had disappeared.

"This is how he left it."

Leah turned to her mother. "This is how it always looks, Mom. And who's *they*? You have to start from the beginning."

Mary's hand shook as she reached out for the brandy snifter sitting on the silver tray. She filled her crystal glass with the amber liquid and knocked it back as if she was auditioning for the role of 'Drunken Sot #3' in some ridiculous *Animal House* remake. "I don't know who they were! If I did, I would have immediately called the police, wouldn't I?" she shouted.

Leah stopped her sigh from coming out and practically threw herself down in the desk chair. "Mom . . . please."

24

Closing her eyes and taking a deep breath, Mary's voice turned into a monotone, as if relaying the facts for the millionth time, "We were having a nice New Year's Eve. New Year's has always been so hard on David, but this year was different. We seemed to be finally celebrating our life . . . together. Then the doorbell rang. When I went to open it, there were three men just . . . standing there."

"Can you describe them, Mary?" Gareth said softly. He sounded like a doctor who was guiding a patient through some type of hypnotic journey.

Turning her gaze to the handsome man, she nodded. "They were dressed in suits—fine silk suits and ties—like rich businessmen." She gazed at Leah. "Just like your father."

"Do they work for Dad?"

Mary shook her head. "No. Your father had never seen them before. I know, because when he came up behind me he asked them who they were." Her speech slurred, "The smaller one took a step. And…even though his shoes were shined, when he crossed his hands in front of him I suddenly felt like I was looking at a wealthy mob boss. The one in charge, flanked by men who did his dirty work. He took off his hat and walked right in . . . *uninvited*."

Leah stared at the stranger before her who was throwing back brandy and stumbling across the carpet.

"He was bald," Mary continued, her voice raising and lowering as if her brain was on a roller coaster. "The chandelier made his head glow like a stubby candle." Her eyes glossed over as she stared out the large den window, as if searching for any explanation that the darkness could provide. "The short one bowed, like some kind of gentleman. But then I saw this thing . . . this drawing on his hand . . . and I got scared. I wanted to yell at your father to run, but the man stood up straight and gave me an evil . . . yes, *evil* smile. Then he walked right into the den. Again . . . uninvited. Your father, of course, ran after him and demanded to know who he was and why he was here."

"What happened to the other two? Did they just stand there by the door?" Leah's questions came out like that detective who wasn't going to stop badgering the woman until all the answers were given.

Mary waited for a moment before slowly answering, "No," she

said, choking on her brandy. "They came up behind me and took me by the arms. They wouldn't let me go. Your father turned around to race back to me but the bald man pulled a gun from his jacket and told your father to go into the den with him, or he'd be forced to let his partners do . . . damage to me."

Revulsion rose in Leah's stomach as she listened to her mother's hiccups of fear. None of this made any sense. If it was a business deal gone wrong, wouldn't her father have known them? Why on earth would a gun be necessary? Leah spoke, "Did you hear anything else? Anything at all before they went into the den?"

Mary wiped her red eyes with the back of her soiled robe "The man told your father that he should have 'left things alone.'"

"Left what alone?" Gareth chimed in.

Thankfully, the man was aware enough to duck, as the heavy crystal glass flew across the room and smashed into the bookshelf behind his head. "Look at me!" Mary yelled. "If I knew that do you think I would be like . . . this?"

Gareth raised his hands in the air. "I'm sorry, Mary. It was a stupid question."

Her eyes grew black. "Then I suppose you do belong with my . . . Leah. You make the perfect couple. You're both smart-mouthed jerks!"

Leah remembered the family dinner that seemed like only yesterday. Mary Tallent's eyes had positively sparkled when she'd come face-to-face with Gareth Lowery for the first time. She'd even presented Leah with a cell phone that rang out, 'Here Comes the Bride,' at the most inopportune moments. Looking at her mother now, it was amazing how fast a world could come crumbling down. "What else did they say?" Leah asked.

Mary spoke through gritted teeth, "That was it. They came in here and shut the door. When they came out ten minutes later your father was completely pale." Her voice quivered, "He looked like a ghost from the past had appeared in that den and taken him away from me . . . again."

The silence soon became frightening as the big house seemed to stop and wait for the mysterious ghost to show itself.

Leah couldn't bear the silence. "Dad just . . . left with them?"

Mary looked across the room at her daughter. A shiver ran down Leah's spine when she noted the vacant look of a mother who was now completely and utterly done with her child.

"No," Mary replied. "The phone rang and it was you. I talked to you . . . remember?"

Leah nodded. "Then I called back and got the stranger on the phone."

"He told you something about finding your father at the bottom of the ocean." Mary's chest heaved as if a giant weight was crushing her, causing her to struggle for every single breath she attempted to take.

Standing up, Leah stared at her. "I'll find him, Mom. Gareth and I will find out what's going on and bring Dad home."

Without missing a beat, Mary stood up, tumbled across the room and slapped her across the face.

Leah fell back into Gareth's outstretched arms that always seemed to appear like an angel offering protection. Righting herself, she followed her mother's departing figure into the hall. "Mom! The drawing on his hand? What did it look like?"

Shouting back over her shoulder, Mary raced up the stairs as if she was desperately trying to escape her daughter's unwanted presence in her home. "It was an apple! A big, red apple with an arrow running through it."

"An apple?" Leah whispered. Reaching down, she rubbed the back of her hand through the leather glove she wore. In their most recent adventure, Leah had come away with a drawing all her own, an all-seeing eye that marked her as protector. Although others she'd met along the way bore the same tattoo, theirs had all been emerald in color, marking them as guardians of secrets that Leah had never once imagined were actually real. Her 'stamp' however, was the same color as her own sapphire eyes. She'd yet to come across a red marking. And an arrow? What the hell could that stand for?

Raising her head, Leah shouted at her mother, "Was that it? He didn't say anything else?"

Reaching the top of the staircase, Mary Tallent stopped and whipped around, clinging to the banister so that she wouldn't take a deadly fall in her drunken, weary state. Her voice echoed off the marble walls, "They told me that when *you* arrived, I should tell you that, 'Leah has exactly seven days before the walls come tumbling down.'"

CHAPTER 3

The bedroom door slammed shut behind her mother and shook the empty house from floor to ceiling. The tinkling of the chandelier above Leah's head sounded like it was making the announcement that a million angels had suddenly received their wings.

Leah looked up as if waiting to see those angels floating above her, commanding her to go forth and find her missing father because this was the punishment she faced for her sins.

Turning, she walked back into the den and stared at Gareth's worried face.

He immediately reached out for her. "She doesn't mean what she says, Leah. She's just upset."

"No. She means it." Clinging to him tightly, she stared over his shoulder. Leah half-expected to see her mother reappear with a shotgun and make sure that Leah paid a far bigger price than just her angry words.

Taking a step back, she stared into the brilliant green eyes. "But I know there's something more. This isn't just rage at what happened to Dad, or anger with me for getting him interested in having an adventure. This is personal somehow."

"What do you mean?"

She shook her head. "I don't know . . . yet. But she seemed almost bitter about this. That look, that anger—all of this goes way deeper than just me being a disappointment in her life because

I'm not married or a member of the Country Club like my sisters."

Gareth remained silent as Leah began to pace the plush carpet in the den. Her eyes scanned the bookcases and the desk, searching for anything that was even the slightest bit out of place that would point her in the right direction.

"And what was that speech about New Year's Eve? My father was never moody on New Year's. He always took me out to dinner and we watched the Ball drop together." Leah threw her arms up in the air in frustration. "She made no sense!"

"She's been drinking . . . heavily," Gareth reminded her.

Leah turned and stared at him. "That's another thing! The lady of our manor was never sauced. She wouldn't permit it. She used to preach about how oxidants dry up your hair and how alcohol causes wrinkles. Not to mention, God forbid, someone could see you and knock you right out of the society pages in this small town. Now all of a sudden this preacher of the 'right' things to do in order to be a lady has turned into a lush?"

Gareth's voice came out like a soft, comforting purr in the room, "Her husband was led out of this house at gunpoint, Leah. I think that allows her to have a breakdown and get wasted on the brandy."

"Oh, really? Siding with her now? This *is* all my fault, I suppose?" Leah could feel her own eyes flash with resentment. She could taste the bitterness on her tongue for allowing her mother to once again make her feel inferior.

Putting his hands in the air to stop the tirade that was about to be unleashed, Gareth spoke quickly, "I stand for you and with you always, Leah. You know that by now. I'm just saying that this must've been quite a horror show for her."

Dropping her head into her hands, Leah sighed. "I'm sorry. I know. But what the hell am I going to do?"

———

Gareth leaned against the oak paneling and stared at the woman he loved more than God loved Man. He so wanted to turn back the clock and return to the Jordanian paradise they had just left behind.

He felt horrible. Leah had already been through so much. First, because of him, she'd faced Heaven's Gate and met evil head-on. Then, because of his own sister's plea, Leah had gotten embroiled in a roller coaster ride through the ancient life of Moses, stumbling from one dangerous location to another at the expense of her own safety in order to save his sister's life. And now . . . this.

Gareth stared at those sapphire eyes set in the most beautiful face he'd ever seen and begged Heaven to give her a break. She didn't deserve all the pain, and he felt so unbelievably guilty. Since the first day she'd teamed up with him, Leah Tallent's life had fallen apart.

Pacing the room like an angry lioness, he remained quiet and simply watched. Her brows furrowed on her forehead, like she was reaching deep inside her brilliant mind for any piece of this odd puzzle that would create even a small spark of an idea.

Gareth joined her, walking around the room and looking for anything that might seem even a little out of place amid the comfortable setting. "Your dad sure likes Egypt," he commented, picking up one of the huge books from the shelf. Its glossy, color pages offered pictures of stunning jewelry, unearthed artifacts and tales of legendary people who'd once dwelled in the mighty world of Alexandria.

Leah nodded at his words. "He dreamed of going there one day. He and I always wanted to excavate the area where the old Library in Alexandria once sat. When I was a kid we'd sit in here and talk about how wonderful it would be when we came across the ancient scrolls buried in some unknown vault alongside the wealth of Cleopatra."

Gareth smiled at her. "That would be cool."

Sitting down in her father's chair, Leah swiveled back and forth. "He knows so much, Gareth. He has a love . . . an obsession really, with ancient Egypt. Always has."

"There's a lot here—Egyptian, Roman and Greek," Gareth noted. He ran his hand along the old first-edition spines that were filled with the words of the greatest philosophers who'd ever lived. Moving on to the next shelf that was made entirely of glass, Gareth's breath stopped as he stared at an entire set of books and programs from the Olympic Games that dated all the way back to when they were held in the ancient city of Olympia. "Wow," he whispered, absolutely amazed at the sight.

"What?" Leah looked up.

Gareth ran his fingers across the glass. "Impressive."

Leah's sapphire eyes filled with frustration. Her hands clenched into fists on the armrests of the desk chair and she began turning in circles, staring up at the vaulted ceiling. "Seven days?" she shouted, causing Gareth to nearly jump out of his skin.

"What does that mean?" she continued, apparently believing that the louder she got, the ceiling would split, and a Divine moment would occur that would lead her in the right direction. "I don't know anything about what my father was sticking his nose into. How am I supposed to rescue the man when I don't even know where in the hell they took him, or why?"

"Do you think it has something to do with where we just came from?"

Leah shook her head. "I don't see how. We finished all that. We buried everything and the bad guys were literally crispy critters when we got out of there."

Gareth smiled, reveling briefly at the sound of the familiar sarcasm that was beginning to creep back into his lover's voice. With Leah, her jokes were part of her power; they were part of the enormous strength that allowed her to lead everyone safely through the darkness.

"Besides," she continued, bringing the swiveling chair to a stop. "I never told him where we were going. We haven't had any contact with him at all. All I remember is, at the holiday dinner, he said he was 'on to something.' "

Gareth walked toward her. "What?"

Her eyes closed, as if calling the memory to the forefront of her mind. "We were in the den talking about you." She smiled. "I told him about what we'd found in Glastonbury. When I was finished, he said that he'd been studying a mystery too, and had come across something . . . strange. He said it wasn't as big as finding Heaven, but it was close."

Gareth sat down on the desk and stared into her now open eyes. "So the men who came and took him must have found out what the strange something was."

"But he never told me the specifics. He changed the subject and talked about what he always talks about. He was planning a trip for him and Mom to go to Athens and visit ancient Egypt while they were over there."

Gareth remained completely silent as her words raced through his skull. "And?"

"And . . . then we joked about how Mom would hate it there because she'd be jealous of Cleopatra's beauty." A smile spread across Leah's face. "Dad and I are always on the same page."

"Exactly!" Gareth's voice came out like a missile. "That's exactly how you're going to find him. Your brains work the same way. I have no doubt that you'll figure this out." He smiled wide. "Must be those sapphire eyes you share. Nothing in the world can hide from them for very long."

Leah swiveled in the chair and moved to face the window. "I could sure use another pair right now."

Fear exploded in Gareth's chest when Leah's chair came to a dead stop with a sudden jerk and she let out a blood-curdling scream.

He raced to stand between her body and the large window, wondering if he would see a strange man with a red tattoo pointing a gun at the woman he loved more than life. But the reflection that stared back at him erased the fear immediately and allowed complete confusion to take over his body.

"Jesus," Leah breathed. "What the hell is *she* doing here?"

Blinking quickly, Gareth focused on the ghostly image of a pale and frightened Anippe staring back at them with wide, sapphire eyes. "Well . . . you asked for another pair," he said. "Something tells me an explanation has just arrived."

CHAPTER 4

Leah raced to the front door and threw it open. Rushing down the icy cobblestone steps, she looked off to the side of the house at the cold, shivering figure standing in the pale green glow of the den lighting.

Leah's mind raced back to her first meeting with Anippe inside the amazing walls of the Coptic Museum in Cairo. There, Leah had not only suffered an extremely bruised nose, but she'd also been completely turned off by Anippe's more than condescending attitude. But the woman had been with she, Gareth and Kathryn when they went on their hunt for Emmanuel, leading them through the ancient city of Petra and discovering crucial information that opened the doors to not only a Divine secret, but also to a group of guardians whose only mission was to protect the most unbelievable treasures from a world that would literally bring about war if they fell into the wrong hands.

Anippe had known about the Sapphire Staff long before Leah had stumbled into the cave where Emmanuel sat, waiting for his friends to arrive. She was also the last person Leah had seen before leaving the adventure behind.

Their last conversation still haunted Leah, as she remembered Anippe questioning her during Kathryn and Emmanuel's wedding reception about the emerald pendant that hung around Leah's neck. She'd been very strange that day, hugging Leah and telling her that they would one day see each other again . . . very soon.

Now seeing her here, shivering on Leah's doorstep that was a far cry from Egypt, she knew that Anippe's prophecy had come true.

Staring into sapphire eyes that were full of fear, Leah pointed at the open front door. "Are you coming in, or do you just want to stand out here and freeze to death?"

Anippe stared at the door where Gareth stood. Nodding at him, she turned back to Leah. "There's been an emergency. A . . . kidnapping."

Fear burst in Leah's body. "How the hell do you know that?"

Anippe offered a confused glance at Gareth before turning back to her. "What?"

"Both of you get in here now!" Gareth called out. "If we have just seven days neither of you can afford to get pneumonia."

Anippe walked toward him quickly, marching her tall, lithe body over the threshold of the mansion. "How do you know I only have seven days?"

Walking in behind her, Leah stared at Gareth's astonished face. "I think we're about to begin."

Nodding, he hustled Anippe across the foyer and into the warmth of the den. Taking off her wet coat and gloves, he stared briefly at the tattoo on the back of her hand. Unlike Leah's sapphire insignia that mirrored the glow of the staff, Anippe's was an eye of emerald that was adorned with two eerie holes that went straight through her flesh—a leftover gift from the fangs of a snake that'd tried to take her life.

Anippe followed his stare. She rubbed her cold hands together, unconsciously covering the two blood red wounds and crept closer to Leah. "Did you ever find out where that pendant came from?"

Leah's hand automatically moved to her neck to grasp the emerald teardrop that Gareth had given to her on their first adventure together. She wanted to be helpful, but as she stared at the pale-faced woman whose straight, dark hair looked like wet asps writhing down her back, Leah decided to wait until Anippe revealed her true intentions for being there.

She settled for the obvious question. "What are you doing here?"

Clearing her throat, Anippe shot a desperate gaze at Gareth.

"Please. I need to know where that pendant came from."

Gareth studied her face for only a moment before answering, "Athens."

Leah let out a loud sigh, offended at his overly trusting personality. "Man!"

"Leah, I think we should listen to her," he said.

Feeling the color rise in her cheeks as she watched Anippe move closer to his side, Leah balled her hands into fists at her sides. "I asked what you're doing here."

Walking over to the leather couch, Anippe removed a strange looking package from inside her coat pocket and held the object in the air.

Leah stared at the familiar metal horseshoe; the quarter of gemstones embedded in the metal frame glittered in the light. Immediately the card catalogue opened inside her head and shot out the exact memory of standing in the Coptic Museum and staring into the small glass case that'd held the mysterious artifact.

Moving closer, Leah could now see that it wasn't a horseshoe, but an olive wreath. Trapped inside the opening of the wreath was what looked to be an old rolled-up piece of parchment held in place with a small, gold clamp in the shape of a teardrop.

"So?" Leah looked at Anippe.

"I want you to open it," she answered.

Leah smirked. "I'm supposedly a descendant of Moses, remember? Not Houdini."

Anippe's eyes immediately sparked with anger. The twin sapphires glowing in her pale face suddenly mirrored the cold eyes of the serpent that'd once attacked her. Without speaking, Anippe took a step forward and ripped the chain from around Leah's neck. With the speed of a runaway train, her thin, graceful fingers pressed the pendant into the teardrop-shaped lock. With an audible click, the mechanism flipped open and sent the rolled-up piece of parchment to the floor.

Rubbing the raw skin on her neck, Leah watched the scroll roll across the deep green carpeting to stop at the foot of her father's desk.

"Sorry about your pendant."

Leah barely registered Anippe's apology as she stared down at the olive wreath she still had clutched in her hands. Leah's pendant had broken in half when the lock opened, snapping the gem in two along the bright blue line that'd run through it ever since her experience inside Chartres Cathedral. At the very bottom, however, the pendant was still soldered together; the two green halves looked like small leaves that were waiting for a beautiful flower to grow up between them.

Leah's mind was spinning. She watched both Gareth and Anippe take a step toward the mysterious parchment and placed her body solidly in front of them. She held up her hand. "Not a chance."

Glaring at Anippe, her voice lowered like a judge about to issue a death sentence, "You'll tell me what the hell you're doing here, or you will leave my house right this second and go do whatever it is you need to do by yourself."

Without a word, Anippe walked back to the couch and sat down. Although Gareth stopped moving as well, he continued to stare down at the scroll like it was the 'missing link.' Leaning against her father's desk, Leah blocked the scroll with her boot. "Now."

Taking a deep, quivering breath, Anippe began, "My uncle, the man you met?" She stopped, staring at Leah for confirmation.

She nodded. "I remember him. Aaron, right?"

"Right," she replied, clearing her throat as if she was being pounded by a sandstorm and was trying desperately to breathe. "He was kidnapped right after the wedding when we returned to Cairo. He wanted to take a break from the dig in Petra and go home for a while . . . get some rest."

Leah could relate.

"I left the museum one day to get us something to eat in the marketplace and when I returned," she continued, her body trembling, "there were three men, standing in the museum . . . Their leader, I suppose you could call him, held a gun to my uncle's head and smiled at me. He bowed like a gentleman, but his voice was cold . . . evil."

"Was he bald?" Gareth asked, trying to avert his attention from the unknown parchment.

Her eyes grew wide. "How did you know that?"

Leah answered, "The same men visited this house. Cairo after Christmas; Connecticut on New Year's Eve . . . these guys certainly get around."

"Can you tell us anything about the bald man?" Moving across the carpet, Gareth sat down beside the visibly frightened woman.

Anippe looked into his comforting face. "Short . . . stocky, as you Americans say. His guards were Greek. I heard them speaking the language but couldn't make out the words. But the leader's accent was German, and there was something about him . . . he made me feel like a very small rat in front of a very large, hungry python. I was petrified."

Gareth put his arm around her shoulder as she continued, "They were all dressed in expensive silk suits and they carried guns . . . big guns, in their belts."

"What else?" Gareth prodded.

"The man, the leader, he had a bright red mark on the back of his hand."

"An apple," he nodded.

"No." Anippe shook her head. "It was an eye, like mine . . . like Leah's. But the drawing also showed an arrow shot through the pupil of the eye."

The color drained from Gareth's face, as Anippe continued, "I believe it's called the 'Eye of Blood.' "

"You know about this mark?" Leah's voice broke through their conversation.

Anippe turned to her. "I have heard about it, but I've been searching everywhere to find it . . . some clue about where it perhaps originated . . . anything! All I remember is that it was mentioned in an old fairytale my uncle told me when I was a kid." She dropped her head in her hands and began to cry, "I don't know what to do. He said I have only seven days before they kill him."

Leah's mind grew dark, and the slight twinge of jealousy at seeing Gareth hover around the woman was affecting her, but she had no idea why. Her mind was literally whirling out of control. Not only had her father been taken by thieves in the night, but now Anippe's uncle had been kidnapped by the exact same thugs who were apparently racking up frequent flyer miles as they raced back and forth across the globe. "But seven days for *what*?"

Anippe looked up. "I have no idea. All he told me was to come to America and find you." Her eyes grew weary as she continued, "He informed me that the Hero's Companion would know what to do."

"The Hero's Companion?" Gareth asked, moving his gaze to Leah. "Why does that sound so familiar?"

Sitting down slowly at the desk, Leah glared at Anippe. "You put a picture of the Goddess Athena in my coat before you left the wedding reception. Right after I found it, I received a call from a man who took my father—for what god-awful reason, I don't know."

Anippe interrupted, "The pendant you wear is from Athena."

"What?" Leah could hear the pure frustration building in her own voice.

"There's a statue of Athena wearing the exact same pendant," Anippe said. "Not to mention, Athena also wears a symbol of the olive wreath." She pointed at the metal artifact. "When you were at my museum you were struck silent by that. You stared into that case for a long time. I watched you. It was almost as if you knew or saw something that no one else could. And then when I noticed your pendant exactly matched the size and shape of the lock, I knew it was the key that would free the scroll. That wreath was found in Athens by my uncle years ago, buried inside a small chamber next to the Parthenon."

"Okay." Leah rubbed her tired eyes and continued, "So you put two and two together with my pendant and the wreath. It worked and opened the lock . . . but what makes you think that I'm this, Hero's Companion?" Leah stared at Anippe, looking for any sign of dishonesty to appear in the woman's eyes.

"Leah," she began slowly, as if she was only a lamb trying her best not to anger the hungry lioness in her midst, "Athena was called the Hero's Companion by the Greeks. She gained that title when she helped Perseus defeat Medusa. You," she continued, swallowing hard, "When I met you, I'd already heard about what Gareth had done inside that cave in Glastonbury. I told you that the story had circulated among our group. Gareth's largely considered a hero for what he did in there; the heroic choice he made not to open the Gates. He honored the Father."

Leah felt her empty stomach churn when she watched Anippe stare up at Gareth like he was the 'second coming' in the flesh. "And *I'm* his companion," she said clearly, asserting her rightful position in Anippe's mind.

The woman blushed as she stared back at Leah. "Of course you are. But when we met and I found out who you were descended from, you became much more than just Gareth's companion. As Gareth did in Glastonbury, you sacrificed your own safety in France to make the right decision and honor the Son. You have become a model of—"

"Stop," Leah shouted. "You're blowing what I did way out of proportion. I didn't ask for any of that. Hell, I've seen things with my own eyes, and I *still* don't believe in all the religious 'who-hah' the two of you believe in. I'm a librarian who misses her father. Nothing more, nothing less."

Anippe shook her head at Leah's words. "Just like Athena was to Perseus, a man who would not have been a hero if it wasn't for her strength—you, Leah, are the Hero's Companion."

"No, I'm not."

Anippe's eyes immediately filled with tears, and her voice turned desperate. "I have nothing but my uncle, Leah. He's all the family I have; the only person who cares for me in this huge world. I need your help."

Taking a deep breath, she continued her plea, "I put that picture in your pocket at the wedding because I thought it would become clear to you. After I saw the marking on your hand—the sapphire eye—I knew you must be one of the leaders of our group who was chosen to protect the truth." She turned to Gareth. "Working at the side of her beloved hero."

Anippe kept her eyes locked on Gareth's face. "But other than the Athena connection, I still cannot understand what this is all about. I have no idea what my uncle could have done. He is not a bad man. Perhaps it was someone who heard about the Staff? Or your experience at Heaven's Gate? But whoever's behind this and whatever they want, I know the two of you can solve it and save my uncle in the process." Glancing back at Leah, the tears streamed down her cheeks like a waterfall of pain. "I just don't know where to go next."

Sighing heavily, Leah stared at the petrified woman and offered her the answer, "Athens."

CHAPTER 5

Gareth turned his attention away from Anippe and stared over at the beautiful owner of the definitive voice.

Leah was sitting at the desk, now holding the unrolled scroll daintily between her fingertips. Gareth could barely breathe as particles of paper fell to the desktop like snowflakes, as the antique document literally disintegrated in her hands.

He raced toward her. "Jesus, Leah. Put it down!"

Leah looked more than annoyed, as anger danced in her sapphire eyes. Her lips twisted into a wry smile. "Don't worry, Lowery. I saw what it was before it fell apart."

He waited. "Well? What was it?"

Leah held out her palm and let Gareth stare at the last scrap of paper. An eyeball had been stamped into a layer of dark red wax.

Leaning over, he was careful not to breathe for fear of destroying the one remaining clue. "What is that?"

Leah simply smiled at him. For a brief moment, Gareth wondered if she was going to withhold the information. He saw a strange spark of jealousy flash through her eyes when Anippe stepped up beside him. And as the realization dawned, Gareth tried to suppress the laughter that welled up inside his soul.

Staring back at her, he challenged his love to state her ridiculous thoughts out loud. "You have *got* to be kidding."

Lowering her eyes quickly, Leah's cheeks turned scarlet with shame when his sarcastic tone met her ears. She shook her head. "I'm sorry. It's been a really long day."

"Brace yourself, darling." He leaned forward and kissed her full, red lips. "Because you're looking forward to at least seven more of them."

Her eyes grew wide. "God that's right. We only have seven days to find my father, and with this clue leading to Athens . . .," her voice filled with panic, "we'll waste three of the days just traveling. We'll never have enough time to figure this out."

Gareth touched her cheek. "I'll take care of that part."

"What clue?" Anippe interrupted, pointing at the ancient logo. "What is that thing? What was on the scroll?"

Gareth saw a brief look of satisfaction pass through Leah's eyes. She was obviously happy that Anippe was less knowledgeable than she was. Gareth smiled down at his companion. He could almost hear the 'whooshing' sound inside Leah's brain as her personal card catalogue shot out the data she needed.

Heading back to the soft, well-worn couch, Gareth sat down and nodded at Anippe to join him. His heart leapt in his throat when Leah's beautiful lips parted and their next journey began.

———

"Are you familiar with the life of Plato?" Leah asked.

Gareth shook his head. "Not much. Just the words of his teacher, Socrates."

Leah tilted her head. "What were they?"

" 'I drank what'?" He smiled wide. "That's a really old joke."

She rolled her eyes, as Gareth let out a bellow of laughter.

"I don't get it," Anippe said, staring at the duo in utter confusion.

Leah waved her hand in front of her face. "American humor. It's an acquired taste." She cleared her throat. "Anyway . . . Plato was a great philosopher in Athens."

Anippe exhaled and her voice took on a slightly haughty air, "I *know* who Plato was."

Leah smiled. "Of course you do." She stared at the small wax seal that'd been centered at the top of the now disintegrated scroll. "Plato founded a school called 'The Academy' in Athens. All the people who wanted to go went there to attend his daily lessons.

Plato advocated a great deal, but he was most widely known for his skepticism."

"What was he skeptical of?" Gareth asked, still grinning from his ridiculous joke.

"He believed that a philosopher cured men's minds like a doctor cured their bodies. And, Plato thought that the worst disease known to mankind was ignorance."

"Well, he *was* a philosopher, after all," Anippe interjected. "He's still counted among the geniuses who once walked the earth."

"But was he a genius in his day and age, or only ours?"

Worry lines accumulated on Anippe's brow. She sighed loudly. "Is this a test?"

Gareth laughed. "Leah believes she's the only living genius."

She stuck out her tongue at him and continued, "No, I don't. But I do actually agree with most of Plato's words. Ignorance is rampant now and that's frightening." The librarian in her made her thoughts known. "Of course, he was also quite creative. Plato was actually the one who made up the story of *Atlantis*."

Gareth leaned forward in his seat. "Who says Atlantis is made up? There are quite a few people who are still looking for its location all across the globe."

"Whatever," Leah mumbled, rolling her eyes. "Trust me, when it became a children's bedtime story it was no longer in the realm of truth."

Sitting back against the leather, Gareth waited for her to continue.

"Anyway, like I said, I agree with Plato's belief that ignorance will be Man's downfall. There's way too much of it in this world, and that's where all of our problems come from."

"Spoken like a true librarian," Anippe offered.

"Maybe," Leah said with a nod. "Unlike the Atlantis myth, however, Plato is quite famous for other writings, especially 'The Allegory of the Cave.'"

"You lost me on that one," Gareth said.

"Really?" Leah grinned. "I believe it was your favorite, Socrates, who was the first to come up with it and then told his favorite student about his theory. The manuscript was written by Plato but the words are what Socrates preached. 'Platonism' is actually a term that scholars use nowadays to describe what these men both believed a long time ago.

"Socrates hated people who thought that something had to be 'right there in front of them' to be real. He believed that people who lived without knowing Divine inspiration would never have access to the real truth."

"So . . . it's like believing in God?" Gareth said.

"Not exactly," Leah replied. "Plato stated that human beings live in a world of visible things. Like this desk, these books," she sent him a wink. "Your ridiculously large bank accounts. You know . . . the things that surround you every single day? If we can see it, hear it and touch it—we know it's there. On the other hand, Plato also said that there's an intelligible world that's made up of human reason, and *that* is the world of the philosopher."

Gareth stared at her; a grin was affixed to his face. "Maybe one day there will be a group that practices 'Leahism.' "

Rolling her eyes, she continued, "The theory that Socrates told Plato was that life was like being in a cave. Say you're in a dimly-lit area and the image of a . . . wolf is projected onto the wall. It's just a shadow, but you know it's a wolf. Why? Because you were brought up to know what a wolf looks like. But to say it's *just* a wolf is wrong."

"Then what is it? What's the shadow?" Anippe asked.

Leah put her hands in the air. "That's the point. You're not really going to know unless you come out of the cave and into the light. What we see every day *is* real in the visible world, but it's also an illusion in the intelligible world."

Gareth stared back at her; a blank expression was all he offered.

"Okay." She smiled. "Let me put this into vernacular you understand. You have a million dollars in the bank."

"Billion, actually," he grinned.

"Whatever," Leah sighed. "That's real. You can see it and you know it's there."

"It better be."

"Exactly!" Leah smiled wide. "You see? Just by saying those words means you're one of the people who Plato would have liked. You never know when that billion will be all gone. There could be some major catastrophe, or a slimy bank teller who wants to see if he can get away with theft and, 'poof!' your billion is history—a figment of your imagination. The 'intelligible' world tells you that money is only an illusion.

"With the wolf scenario, in the 'intelligible' world you know the animal can change. You know that wolves come in different sizes, shapes and colors. In other words, a wolf is the correct answer to the image you see in the cave, but only on a very basic level."

"Like your 9/11 here?" Anippe chimed in.

Leah stared at her. "I'm sorry?"

She continued, "I heard people say that America was never really safe. That because of your victorious history, your people were under the illusion that nothing could happen to them—certainly not from such a small, unknown enemy."

"You got it," Leah said. "Plato wanted everyone to get out of their 'cave of ignorance.' He wanted them to not take things at face value, but delve further. He said that few people ever climbed out of their cave, and those who did, became the objects of scorn and ridicule because of their 'strange' beliefs. But he just didn't want people to live in the shadows. Good or bad, he thought people should open their eyes."

"Was that scroll 'The Allegory of the Cave'? That's why you brought this up?" Gareth said, pointing at the pieces of parchment littering the desk.

Leah nodded; her heart was full of sadness. "I think it may have been the original," she said in the librarian voice that truly wanted to cry for losing a historic document of such magnificence.

Gareth blanched; he suddenly looked as ill as Leah felt. "Well . . . no one knew it even existed. I guess it won't be missed."

Leah thought back to the journals of the Son that she'd held in her hands not so long ago, and felt the tears choke her throat.

Gareth continued quickly, "It's okay, Leah. We have seven days. We didn't exactly have enough time to get the scroll into a lab for preservation. You did what you had to do . . . for your father."

"So the 'Eye of Blood' has something to do with Plato?" Anippe asked.

"It's not a widely known fact, but I remember learning a bit about Plato's Academy." Closing her eyes, she read the data that'd collected inside her brain. "It was a public grove; a garden located in the suburbs of Athens. I believe that someone left it to the city for their athletes to use for training. The Olympics originated there, of course.

" 'The Academy' was supposedly surrounded by a wall, and had statues and figures of all the illustrious men and gods who'd lived in their world.

"There were olives trees everywhere in the gardens. According to a story my father loved, the trees had been grown using layers from the sacred olive that belonged to the Goddess Athena."

Leah opened her eyes and aimed her gaze at Anippe. "The students of 'The Academy' sat in an area of this beautiful garden where Plato would teach them. His followers were said to be marked with an all-seeing eye that stood for the belief that there was something out there . . . a real world just waiting to be found. Why it's blood-red though, I have absolutely no idea. And I can't remember anything being said about an arrow running through it."

Leah stared at Gareth. The look of extreme love and respect that flowed through his emerald eyes made her heart skip a beat.

He smiled. "Maybe someone defiled the marking on purpose. Maybe there's a group out there that has twisted Plato's thoughts and beliefs into something evil and sick."

"Wouldn't be the first time," Leah said, thinking about the tragedies of the past. "Plato stated in his 'Republic' that: 'Until philosophers ruled as kings . . . cities would have no rest from evil.'"

"Plato didn't condone power?"

"No. Only intelligence," Leah replied. "The only power he believed was real and would help the human race was, in fact, philosophy. He believed that only when philosophy and political power combine, will the world survive. This is where the term 'philosopher-king' came from.

"Plato and Socrates believed that a truly wise leader is the one who accepts the power that's given by the people, *not* the ones who achieve it by using brute force."

Gareth nodded. "Which is pretty much every single person in power today."

She nodded. "Pretty much."

Anippe wrung her hands. "But what does Plato and this 'cave' thing have to do with getting my uncle and your father back alive? Do you think they're in Athens buried in a cave? Why would they be there?"

Leah shook her head. "I don't know, Anippe. I'm just telling you what I know about Plato. Not to mention, you thought Athena—the Hero's Companion—was a reference to me. That's two votes for Athens."

"But where will we look when we get there? The ruins of Athens are substantial, Leah. We only have seven days!"

Leah dropped her exhausted head down on the edge of the desk, sending the last small piece of paper fluttering to the floor below her. She sighed, staring down at the wax eye through her folded arms and wondering what the answer was to Anippe's really good question. She wanted to scream at her—tell her to go home—but Leah just couldn't. Locked in the woman's eyes was the same painful heartache that Leah had deep in her own soul.

Bending down to retrieve the small clue, Leah caught sight of a large, rolled-up piece of paper hidden under her father's desk . . . and her heart dropped.

CHAPTER 6

"What the hell is this?" Leah whispered from under the desk.

"What the hell is what?" Gareth asked.

Sliding off the chair to her knees, Leah carefully pulled the tape from both ends of the large piece of paper and took it in her hands.

When she lifted her head, Gareth was standing above the desk staring down at her like she had finally gone insane. But when he caught sight of the item in Leah's hands, his smirk disappeared. "What's that?"

"No idea." Leah shrugged. "But it sure would be great if Dad left us detailed directions to where he went."

"Would certainly be a time-saver," he agreed with a smile.

Carefully unrolling the heavy paper, Leah held her breath. Thankfully, unlike the priceless words of Plato, her father's mysterious scroll was made up of four pieces of strong construction paper that had been taped together to form a large, rectangular mat. Leah felt a jolt of excitement race down her spine when she saw the familiar handwriting. "My father made this."

Gareth's voice was a whisper in her ear, "Looks like some sort of odd map."

Sitting down quickly in the chair, she scanned the strange combinations of words and pictures.

Anippe walked quickly to the desk. "Will it help? Let's follow it! Let's go!"

"Slow down." Gareth raised his hand. 'We don't even know what we're looking at yet."

Leah stared at the large painted drawing that sat smack dab in the middle of the mat. A huge tree had been created, with twisted branches reaching out on each side that were filled with bright green and silver leaves.

"Maybe it's just a genealogical thing . . . your family tree, maybe?" Gareth asked.

"Why would he hide our family tree under his desk?"

Gareth shrugged. "Maybe he found out about the whole Moses thing before you did and didn't want anyone to know about it. Maybe this is written in some kind of code."

Leah moved her eyes to the first picture on the left hand side of the map. "No," she whispered. "This has nothing to do with Moses." She pointed at the drawing.

"What is that?" Anippe asked, staring at the map that was upside down from her vantage point.

Leah turned the paper so she could see. "Looks like an owl."

"An owl?"

Leah nodded. Moving her finger across the page to the next drawing, she followed the small owl's journey. "See? The little guy starts here and then he's all over the place. I think it's like footsteps; you have to follow the owl from one point to the next on the map."

"Like those kid's maps that come with crayons?"

Leah lifted her head and stared at Gareth.

"You know?" he said. "There was a place when I was younger where we would go for ice cream, and the placemats had these mazes on them where you'd take the crayon and . . ." He stopped and stared at Leah whose eyebrow had lifted into the air at his suddenly excited, childlike voice.

"Forget it," he mumbled.

"I'll make you a promise," she smiled. "When we're done with this I'll take you for a hot fudge sundae and you can play with the placemat."

"Really?"

"You bet." She laughed at the handsome man who'd suddenly become the spitting image of an overeager ten-year-old.

Anippe tossed her long, black hair over her shoulder and let out a deep sigh. "Can we get on with this? We're wasting time!"

"We sometimes use sarcasm to help us get by," Leah's response came out loud and strong. "If you don't like it, feel free to leave at any time. There's the door."

Anippe swallowed hard and her chin inched toward the ceiling.

Gareth ignored her completely and pointed to the owl's starting point. "Isn't that Athena?"

Leah squinted at the small picture of the statue. "I think so. Wait!" she yelled, pulling open the middle drawer of the desk and grabbing the magnifying glass that she knew lay inside. "That's better. Yup, that's Athena, alright."

Anippe spoke softly in an apparent attempt to not ruffle any more of Leah's feathers, "Athena's bird was an owl."

The librarian lifted her head. "Excuse me?"

"On all of her statues . . . Athena had an owl on her shoulder. It was the messenger of wisdom. One of the names the Goddess bore was 'Glaukpis,' which means 'Owl-Eyed,' because she could supposedly see anything day or night."

"Look what's beside her," Gareth cut in; his voice sounded excited.

Leah moved the magnifier to look at the bright red eye that had been drawn at the bottom of the weapon in Athena's hands. "The eye is bloody because Athena stabbed it with her spear."

Gareth thought about the description of the strange tattoo. "Coincidence?"

"What?" Anippe begged. "Do you think the kidnappers are followers of Athena?"

Leah shook her head. "No. Nothing's ever that easy. Look at the map. Athena is just the first clue. My father obviously found a way to get to . . . something, and Athena was only the starting point." Leah tapped her teeth with her fingernails, moving her gaze back to the large tree in the center of the map.

Tracing the owl's flight, Leah saw that the small bird soared from Athena's shoulder, through a small courtyard of tiny trees, and then across an area that looked as if it was a bright blue ocean. From there, it once again crossed dry land to a new picture, taking a seat on top of a large skull. The black eyes stared back at Leah from the page and filled her with fear. It looked almost like the skeletal face was laughing at her, daring her to come and sit down beside the owl . . . at her own peril. Surrounding the skull on one side was a large mountain; on the other, a grove of trees had been drawn with a golden cross sitting inside a green and silver cluster of leaves.

The bird then took flight, leaving the frightening skull behind and flying across the map, hovering over something that looked like an actual torture device. A mammoth handle was being brought down on a large, round object. *Someone's head?* thought Leah. *God, what the hell has my father gotten himself into?*

Beside the eerie looking device was a hole dug deep into the ground, creating a large cave with hundreds of yellow eyes drawn into the walls. Leah felt her body shiver at the large 'X' that'd been drawn inside the hole. Her father's handwriting was right beside it, and the statement was beyond troubling. It read, "Could it still be here?"

Forcing herself to continue along the painted line of the owl's flight, Leah was led to a picture of a huge castle—a palace sitting all by itself in the bottom left hand corner of the map. Turrets, pools— even a large hall had been drawn inside the grand building. Leah's fingernail caught on a raised corner and she suddenly noticed that this one image had a thin piece of parchment taped over the heavy construction paper. It looked almost like an advent calendar, where you needed to open the small square door in order to reveal what was underneath.

Holding her breath, Leah carefully removed the tape at the bottom of the picture and lifted it up. Hidden underneath was the same painted palace, but the pool was no longer colored in with clear blue ink. Instead, small drawings of people had been placed where the water had once been and the bodies open wounds were leaking red ink. The pool had turned into the sight of a massacre. Beside the horrific scene was a lone stick figure lying down, painted in with a dark red color that looked like dried blood.

Leah took a deep breath and went back to the path of the friendly owl, but there was nothing more to see except the large tree. The owl had ended his journey on the lowest branch, staring up through the silver and green leaves like it was searching for something. Inside the brown trunk a set of gray stairs had been colored in that led right off the bottom of the map. There was no treasure, no sign of a pot of gold, no words of ancient wisdom at the end of the owl's flight—the only thing that appeared was the number *64* written on the bottom step.

Leah focused her attention on the other two people who had gone absolutely quiet in the room. She stared over at Gareth's wide eyes. He was on his knees at the corner of the desk; his head rested on his hands. "It's certainly a map," he whispered.

Leah agreed but Anippe remained silent. She studied the map like an artist studied his model. Her eyes seemed to be collecting and memorizing every detail so that she could begin the long and arduous task of finding her beloved uncle.

Gareth pointed to the bottom. "Is that your father's signature?"

Leah moved the magnifier. "No. It says: 'Plant the seeds to find the tree.'"

"What tree?"

She shrugged. "I assume the big one in the middle."

Anippe broke through the quiet consideration of the longtime partners, "That's an olive tree."

Leah raised her head. "An olive tree?"

"Yes. You can tell by the silvery-green leaves, which is yet another reference to Athena."

"Athena?"

She nodded.

Leah noted the familiar smirk of self-satisfaction on Anippe's face. She was blatantly happy that she possessed knowledge that Leah didn't have. And, not wanting to burst her bubble, Leah decided to let the girl have this one round. She watched Gareth stare at Anippe; his emerald eyes were focused intently on her face.

Leah sighed. *Nope,* she thought. *Sue me God, I'm only human.* Sitting back in the chair, she spoke, "Are you talking about the fight Athena and Poseidon had?"

The light immediately faded from Anippe's eyes. "You know the story."

"Some of it. Athena won the battle . . . with her olive tree."

"What?" Gareth said, shifting his gaze from woman to woman.

Leah, not liking the feeling of jealousy that seemed to crawl underneath her skin and turn her into a woman she truly didn't like, moved on. "Forget it. We don't have time." She looked up at Anippe and pointed to the writing on the map. "Maybe the seeds they refer to are olives?"

The light came back to the Egyptian woman's eyes, as if she was grateful that the Hero's Companion was including her in the puzzle-solving. "It would make sense. But I know of no famous olive tree that would be important enough to kidnap somebody over."

Leah stared down at the map. "Maybe Athena knows," she whispered.

Gareth pointed at the sentence under Athena's picture, "This says, *the seed of the warrior for strength to defy all armies, including breaking the chains of Paradise.*"

"And this one," Anippe said, pointing to the small group of trees growing beside the hideous skull. "It says, *the seed of the one who'll bind your wounds and lead you to Temptation.*"

"You mean *through* temptation," Gareth corrected.

Anippe shook her head. "That's not what this says. It reads, 'to Temptation' . . . with a capital 'T.'"

Leah moved her own gaze to the picture that seemed to burn through her very core. The small piece of unsecured paper literally offered a pool of death that Leah had no desire to find. Under the bodies was yet another small sentence. She swallowed hard. "This one says, *the seed of Hell's King that will show you the innocent reality of who will come again.*"

The room went silent. Leah suddenly rolled up the large map and flattened it with her fists. Standing, she dropped it in the deep pocket of the long leather coat she still hadn't removed from her body, and turned to Gareth. "What time is it?"

"It's almost dawn, love," Gareth whispered, staring at the clock behind her head. "You need sleep."

"No!" Anippe shouted. "We need to go now! The time has already started."

Leah closed her eyes and buried her face in Gareth's muscular chest. "She's right." Breathing deeply, she drew in Gareth's familiar scent of soap and musk, offering her a moment of blissful calm before the storm.

Gareth's arms tightened around her. "I think I have an idea on how to speed things up, so to speak."

Leah took a step back and stared into the green eyes filled with love for her. "How?"

His response was drowned out by the sudden sound of the large door crashing against the wall, followed by Mary Tallent's shrill scream, "Get the hell out of my house!"

CHAPTER 7

The angry voice made Leah's teeth grind together as she stared into the bright red face of her mother. Not only did her cheeks resemble a volcano that was gearing up to release a deadly fire onto the rest of the world, but her brown eyes looked almost black inside her skull, as she pointed her shaking finger at Anippe.

Leah's gaze moved to the woman's extremely confused face. Anippe had literally jumped backwards and landed on the couch, looking completely scared out of her wits, as she stared up at the enraged stranger.

"Mom?" Leah began, slowly. "This is Anippe. We met her in Cairo." She added softly, "You don't know her."

Mary Tallent didn't move and never turned her blazing gaze away from Anippe. "Don't tell me what I know. Get out of my house . . . now!"

Looking from mother to daughter, Anippe scanned the faces in the room as if hoping someone would explain what was so terribly wrong about her presence.

"Mom." Leah took a cautious step forward as Mary Tallent backed away. "Mom?"

Turning on her heel, Mary raced from the room with Leah on her trail. Reaching out, Leah grabbed her shoulder and tried to calm her down. "Mom, what's wrong with you?"

Whipping her head around the bloodshot eyes glared into her

soul, making Mary Tallent look as if she wore the mask of a true demon. She seethed through her teeth, "No matter how much you hate me, I do not deserve this."

Leah released her mother's arm in complete and utter shock.

Backing across the floor, Mary Tallent's eyes never wavered from Leah's face. Shaking her head, she turned and stumbled back up the grand staircase.

Leah heard her repeating the same words over and over again in a truly exhausted voice, "I do not deserve this. I never deserved this."

A waterfall of tears fell on the marble as Mary disappeared to the second floor. As the bedroom door slammed above her head, Leah could swear the last words her mother said were, "And you don't deserve this either."

———

The wind at JFK was cold. As Leah stepped out of the limo, the gusts whipped through her jacket and pierced her skin with its unforgiving needles of sleet. It reminded her of the world of the self-proclaimed Devil, Aleister Crowley, when she and Gareth had made their way to a sub-zero house on the shores of Loch Ness to hunt their very first monster.

Taking a deep breath, Leah closed her eyes and willed the image of her mother's devastated face from her mind. She couldn't even fathom the pain and fear she'd seen swimming in Mary's eyes, but the shock was still sitting in Leah's stomach like a ball of iron. She'd wanted nothing more than to reach out and pull her into a hug—tell her she was sorry for the horrible words that they'd exchanged with each other . . . but she couldn't. Leah could tell her mother was too far gone to hear her apology if it was voiced, let alone accept it. It was as if the woman had been stuck in some horrific nightmare, unable to wake up.

Leah grunted. She couldn't blame her. After all, that's exactly what this was . . . a nightmare.

She tried not to notice the woman staring at her with confusion still blazing in her eyes. Yes, she felt bad for Anippe and knew she was searching for some explanation as to what had happened back in the house, but Leah held no answers to this strange day. She had no idea why her mother had attacked a stranger so viciously. So she chose to remain silent.

Suddenly the flutter of happiness that was like an eternal flame inside Leah's soul burst to life when Gareth appeared in her line of vision. Putting down his cell phone that was probably filled with more data and contacts than the President's, Gareth offered a sly smile that could have the entire female population falling to their knees.

Making his way over, he kissed her on the cheek. "Everything's all set to go."

"Private jet, Daddy Warbucks?" Leah smiled.

"Sort of." Gareth winked.

"So tell me," Leah began, as she and Anippe followed behind him. "How exactly are we standing here, on the tarmac no less, in one of the most protected airports in the world without having to pass any security checkpoints whatsoever? You own JFK too, is that it?"

He sent her a look over his shoulder. "Security? Do I *look* like a terrorist?"

"Looks can be deceiving," she reminded him.

Leah spotted a pair of baggage handlers sneaking cigarettes and basically looking as if they wanted to be anywhere but where they were. Slowly but surely, taking care not to slide and fall face first on the ice, their group rounded the corner of the very large terminal.

Anippe immediately gasped at the sight that met her eyes. "Is that what I think it is?"

Leah stared over Gareth's shoulder toward the object that'd turned Anippe's eyes into sapphire saucers, and before she knew it, the laughter burst from her throat. Doubled over, tears running down her cheeks, Leah could barely speak. "No…way… No WAY is that the fucking Concorde!"

Gareth turned to her with a twinkle in his eye; he looked like a young boy who'd just scored his very first touchdown. "Of course it's not," he replied with a grin. "Even *I* don't have that much money. This is my own creation; however, I had some alterations made to it after our first adventure together. I had a feeling that with you by my side, Ms. Tallent, that speed would be of the essence."

"For you to make a quick getaway?"

"Actually, I assumed you would try that…not that I'd let you go."
He winked. "It does have all the bells and whistles of the Concorde
though, yet not an original I'm sorry to say."

Leah shook her head, wiping the frozen tears from her eyes. "I
have to know . . . exactly how much money does it take to build an
exact replica of the Concorde?"

"You don't want to know," he shook his head and laughed.

Anippe broke through their banter; her voice was filled with
wonder. "This is spectacular."

Gareth grinned. "I had it modeled after the Alpha Delta, which
made the fastest Atlantic crossing ever. It took just two hours and
fifty-three minutes, or something like that."

Anippe's eyes grew wider. "It really is unbelievable."

The trademark grin of satisfaction appeared on his handsome
face. "If you have enough money, Anippe, you can create almost
anything." Clapping his hands together, he bowed at the waist. "Shall
we board, ladies? We're wasting time."

Anippe walked past him, offering a look of pure awe at the
incredible man.

Picking up her bag, Leah shook her head and followed. Kissing
Gareth on the cheek, she smiled wide. "You're something else,
Lowery."

"Why thank you, Ma'am." Bending down, he took the suitcase
from her hands. "I'm digging my own grave, though."

"How's that?"

Wrapping his arm around her waist, he led her to the red-
carpeted staircase. "If I keep doing all these amazing things, I'm
gonna run out of miracles one of these days. How will I possibly
impress you then?"

Leah's voice grew serious, "Sweetheart, you are a miracle."

The kiss was passionate, melting Mother Nature's strong attempt
at making them freeze. Leah was still astounded that the feelings
they shared were so strong that they were almost surreal, making
the world around them and the problems pressing down on their
shoulders absolutely disappear.

Anippe cut through their moment of bliss and shouted from
the top of the stairs, "We have to go!"

Pulling away, Leah let out a sigh. "She's a nice woman and all, but extremely annoying."

Gareth laughed. "Actually, she reminds me of you a bit."

"What?"

He held up his hands in mock surrender. "I only said a bit."

Leah grunted and walked up the stairs. "It's just the eyes."

The wind delivered his magnificent voice to her ears, "No . . . it's more than that."

———

As they stepped into the luxurious plane, Leah let out another deep, rich laugh. Circling around them were four attendants . . . male attendants. Each extremely handsome, they smiled wide and welcomed her aboard.

A lovely young man who looked like he should be on the cover of *People's, Sexiest Man Alive* issue, stepped forward immediately. "Good morning, Mr. Lowery."

Gareth smiled and looked at Leah. "Stewardesses seem to rile you up, so I thought these guys would make the trip more bearable."

Leah kissed him hard on the lips. "You're everything."

"And smell that?" he whispered.

Taking a deep breath, the strong, rich scent of very real, very extravagant coffee hit her brain. Her stomach began to do a happy dance as Leah clapped her hands. "Real coffee?"

Gareth shrugged. "Well, I do try to think of everything."

Leah beamed as Gareth followed the young steward down the aisle to introduce himself to the pilot and get the show on the road.

Anippe stared at his retreating figure. "You are a lucky woman. He loves you very much."

Hearing the strangely somber tone ring out in the woman's voice, Leah replied, "I am lucky. Wasn't even looking and then—'boom!'—there he was." She smiled, remembering the actual 'boom!' that exploded in the basement of her beloved library where she'd discovered the handsome miracle-worker digging up history from inside the cornerstone that Andrew Carnegie had put in place. It seemed so long ago, that moment. Even though it'd been barely anytime at all that she and Gareth had been together, Leah felt as if they'd already lived two lifetimes with all the adventure, excitement and sheer danger they'd faced.

Anippe slowly nodded as tears appeared in her eyes. "I thought William was the one for me."

"The nice man who tried to kill me? Who tried to kill *you*?"

Anippe's voice grew soft and sad, "I was taken in."

"Sorry," Leah sighed, seeing the loss and loneliness register on Anippe's face. "I'm not exactly what you would call a comfort friend. I don't even have any female friends, really. Just ask Skylar. She's a fellow librarian who works with me and wishes she didn't. She'd be more than happy to tell you what a sarcastic pain in the ass I am, so please don't take me personally."

Anippe remained silent. Her sapphire eyes stared into Leah's.

Suddenly nervous, Leah shifted in her seat. "William Knight was a jerk, Anippe. But that's not your fault; there are thousands of them. Gareth can be a jerk, too . . . if that makes you feel any better."

"But he would never hurt you."

Her statement sounded more like a question to Leah, and she gave her an odd stare. "No. I don't think he would. Not without help, anyway."

Anippe turned away, staring out the window at the dark sky filled with threatening clouds of snow and sleet. "Everyone's tempted."

Leah thought on that for a moment. "I suppose. Everyone has their Achilles' heel, but females aren't Gareth's."

Anippe turned slowly to face her. "What is . . . do you think?"

"Why?"

"He seems too perfect." She shrugged. "It's hard to find a fault."

"What's yours?" Leah turned the tables on her, feeling more than a bit uncomfortable with her haunted voice.

"Love," Anippe answered immediately. "I have never had a family . . . someone to care for. It has just been my uncle and me for so long. My mother died when I was young and I do not remember her very well. I have this picture in my mind, but I know it must be wrong. My father died, as well. My uncle believes they were lost under an avalanche of rock when they were out on an expedition. Don't get me wrong, I love my uncle. He's a wonderful man, but I have lived a very lonely life."

Leah remained silent. She thought about her beloved basement in the New York Public Library, and how she would sit down there and enjoy her silent Sunday afternoons. She would make some coffee in the pot that looked like an ancient artifact from a different time. There, she would while away the glorious hours reading the words of true artists. Being alone had never bothered Leah. In fact, with everything she'd gone through, she actually missed the solace of living in a world that made complete and utter sense; a place that was structured, reliable and safe. She certainly didn't want to ever lose Gareth, but there was a part of her that strongly wished she was back in her comfortable basement, safe and sound,

Anippe's voice broke through Leah's thoughts. "Your Achilles' heel is quite clear."

"Excuse me?"

"You crave knowledge. I have seen your brain work . . . how it pumps information. Watching you solve the puzzle in Cairo—finding Emmanuel, locating the Ark, making the right choice with the words of the Son—it was spectacular from a bystander's point of view. You are brave, but your mind is the true gift."

"You can never learn too much," Leah stated.

"Perhaps you can." Anippe disagreed. "Although, in your case knowledge has helped you and your hero survive. And your hero is certainly courageous. He is also very smart, although he bows to your brilliance. You make a good team." Her voice faded as the last statement slid from her lips.

"Gareth craves the adventure, I think. He believes that it's his destiny to find the truth. Maybe he thinks he can save the world." Leah shrugged. "Who knows? Maybe he can."

"He's certainly proven himself worthy. There are very few genuine people in this world, and you're honest with one another. That's the key." Anippe laid her head back on the soft-as-butter leather and closed her eyes. "Just continue to always be honest with each other."

Leah moved her gaze up the aisle and watched Gareth saunter toward her with the largest mug of coffee she'd ever seen, and sighed happily.

Offering a big smile, he handed it to her. "Your beverage, my lady."

Placing it on the tray, Leah pulled him down to sit in the chair beside her and wrapped her arms around his neck. "I love you. You know that, right?"

His face turned into a mask of confusion. "As a matter of fact, I do know that. And . . . I love you right back."

She smiled. "Good. As long as we're on the same page."

His laughter was deep and intoxicating. "Do you honestly think I'd spend millions to create a Concorde for just anyone?"

Her eyes grew wide. "*Millions?*"

Gareth waved his hand in the air, as the four Rolls Royce engines of the magnificent aircraft roared to life. "Money is just a shadow in a cave, remember? You're the only real thing in my life."

Her heart exploded with emotion, mimicking the thrust of the plane as it shot from the strip like a bullet out of a rare gun. All she could think to do was send a prayer up to the heavens asking them to let the hero and his companion solve this one last puzzle in time to save her father's life.

CHAPTER 8

"She comes on gilded wing."

David Tallent stared at the sterling tray, attempting to ignore the wretched bald man standing by the large glass doors. The line of bright platters that lay before David were covered with silver domes, hiding the sustenance that he needed to stop his head from swimming. Although every time his captor opened his mouth, the craving for food went right out the window.

Aaron sat beside him completely silent. David could just make out the angry face mirrored in the polished dish. Their side-by-side images were contorted into hideous masks from a fun house mirror.

"Did you hear me, Herr Tallent?" The terse German accent reverberated in the air. It seemed so out of place in the luxurious room created for comfort . . . not pain.

David nodded. "I heard you."

"She's something . . . your daughter." The bald man continued, "I don't believe I've ever seen anyone who could solve a problem so quickly. She must be very intelligent. Like her mother, perhaps?"

David kept his mouth shut. There was a large part of him that'd prayed Leah wouldn't discover the map that he'd hidden away. He had prayed that his last seven days on earth would simply go by, extinguishing his life with no fanfare or fear. But, of course, his daughter had proven that there was nothing that could stop her brain from finding the answer. And, with Gareth Lowery by her side, he knew that there was no chance she'd stay away and let Fate takes its course.

David did thank the Lord for Lowery's presence, however. Perhaps he would figure it out first, considering what he'd once been searching for himself. Maybe he would understand what David had found and stop Leah from going any farther on the journey; convince her to turn the plane around and deliver her back to the safety of her precious library.

His wretched keeper interrupted his wishful thoughts. "I am wondering how she worked it out so quickly." The man reached up with his black glove and rubbed his head, as if he were polishing the bald spot so it would shine more brightly in the desert sun.

Aaron Cain finally spoke; his voice was full of anger and frustration. "I don't even know what's going on here, and neither does my daughter. This is obviously something between you and the Tallent family, so why am I here? I demand to be released."

Vicious laughter met his ears; a violent sound like a vampire stalking his next piece of flesh came from the man, as his beady, black eyes shone with an evil light. "You are Anippe's uncle, are you not? That is what she calls you. Why do you refer to her as your daughter?"

"I might as well be her father. I raised her!" Aaron's testimony was fierce, as though he could rip someone's head off for ever questioning his legitimacy for being Anippe's only family.

The man nodded; his voice transformed back to the false, polite tone. "And, if I may say, you did a wonderful job. But I needed young Anippe to bring something to Ms. Tallent in the states. I knew she had possession of the artifact, and I knew that Anippe understood what she needed to open it. Whatever was in that wreath will lead her to discover what I need. And when I get what I need, you can all go home. No hard feelings."

David Tallent snorted, "You're going to kill us."

"Why would I do that?" He walked forward and stood in front of the two angry men. "If you'd just told me what you knew back at your house I would have left you alone then, Mr. Tallent. But instead, you decided to hide the secret from me. Now, it's your daughter's life that hangs in the balance . . . not yours. You should feel an extreme amount of guilt for that."

David could feel Aaron's body tense beside him.

"You *know* what's going on?" Aaron clenched his fists and turned on David. "You *know* what they're after? Tell them!"

David remained silent.

The bald man stepped forward and lifted the small silver dome off the plate. David stared down at the bowl of black and green olives. The sour stench rose into his nostrils, and he raised his head to glare at the evil little man. "Who are you?"

He grinned. "You may call me . . . Max. That will be easy to remember. I've watched the Tallent clan for some time now; ever since 1972, in fact."

David felt the ball of fear form in his stomach. "What?"

Slamming his fist down on the table, Max shouted, "You are not the only ones who knew about it! All we needed was a place to start and your daughter found that. Anippe has brought it to her. I know she has. And together they will uncover the path that you were once too scared to walk."

"Tell me who you are!" David Tallent screamed back as he stood from the couch, ready to smash the man in the face no matter what the consequences would be. "What do you know about 1972?"

The door flew open, allowing the two tall, greasy guards to march into the room; their large guns were pointed directly at David's head.

Smiling, Max reached down and popped a ripe olive into his mouth. "I thought this would be a fitting appetizer for you. As the worthless French say, *Bon Appétit.*"

David's chest heaved with disgust, as the men walked out the door.

When the deadbolt was thrown, Aaron Cain turned on him. "What the hell did you mean by that? If you know what these morons are looking for tell them for crissakes so we can save the girls!"

"You don't understand," he replied, shaking his head in defeat.

"Oh, please!" Aaron yelled, "What is it? Some treasure you just *have* to have for yourself because you don't have enough already? You are risking your own flesh and blood!"

David released his rage, pushing against Aaron's chest as he knocked the man backwards with all his might. "You think I don't know that?!" Picking up the silver dish, he threw it across the room. The plate slammed against the window sending olives scattering across the carpet like foul-smelling raindrops.

"You don't understand," David repeated. "What I know . . . I have to keep away from them. If the pieces of the puzzle are brought together it could be catastrophic."

"What are you talking about?" Aaron rolled his eyes. "Overdramatic as usual."

"These men are after very explicit items which, when brought together, could literally bring about a massacre. I didn't understand until the night they took me from my home. I thought I'd uncovered an ancient treasure—*one* ancient location." David stopped and looked at Aaron's hard gaze. "You wouldn't believe me if I told you. Let's just hope Leah doesn't figure it out. Or if she does, let's hope she leaves the other items right where they are."

"You're not making any sense." Aaron sighed deeply. His eyes were filled with pain, showing David how much he needed to understand; how much he wanted to figure everything out before his beloved Anippe was harmed in any way.

Throwing himself on the couch, he dropped his head in his hands. "Leah will figure it out, David. And she will come. I've never seen such determination in a person before. Well . . . maybe once." He lifted his head and gazed out the window. "But Leah won't give up and she won't walk away."

"I know." David nodded. "But maybe the man with her will understand the artifacts that are at each site and leave at least one behind. If one is not brought here, the rest will be useless. The power will only come from them if they are placed together . . ." he shook his head and sighed, "And that power will be impossible to stop."

"And these . . . artifacts? You know what they are used for, and where they are located?"

"I found all but one," David replied. "The one I was looking for back in '72 is still a mystery. It remained beyond my grasp." His voice turned into a whisper of fear, "I found out what it could be used for and I pray that it's already been destroyed. I believe I found its location, but I could never find out if I was right. I was missing . . . something."

David turned and stared at Aaron. "Something that Anippe obviously had with her at the Coptic Museum. Whatever that was is most likely the clue that pinpoints where to begin. Without it, Max and his goons had nowhere to go. If Leah begins the journey she'll end up giving them exactly what they needed—the place to start."

"What do they want this stuff for?"

David swallowed. "Whoever owns these things will possess a power unlike anything that you've ever seen."

Aaron leaned forward and stared up at the desperate man. "How do they know about 1972? Max seemed awfully smug about that little nugget of information."

David stared at the carpet. His eyes followed three large olives that led to the glass doors, like an arrow pointing the way. "I don't know. Let's take one nightmare at a time.

CHAPTER 9

"Ouch!" Leah screamed when the large group of children raced by and smashed her foot into the ground.

Gareth laughed as Leah seethed, "Must they allow these little monsters to go everywhere?"

Anippe smiled as she, too, sidestepped the herd of tourists who were roaming the Athens Acropolis. "They are only children, Leah. They, too, have the right to be educated in regard to humankind's history."

"Bullshit!" Leah stated, feeling the burning pain in her toes. "They don't want to be educated. They want to touch things, move things and destroy. Look at the faces of the guides, if you don't believe me!" She pointed at the tour guides dressed in mauve that were barely holding on to their masks of civility in order to get their paycheck at the end of the week. Their smiles were stretched taut across their red faces, watching in agony as the tourists manhandled everything they saw—wiping their grubby hands on true artifacts that were irreplaceable.

Gareth couldn't help his continuous stream of laughter. "I'll admit, they don't look very thrilled."

"Come on." Anippe waved at them, forcing the duo to follow her through the entrance in order to join the next tour. "Hopefully they'll tell us something that will help lead us in the right direction."

Pulling on Gareth's arm to stop him, Leah pointed toward a

group of senior citizens waiting patiently to begin. "I want to go with them."

Nodding, Gareth smiled at the small group of elderly people with cameras hanging from around their necks. Not a child in sight. "Anippe!" he called after the practically speeding woman. "Over here. We're going with these guys!"

Sighing, Anippe moved away from the large family gathering with the pack of squealing children, and rolled her eyes at Leah. "You're being a little ridiculous about this."

"I detest children," Leah said. "Obviously I've hidden my feelings on this subject really, really well. I'll make sure not to be my 'oh-so-subtle' self in the future."

Gareth immediately brought up the subject of Mary—Leah's newly acquired pen pal from France. "That's not true. You do like one child."

Leah thought about the little ten-year-old girl whose life she'd saved back in the basement of Chartres. "Yeah, well, jury's still out."

Letting the point rest, Gareth watched the guide raise her hand for silence so they could begin the tour of one of the most wondrous sites ever created.

"As you walk through the Propyla," the guide began, "you are entering the Acropolis, which is a fortified hill that was home to statues and temples dedicated to the Greek gods and goddesses. Many of the original buildings were destroyed during the Persian War, but the citizens of Athens chose to rebuild the roads and temples. Speaking of which, to your right is the *Temple of Athena Nike*, erected to honor Athena, the bringer of victory. 'Victory' means Nike in Greek . . . which fit the Goddess well."

The guide brought all eyes forward. "In front of you, during the time of Plato and Socrates, sat the statue of *Athena Promachos*. Extremely gigantic, the statue was said to be over thirty feet high and could be seen by all the ships at sea. Crafted of ivory and gold, this was yet another Greek tribute to Athena, for the work she did fighting for and protecting Promachos—which is, of course, the name for Athens."

Leah let out a low whistle as she glanced around at the other ruins, and whispered to Gareth, "Gonna' be hard to narrow this down if every building was dedicated to her."

Taking her hand, Gareth replied, "We'll get there."

On past the Chalcothece they wandered, searching the exterior for possible clues, as the learned guide explained how the building was used long ago as a storehouse for bronze artifacts that were offered to Athena by her people.

Leah took note of how well the woman bypassed the huge, well-known Parthenon in order to continue the group's circle of the Acropolis. She supposed the guide was saving that building—what most would consider the best part—for the grand finale.

She listened carefully as sanctuaries that were dedicated to entities other than the beloved Athena were finally introduced. Thankfully, Leah was able to begin deleting at least some of the historic sites off the list she was keeping in her mind of places she'd need more information about in order to figure out their next steps.

The tour guide was well-versed and the group was polite and listened attentively, allowing Leah to soak in the data and block out the noisy chatter of the group of children who were now in the 'complaining' mode. Their small voices wafted across the ancient ruins so loud and clear that Leah was sure they were disturbing the sleeping gods. She rolled her eyes. A part of her truly wished that Poseidon would rise out of the sea with mighty trident in hand and put them all in a time out.

Trying to shake the mean thoughts, Leah took in the breathtaking sanctuary of the mighty Zeus, as well as the lesser-known temples dedicated to Asclepius, the son of Apollo and God of Medicine; Artemis, the protector of women about to give birth; and Pandion, the father of Erechtheus.

Following the tour guide's instructions, their group finally came to a halt before the steps of the incomparable Parthenon. Her commanding voice turned almost reverent as she began her memorized speech: "Of course, you all know what this building is. The Parthenon has stood in this ancient spot since 438 B.C. Pericles ordered the monument to be erected and it took ten years to rise from the Acropolis. Underneath the base are two earlier temples to Athena that were destroyed by the Persians.

"Pericles told the architects that he wanted the Parthenon to

AMY LIGNOR

be built in Athena—the Virgin's—honor. Here, it would sit atop the Acropolis for all Athenians to see. The temple was built at the height of the Athenian power when they were not only regarded as the heart of Greek defense, but also master over all the Greek States. They even moved the wealth of the Greek league into this temple and placed it in the back chamber called the, *opisthodomos.* That was where the treasury resided.

"Now, the larger room inside the stunning Doric temple was where Ictinus and Callicrates sculpted the statue we spoke about. The huge figure was plated with over forty talents of pure gold which, of course, could be removed if there was a financial need that Athens simply couldn't meet." The guide stopped and looked over her shoulder as if the Goddess, herself, would still be there looking back. "I am told that Athena was a stunning sight to see."

Leah climbed the front steps and watched the guide stare up through the roof of the idyllic monument. It was as if she had become unaware of the great holes in the building or the ruins that surrounded her feet. Her face was a mask of pure joy, as if she was staring up into the actual golden face of the Virgin who had long since disappeared.

The guide continued in an almost haunted tone, "She held her mighty spear in one hand and her shield in the other. Her helmet rested upon her head; a helmet that when worn by Athena had the power to make her invisible to all eyes. This power was very useful, allowing Athena to sneak up on Athens enemies and destroy them."

Anippe's voice suddenly rose over the almost sermon-like speech, "I heard that a snake sat beside her feet."

Turning back to the present, the woman looked at the source of the interruption, and smiled. "Yes. I am told that the serpent, which was seen as the 'Enlightenment of Mankind' by the Greeks, was always by Athena's side. In an old myth, in fact, a young man named Tiresias stumbled on Athena while she was bathing. She was so beautiful that he was immediately struck blind—a curse sent down by the gods. That was his punishment for a mortal seeing a sight that not even the gods were allowed to partake of. But Athena was troubled by this sentence and sent her trusted serpent to lick the man's ears, giving him the gift of prophecy. He became a great man in his time because of the gift of a different kind of 'sight' that Athena had bestowed upon him."

Anippe simply nodded, as Leah stared into the tour guide's face. The middle-aged woman was illuminated by the sun beating off the marble columns, which seemed to infuse her tired limbs with both youth and peace. Leah began to wonder if the goddess Athena had the power to make the whole world beautiful, and somehow stop the horror of war and terrorism from escalating any further.

Pulling her gaze away, Leah stared up at the frieze that ran in a continuous line around the exterior wall. She followed the broken and battered tiles, watching a picture unfold of a procession that included both horses and people carrying baskets and gifts around the building's façade.

The guide must have followed Leah's focus, because her mouth soon opened and the information Leah wanted flowed from her lips like rain from a cool, refreshing cloud. "Above your heads, if you follow it around the building, there are one hundred and twelve plaques depicting the Panathenaia. This was the Athenian's most important festival that honored their patron deity."

She pointed over the edge of the Acropolis to a small dirt road that wound its way around the ancient hill. "They would walk down the Panathenaic Way to the Acropolis. Maidens came first with their offerings, then priests, attendants, matrons—followed closely by men carrying olive branches as a symbol of both ability and intelligence. At the end of the line came the armed warriors and the cavalry. They all brought with them gifts for the great Athena."

The woman suddenly stopped. Her face flushed, as if she was now embarrassed by her over exuberance for a mythical being. Changing her tone back to that of an uninterested guide who was looking for nothing more than a paycheck, her words came quickly as she waved her hands in the air and walked down the steps. "Feel free to take any pictures you like. We'll conclude our tour here."

Moving quickly, Leah followed the woman and left Gareth and Anippe to stare up at the frieze for any clue that might lead them to the treasure of Athena.

"Excuse me?" Leah yelled at the woman's retreating back. "Ma'am? Excuse me? May I have just a word?"

The guide suddenly turned on her heel, and Leah plowed directly into her. "Sorry," she mumbled, as she tried to regain her balance.

The woman winced from the pressure of Leah's boots on her toes, but tried to cover her face with the smile that was obviously taught to her a long time ago. "It's fine. I hope you enjoyed the tour."

"I did, but—"

"It's over," she snapped, causing Leah to take a step back.

"I understand," she replied just as quickly, trying to maintain what little communication skills she possessed. "It's just that . . . I'm a librarian with the New York Public Library." The guide's face remained a mask of annoyance so Leah hurried on, "I know exactly how you feel about these tours. All these people touching stuff . . . I can sympathize."

As she heard her own tone fill with sarcasm, the guide offered a small smile that pulled at the corners of her mouth. "It's like they think they're at the local zoo or something. No respect at all," Leah added.

The woman nodded her head in agreement.

"A library is my church, you see," Leah continued, trying to find common ground that would perhaps urge the guide to speak more about the Goddess that seemed to be holding the reigns of Leah's life. "It's a precious monument that someone built to teach the world. It's not to be manhandled by those who don't have the intellectual capacity of an . . . olive branch."

Suddenly the woman burst into laughter at Leah's haughty tone. "My name is Katarina," she said, putting out her hand in greeting. "But you may call me Khait."

"Leah," she replied, extending her hand. The woman's grip was hard and spoke volumes about the strength and pride she possessed for everything from her job to her beloved city. "You wore the same look of peace I do when I walk up the stairs of my library. When I pass the lions—Patience and Fortitude—I feel as if I'm entering some Divine home. I know every crack and every speck of dirt that's in there."

Khait folded her arms across her chest and the women began to walk together around the Parthenon, avoiding the children with every precise step.

"I saw the same look on your face when you talked about Athena. You sound like an expert, which is why I would like to ask some questions. I would truly like to know more about the goddess," Leah said.

"Can you not get all that information from the books in your library?" She smiled wide.

"Touché," Leah chuckled. "The facts are there, I'll give you that. But I would like to know about Athena from a loyal servant of Greece, not some author who basically didn't pay attention to anything but the children brought along on the family vacation."

Khait smiled wide and let her hands fall to her sides. "There is so much," she sighed.

"Start anywhere you like." Leah lied, "I'm in no hurry."

Khait grinned. "Well . . . in ancient Greek mythology, Athena was the representation of Eve. Mythology basically tells the same story as the Bible, with the one exception being that the serpent in mythology was the enlightener not the deceiver. But it does not go against the Word of God. In fact, if one truly reads all the Greek stories about the Great Flood, they will see that it directly correlates with Noah. As with many Christian tales, there is a Geek myth that actually reinforces the Scripture because they were told long before the Bible ever came into being."

Leah nodded, remembering that information from one of Kathryn's speeches. "But what about the Goddess, herself? What was she like? Where did she come from?"

"She came from the brain of her father," Khait replied. "It is said that she sprang full-grown from the head of Zeus. She was his valiant warrior daughter and carried his shield, the Aegis, in her hands. She was first called *Pallas*, which means 'the maiden of Athens' and was untouchable by Man. Her spear was infused with the power of the gods and her serpent was her eternal guardian."

Leah listened intently, trying to locate anything within Khait's words that would lead her to find the first clue on the map that was in regards to 'the seed of the warrior.'

"People said that Athena was bright-eyed," Khait continued. "She had gleaming sea-gray eyes, but when she was at war, they turned sapphire blue." Stopping, she offered Leah a smile. "Like yours. I can honestly say I have never seen sapphire eyes before. Perhaps you are a relation of Athena and that is why you have so much interest in the subject?"

Leah tried to hold in her snort. Moses is family so, *sure*, why not Athena? Leah could definitely see a mental asylum in her future. "So why is Athena called the Hero's Companion?"

Khait nodded appreciatively. "You have done some research, I see. Well, it refers to the story of Athena and one of her sisters . . . Medusa."

"The creepy chick with snakes for hair?"

"That description was in a book?" Khait laughed.

"*Clash of the Titans*, actually," Leah said with a shrug. "My significant other has a thing for movies. I end up having to watch at least two a week now."

Khait gazed up at the bodies milling around on the cracked and broken stairs of the Parthenon. "The handsome man with the bright green eyes?"

"You're very observant."

"He is difficult to miss."

Following her gaze, Leah had to agree. In the stream of light that lit his dark blond hair like a golden halo, Gareth was almost a mirror image of a valiant Greek god coming home to roost. All he had to do was take off his shirt and Leah knew there would be a female riot that would rival anything the Persians had ever thrown at Athens.

Khait kept her smile and continued, "Medusa was supposedly just as lovely as Athena. Therefore, Athena made Medusa what she became—a hideous creature who could turn men to stone with just one look. Athena was the one who banished Medusa to the Land of the Grey Women. In that place lived three very shriveled and withered old crones. Some believe they were all Athena's sisters and the Goddess had just gotten them out of the way. After all, she *was* firstborn—the powerful daughter of Zeus—and she was allowed to do most anything she wanted."

"Can't blame her. I've thought about putting my sisters on an island," Leah mumbled, thinking about the gorgeous triplets back home.

"I'm glad I'm not a member of your clan," Khait chuckled. "Anyway . . . a young man named Perseus went to kill Medusa but he had no idea how it could be done. He was aware of the fact that long before his sword could penetrate the scales on her flesh, she would be able to turn him to stone. That's when Athena appeared and handed him her polished bronze shield. Perseus held it out in front of him and walked toward Medusa. You see, just the reflection off the shield could not turn him; only a direct hit from Medusa's eyes would bring him down. With the help of Athena, Perseus killed the mighty Gorgon and cut off her head. Athena then placed the head within her shield, forever carrying it with her.

"But she helped more warriors than just Perseus along the way. There are many stories about Athena, and every hero she assisted spoke of her greatness, her wisdom, and her extreme cunning at being able to take down unstoppable foes."

"I wish she was here," Leah sighed. "There seems to be quite a number of those nowadays."

Khait's face grew serious; her tone turned sad. "I agree. The world needs the Hero's Companion to live again. Unfortunately," she continued, with a small laugh, "I think you have to find a real hero first for her to help. Most of them have gone the way of the Dodo bird."

Leah remained silent, knowing that a true hero was right now standing on the Parthenon's steps doing everything in his power to find her beloved father.

The sun glinted off a small temple in the distance and Leah shaded her eyes from the newfound glare. Focusing, she noticed the odd row of tall, marble women staring back at her. "What's that one? That wasn't on the tour."

"That is the Erechtheion," Khait replied. "That temple played home to the most amazing battle in all of Greek history. However, we do not lead people there."

"Why not?"

Khait shrugged. "Much like your Divine objects, that temple is a true site we wish to keep from other's grabbing hands. Without that building, you see, the world wouldn't even know what olives are."

CHAPTER 10

Hope suddenly shot through Leah's heart. "Um . . . I thought the mighty showdown between Poseidon and Athena was in the Parthenon?"

"You've heard of it?" Khait's eyebrows rose in amazement.

"A little," Leah shrugged, searching the card catalogue that was just waiting to spit out the facts she needed. "Athena gave an olive and Poseidon offered a spring, or something like that."

Khait laughed. "Well, there is a bit more to it than that. Our history is actually quite deep, Leah. As a librarian you should be ashamed."

Offering the warmest smile she could produce from the depths of her exhausted soul, Leah bowed her head and tried to cover the impatient sarcasm that always seemed to leak from her lips. "You tell me, then. That way, I'll know."

Another laugh came from the knowledgeable guide as she finally led Leah toward the strange looking building. "This was an old temple that sat between the Erechtheion and the Parthenon at one time. Of course, both were dedicated to Athena; although, in the Erechtheion, they also celebrated Poseidon and Erechtheus. Inside the temple they placed a statue of Athena made out of wood. This was not carved or made by human hands. The Athenians believed that the likeness had fallen from the sky and had been given to them by Zeus for protection.

"When the Persians came and destroyed the city, they supposedly walked into the Erechtheion and found this coveted statue missing. Many Athenians told the invaders that the Goddess had already abandoned the citadel, making the Persian Army believe that Athena had come to life and flown away before the fight."

"I thought she was the protector of the city?" Leah asked. "Not very valiant to fly away from the town when it's falling into the hands of a vicious army." She stopped quickly, seeing Khait's clearly angry expression, and raised her hands in the air. "No offense."

Khait took a deep breath and offered a small smile, like that of a mother attempting to explain something to her poor, dimwitted daughter. "Athena *had* flown to the 'wooden wall' of Athens, which was another name for the line of ships that made up the Athenian fleet, which sat in the harbor. After she had gone there, the Athenians were victorious and the city was saved."

"Convenient."

Khait blatantly ignored her sarcastic tone. "Quite."

"So did the magic wooden statue ever fly back into the temple?"

"No," Khait sighed. "The statue was never found again. But, as I have said, they later created a huge gold and ivory statue that scared away any and all would-be invaders from Athens shores."

Leah wondered how much time these old writers and philosophers had on their hands, considering the millions of amazing 'feats' they wrote about and then attributed to their gods and goddesses.

Stopping in front of the odd-looking temple, Leah stared at the awesome porch. Six beautiful women stood stoic staring out at the remarkable Acropolis before them. Their heads supported the weight of the porch's roof, and their blank eyes seemed to gaze at Leah with interest as she moved closer.

"The Porch of the Maidens," Khait's soft voice broke through Leah's thoughts. "They're supposedly placed in the exact spot where Athena disappeared. It is said that they step inside their home every morning to pay homage to the holy place where Athena used to reside."

Leah stared through the dark entrance, hoping to see a big neon sign with an arrow blinking that read, 'Solution Here! Solution

Here!'

"Actually, we know hardly anything about the interior rooms."

"Why's that?"

"It is not safe to enter. But it is an intricate piece of work. In fact, it has quite a complex design because the builders had to take into account the particularly uneven patch of ground that it sits on. It's a very delicate temple, unlike the mammoth Parthenon. If we walk around back," Khait continued, waving Leah around on the side of the strange creation, "You can see that the north and west walls drop down much lower than the east and south sides."

Leah nodded as she stared at the strange base. It looked like a condo with a ground floor that'd been built underneath the rocky terrain instead of above it. She stared up at the frieze of tiles that bordered the roof. "This looks so much different than all the other temples."

Khait nodded. "No one actually knows the theme of the tiles or what story they're trying to tell. It is a puzzle to Athenians even today."

"A puzzle?" Leah caught the word and her eyes moved carefully across the white marble figures that'd been carved and then attached to the dark gray marble background. She stared at the maidens holding spears, shields and even large platters that had what looked to be olives carved into their flat surfaces.

She barely heard Khait speaking behind her. "There are testimonials written that say this building was once used for religious rituals, and was actually decorated with colorful paintings, gilded rosettes and many sculptures. It was once bright and cheery; immaculate in design and decoration like the cathedrals in your country."

Leah spoke up, "And the contest between Athena and Poseidon took place here?"

Khait nodded. "You have seen the side dedicated to Athena. Over here," she said, moving to the western face of the building, "inside this wall, is where you can supposedly see the spot where Poseidon's trident struck the stone during their competition."

"But I can't go inside?" Leah prodded, trying with all her might to make the woman toss away her rulebook. "I promise I won't touch anything."

"Not now." Khait shook her head sternly. "This building had more than one level at one time but it's been so badly damaged and rebuilt so many times that most of the original temple is only a memory. Unfortunately, no one possessed those lovely digital cameras back in Ancient Greece. It would have been nice to see what the original Acropolis truly looked like during its heyday . . . so to speak."

"Surely there would be no harm in just peeking?" Leah continued.

Khait stood her ground. "It was damaged almost beyond repair during the war. There was also a major fire that took out most of the interior. It served as a Christian basilica around the seventh century and they had to build new interior walls just to hold up the ceilings." She released a giggle. "They even say during the Ottoman Empire, the Erechtheion was used to house a harem, and they walled up the north porch to offer them . . . privacy."

Leah pointed to a large pit that sat beside the temple. "What's that hole from?"

"That was part of an archaeological dig. They found many statues and things from long ago that are now on exhibit at our museum. Would you like to go see them?"

Leah stared into the large, gaping crevice and wondered just how far it went underground . . . and where it ended. She thought back to Gareth's remarkable 'find' that'd been buried for thousands of years in an underground chamber right below the people's feet that were rushing through their normal, daily lives. "No thanks. We're going to the museum later," she replied. "You've been more than helpful though. I can't thank you enough."

She began to turn away, but Khait wasn't quite finished. "Poseidon struck his trident on the rock and a spring bubbled up from the desert floor. The people were very excited until they realized that the water was filled with salt from the sea. This made it undrinkable, of course, and unusable in any capacity for the growing of crops."

Leah nodded. "And Athena?"

Khait smiled. "Athena sank her spear in the ground and planted an olive which produced trees, foods, shade, timber and oil—which became the major export of Greece. The people were thankful for all the gifts that Athena had given to them."

"And Athens was born," Leah said softly. "You wouldn't think a tiny little olive would play such a large part in Greek history."

Khait shook her head. "Actually, olive groves are considered sacred ground here. At one time only chaste men and virgins were allowed to cultivate them."

"Seems a bit extreme," Leah said with a slight smile.

"I don't know." Khait tilted her head. "Unlike Athena, Eve ate a sacred object and gave it to Adam which caused them to be cast out of Paradise. At least Athena's people knew not to mess around with the power of the gods."

"Did Greek religion also offer its own Garden of Eden?"

Khait shook her head. "No, but we did have the Garden of the Hesperides. It belonged to Hera, the wife of Zeus, and the trees grew nothing but golden apples."

"Break a tooth on one of those."

Khait laughed at Leah's stream of dry comments, "They offered joy, wealth and happiness to good people. There were only two throughout history who stole from that garden, but Athena caught them and returned the apples to their sacred place. She believed that the apples were too powerful and too potent to fall into the hands of greedy, evil thieves, so she placed them back on the tree and warned others that she would defend the garden with her golden spear." Khait smiled. "No one messed with them after that."

Leah laughed with her. "Athena could see everything, huh? Good to be a Goddess."

"Makes sense, actually, considering that Athena was the first all-seeing eye."

Leah's heart sped up inside her chest at the woman's words. "I'm sorry?"

"She was the 'Eye in the Sky.' Athena, with the help of her trusty owl who could see all day and all night, watched over all of Athens."

"Was her symbol a sapphire eye, by chance?"

Khait shook her head. "No. Philosophers said it was a red eye as bright as a fiery sun. I believe Plato used it as a logo for his Academy in Athens, except he added her spear to the picture. If I remember correctly, it was to show the world the ultimate power that comes from the wisdom of the Goddess. Plato was the one who said that the name Athena meant 'the mind of God.' He admired her power and thought that everyone should exercise their brains first, like Athena always did."

"I thought she was known as a warrior?"

"She was," Khait agreed. "But Athena combined her skill and her strength with her unending wisdom in order to make sure that all avenues were exhausted before choosing the path that led to violence and battle. It is what made her a truly great warrior. Therefore, for her weapons to work, one would also have to possess the wisdom to understand and the skill to choose when it is the right moment to fight."

Leah smiled. "Well . . . knowledge is power. That's what I always say."

"Again, like Athena." Khait smiled. "It is too bad the sacred olive is gone from Athens. Perhaps, in your hands, you could work some magic and bring back the heroes—aid them in stopping wars before our world disappears completely."

Leah felt her throat constrict as she stared into the woman's deep brown eyes. "So . . . no one knows what happened to this famous olive?"

Khait shrugged. "Some say Poseidon took it. Others say Athena buried it so that no one would get a hold of its power."

"What power would an old, icky olive have?" Leah asked. "The thing would just be disgusting now."

Khait's eyes grew wide. "It is a sacred object, Leah. I told you that. It is a seed that grows actual miracles."

Feeling the cold sweat erupt on her forehead, Leah quickly shook Khait's hand and thanked her for the excellent history lesson. Turning away, she marched across the Acropolis and made sure not to look back at the strange temple she now needed to get inside of.

Walking quickly up the broken marble steps, Leah grabbed Gareth's shoulder and turned him back toward the entrance. "We need to go."

Anippe jumped at the sound of her voice. "But I think we can figure out these pictures," she said, pointing up at the large frieze of the processional walking around the Parthenon. "Leah, we can't leave here without the Seed of the Warrior."

Leah grabbed her hand, and growled, "Be quiet, for crissakes. If someone overhears you they'll drag us all off to a funny farm so fast it'll make your head spin."

Her brows furrowed. "Funny farm?"

Leah sighed. "It's an American expression. It means you'll be in a straight-jacket by dusk."

Allowing herself to be led across the Acropolis, tears immediately formed in Anippe's bright blue eyes. "My uncle . . . your father."

Not listening, Leah marched under the archway of the ancient gate and glanced back over her shoulder. The wary eyes of Khait were closely observing the group's hasty retreat.

"You know where it is," Gareth whispered.

Leah nodded. "I know which temple it's in, but I don't have any idea how we're going to find the damn thing."

His comforting arm snaked around her waist and his soft voice echoed in her ears, "The gods will help us."

Leah shivered once again under the setting sun. "Uh, huh. Let's just hope the *Goddess* doesn't get mad about it."

CHAPTER 11

Leah felt humbled when she walked through the dark circular theater located at the bottom of the Acropolis. She could barely believe that she was standing in the exact spot where Plato once stood, regaling the crowd with his tale of a lost city in the middle of the sea.

This stage, the Theatre of Dionysus, was where he had once entertained by preaching his story of Atlantis and warning his own brethren not to make the same mistakes that the Atlanteans had—to not hold material wealth higher than utility, wisdom and brotherly love.

Leah remembered her father reading Plato's words to her; the legend of Atlantis—a glorious city where everyone had lived in peace and harmony. Together, the Atlanteans had cultivated the land, raised their animals, and lived off the rich, fertile earth provided by nature. And even though these people had been surrounded by mountains that held gold and silver by the truckload, they hadn't cared. They lived blissfully unaware of the evils that fortune wrought, not requiring or missing the luxuries that wealth could provide.

But then . . . strangers traveled to their shores and the Atlanteans had let them in. The rest of the world had heard about this 'paradise' and wanted it for their very own. They came by the shipload, and the Atlanteans had accepted them with a smile. But the visitors had no desire to work the fields; they simply wanted to eat all that was there. They had no desire to build houses; they simply wanted to be provided with amazing and comfortable lodging. And when they'd stared up at the mighty temple that'd been built in the center of Atlantis, their mouths had watered over its bronze, gold and silver walls. They couldn't believe that the silly natives didn't know what they had, and they began to explain what the Atlanteans were missing out on.

Slowly the people of Atlantis turned into capitalists just like the rest of the world's population, and paradise slowly transformed into a den of evil greed. Their god, Poseidon, became angry when he saw the land dry up and the untended animals die. As the Atlanteans spent more time worrying about what they could buy with their gold, they allowed the earth to be destroyed. So Poseidon sent earthquakes and floods to crush Atlantis, forever burying it under the sea.

Now here she was, perhaps standing right on the spot where Plato, thousands of years ago, had first told of the destruction of paradise—and the thought of that made Leah's heart race.

Gareth tripped and fell into a large stone bench, breaking Leah from her thoughts. "Damn!"

"Careful," she snickered. "Even though you look like a god, I have a feeling you don't want to become a permanent resident of this place."

"I'm too old to traipse through ancient ruins at midnight," Gareth growled.

"There's a cut-off age for that?" Leah chuckled. Keeping a watchful eye on the rocky hill in front of her, Leah climbed over row after row of stone benches; the seats that circled the theatre had been built in concentric rings to allow the audience room to enjoy the evening's artistry.

Listening to the swear words being whispered behind her as Gareth continued to trip his way up the hill, she finally reached the wall that surrounded the Acropolis. Leah stared through a large broken section, searching for the guards who certainly must patrol the ancient spot. She could see the bright lights illuminating the moonlit sky at the entrance. There, she knew, sat a booth that must be home to at least one guard.

Leah smiled to herself. If she wasn't a librarian, she'd probably make a good night watchman. Quiet job, relaxation, no one yapping—the job would be pure heaven. Besides this and lighthouse keeper, there weren't many of those left in the world.

Gareth whispered behind her, "I think we can get in through here." Crawling through the broken rock, his bright green eyes looked almost silver in the moonlight as he reached back through and lifted her to the other side.

As he pulled Anippe in and placed her down beside Leah, Gareth stared toward the small path that was lit up by the guardhouse. "There seems to be only one and he's fast asleep."

Leah smiled. She took a deep breath of the fragrant air; the spicy mixture of citrus and olive trees filled her nostrils. Before them, stood the imposing Parthenon that looked almost like a haunted mansion in the moonlight. The lunar rays seeped into the deep cracks and broken stones, making the jagged lines appear like evil grins in the marble façade.

Taking deep breaths, Leah walked around the building, averting her gaze from its slightly terrifying image. As the stealthy group walked around the corner, they saw the smaller temple that was barely exposed to the moon; sitting in the shadow of the Parthenon, the maidens were wrapped in darkness.

Walking forward, Leah stared up at the blank eyes of the women. In the dark they seemed to be asleep, just waiting for the brilliant golden sun to wake them so they could once again pay homage to Athena.

Leah walked slowly up the broken stairs behind Gareth and when they reached the top of the porch, Leah truly studied a maiden's face. Her head was turned, staring down at the intruders in her midst. Leah briefly wondered if the marble mouth would open and begin to scream for security to come and drag away the trespassers.

But the night remained still and quiet, as Gareth stepped over a wide line of dark gray tiles and through the pitch-black door, entering the inner sanctum.

Anippe let out a small yelp when Gareth suddenly sneezed

within the eerily quiet room; the sound seemed to echo off the walls like a yodeler on top of Heidi's famous mountain.

He offered a smile. "Don't worry. I don't think it was loud enough to wake the dead."

Leah could hear the creak of the marble door when Anippe shut it behind them. Her heart raced inside her chest and she reached out for Gareth, calming her nerves as she found his soft jacket in the darkness and held on for dear life. She practically jumped out of her skin when Anippe placed her quivering hand on Leah's shoulder, making sure that she, too, wasn't alone inside the black pit.

"Well," Leah said, nervously. "Talk about the blind leading the blind."

Hearing the click of the flashlight, Gareth illuminated the space with the harsh industrial beam.

"That's better," Leah exhaled.

A small sob came from behind her and Leah turned around, watching Anippe scan the room quicker than an Amtrak train crossing the railroad tracks. Desperation was prevalent in her voice, "There's nothing here."

Leah tried to smile. "I'm sure this isn't the only room. Khait said there was more than one level in this building."

"But they've rebuilt it over and over again," Gareth mumbled. "I would assume that if there was some sort of legendary olive inside this place, someone would have found it by now."

Leah had to agree. "Yeah, the smell of an ancient olive would be too hideous to ignore."

Anippe answered with nothing but a sniffle.

Hoping that the dim light covered the rolling of her eyes, Leah sighed. "Calm down. My father put this on the map for a reason so it must be here."

"But like you said," Anippe began. "Almost every temple in this place was dedicated to her. It could be buried anywhere on the Acropolis."

"No," Leah corrected. "This is where the competition was held which means this is where the people of Athens stored the olive. It's got to be here. We just have to look."

At Leah's command, Gareth moved forward into the small

empty space. The walls were bare, made of simple marble slabs that were covered with cracks and breaks, weathered over time by the heat of Athens' sun.

Leah tried to tiptoe across the floor, terrified of the creaking sounds that echoed beneath her feet. She slid her body between two large columns that'd separated from one another and looked around at the smaller chamber. Perhaps the renovators for the Basilica had boarded up this alcove long ago, choosing instead to use the much more spacious front room that would have received the light from the beautiful porch.

She could barely make out the feminine figures that were embedded in the tile walls. Heads were missing and the carved robes had been cut off at the knees. Yet Leah could see that the pattern remained the same; the familiar spear or shield was carved into the hands of each one of the young maidens.

Kneeling, she carefully inspected the floor and found . . . nothing. Getting more and more agitated, Leah began pressing her hands against the walls, silently hoping that perhaps a secret door would swing open to allow them access into another hidden level of the temple. Frustration and exhaustion overwhelmed her when absolutely nothing . . . no solution presented itself inside the empty chamber.

"Jesus!" Gareth's sudden shout made her blood run cold. She forced her body back through the columns to get to his side. "What's wrong?"

"You are not going to believe this!"

Leah scanned the dark chamber, following the bright beam of Gareth's flashlight, and her heart leapt into her throat. The high-pitched screech that suddenly erupted from the object made her body tremble. It was as if an evil trumpet had sounded, demanding the dead to rise from their graves.

Her mouth turned as dry as the sun-bleached sands of the Acropolis, as Leah focused on the form that was caught in the flashlight's glare. It barely moved. Only the dark eyes, growing wider as it tried to focus in the harsh light, gave it away.

"You have got to be kidding," Leah said in a confused whisper. "Athena's owl?"

Anippe's snort shot from her throat. "Athena's owl is most assuredly dead by now, Leah. This poor thing probably just flew in through one of the cracks and can't get back out."

As soon as the completely sane statement left her lips, the bird sent out a soft hoot into the room and its eyes immediately bathed the area in a cool sapphire light.

Leah swallowed hard, seeing the resemblance to the cave buried in the red rock of Petra. This owl's eyes glowed the exact same as the remarkable Sapphire Staff had when it'd hovered above the floor of the ancient crypt.

Immediately, Leah felt her knees bend and she fell to the floor, bowing before the owl like it was the first sign of the Second Coming.

Gareth silently sank to the floor beside her and bowed his head, following her lead.

Leah hissed at Anippe, "You have to show her honor."

The Egyptian woman stared at the strange owl that suddenly looked like something out of a science fiction movie. "But . . . it's a bird."

Reaching up, Leah grabbed her elbow and forced Anippe to her knees. "This is the place they worshipped her. You're standing in the most religious place in Athens so show some respect!"

"But . . . it's a bird."

Leah fought the urge to reach up and slap Anippe on the back of her head. It was as if her three sisters were kneeling beside her, bitching because their new designer clothes were being ruined by cobwebs and dust. Leah sighed. "The owl's on the map. Athena's owl has come home to tell us where to go from here."

"That's impossible," Anippe whispered.

Leah turned her head and allowed the sarcasm to leak from her lips, "You mean like me being related to Moses, or people who walk the world with all-seeing eyes tattooed on their hands getting into everybody else's business, or being attacked by a serpent that turns back into a staff, or Noah's Ark being in an underground chamber . . . with Noah still in it!"

Gareth spoke calmly, "Let's not scare the bird, ladies."

Leah brought her frustrated voice down to a whisper, "This

seems to be yet another one of those ironic moments where you need to suspend your disbelief, Anippe. God knows you've done it before. Oh . . . and shut up!"

"Hey!"

"It's moving," Gareth's announcement ended the female fight.

Leah raised her head and watched the small owl soar around the room. She followed the soft, blue beam as it raced through the columns into the inner alcove, then returned to the larger room. Suddenly it twisted in the air as gracefully as a ballerina and shot through a small crack in the front entrance.

Racing after it, Leah pushed the door open and stepped carefully out on the Porch of the Maidens. The owl sat there, perched on a finely-carved platter held by one of Athena's loyal attendants.

Staring into the soft, blue gaze, Leah remained silent. She wondered if Athena would now fall from the sky. Poking her head out from under the porch roof, she stared out into the moonlit night pleading for a spaceship to land, unload everybody's favorite goddess from Greek mythology, and unveil the exact way she could find and rescue her father.

But the small owl simply tilted its head and stared at her. Finally, he laid back his snow-white ears and let out another blood-curdling screech.

Leah stepped back, trying not to upset the tiny, yet ferocious-looking beast. She mumbled, "Sorry, I get it." Leah offered a penitent posture. "That's your dance space . . . this is my dance space."

The blue eyes grew wider, as the owl rose in the air and disappeared through a large hole in the porch roof.

Leah turned to Gareth. "Where'd it go?"

"You probably scared it away," Anippe snapped

Leah turned on her as Gareth held her by the shoulders. "I think we have to follow it," he said.

"Into the roof?" Leah's voice was filled with fear. She wondered how on earth she was supposed to climb *into* the monument. And, more importantly, if there was even enough space waiting in there for her to turn around and get back out.

"She's smaller," Leah huffed, pointing at Anippe's reed thin figure.

Gareth smiled; his straight, white teeth caught a ray of the silver moonlight. "You do have more of a figure, love," he said, as his gaze studied each and every curve.

Leah placed her hands on her hips. "Are you kidding?"

"I know, now's not the time." Gareth offered a slightly nervous laugh and switched gears. "I think the Goddess Athena wants to speak to *you*, Leah."

"I agree," Anippe chimed in.

Leah felt the heat rise in her cheeks as she offered the annoying woman an angry glare. "How convenient for you," she sighed. "Well, even death is better than dealing with her."

No longer wanting to deal with Anippe, Leah chose to place her hand around one of the carved maidens, praying that the ancient statue wouldn't crumble under her weight.

"They've survived wars, Leah. I doubt your one hundred and twenty pounds is gonna' hurt much," Gareth reminded her.

Leah snarled through her gritted teeth, "One eighteen, jerk off."

"My mistake," he said with a wink.

"Actually, in the brochure it said that the real Maidens are in the museum. These have only been here for a short time," Anippe added, haughtily. "So, they just might break. Who knows what these knock-offs are made of nowadays?"

Gareth turned to her. "You can go home at any time, you know!"

Anippe immediately stepped back. "I was just saying."

"Just . . . don't say anything," Gareth snarled.

Leah's heart sang in her chest as she listened to Gareth's frustration, but her muscles clenched in pain as she put her hands into the crevice. Moving from the Maiden statue, Leah hung from the roof for a moment, waiting for it to cave in and send her crashing to the rock-slab porch below. The line of dark gray tiles on the porch's floor looked like a river flowing far below her feet. But no cracking, no creaking—nothing at all happened from adding her extra weight. Only a little cloud of dust rained down on Leah's head as she pulled herself up into the small, dark hole above.

Filling her lungs with one last clean breath of the cool night air, Leah headed into the unknown.

CHAPTER 12

She could hear the soft cooing of the owl and focused on the blue light that beamed from its eyes. Flat on her stomach, Leah pulled her body slowly across the ragged rock. The cold stone slab pressed on her back, as if reminding her that if it did collapse the marble would flatten her like a pancake. Sweat poured off her forehead, and she wondered when the porch roof would crush her spine and make her a permanent statue on the ancient Acropolis.

Leah began to pant, inhaling the dry, sour air into her lungs. The horrible scent assaulted her nostrils. Was it simply rust, or was it the smell of infected blood that'd once poured from a vicious wound?

Swallowing her nausea, Leah closed her eyes and tried to make her head stop spinning. She began to pull her body as quickly as possible through the roof of the Erechtheion as the blue light grew dimmer and the owl's silhouette went missing from her sight. Leah pulled hard, scrambling to catch up with the bird, pleading with the creature not to leave her alone and helpless. The walls were closing in; the obnoxious scent was overpowering, and her mind froze as she suffocated under the claustrophobic weight. She tried to fill her lungs with air to shout out for Gareth, beg him to break open the ancient fortress to get her out.

But gravity suddenly entered the confines of her coffin and sent Leah's figure through a crack in the slab, down into the depths of the ancient building.

Her brain kicked into gear, as her arms and legs flailed in all directions. Reaching out, Leah tried to grab onto anything sticking out of the smooth rock walls that felt as if they were shooting past her.

A splinter pierced her skin, as Leah's body suddenly found the floor. Her muscles and joints cried out in pain as the sudden impact sent the breath rushing from her lungs.

Leah let out a shriek and then lay completely still. Her mind went into gear and worked quickly, assessing any damage that'd been done to her bruised and battered body. A line of warm blood ran down Leah's cheek; the side of her head pounded like a kettledrum, and her right leg felt like she'd been kicked repeatedly by a crowd of angry children that were sick of her comments.

Getting slowly to her knees, favoring the right side, Leah put her hand down on the hard-packed dirt and stood up carefully in the round room. She raised her chin and saw the large hole she'd left in the ceiling. "Someone's going to be really pissed off."

She shook her head, completely embarrassed that she'd broken a true relic from Ancient Greece. But as she stared at the wooden walls, Leah felt a little better. The cobwebs were literally undisturbed. Apparently, no one even knew about this room so hopefully no one would ever discover the mess Leah had made.

Another sudden yelp came from her throat when the owl suddenly reappeared and flew past her head; so close that the wind from its small wings whistled in her ear like a high-pitched siren. She glared at the blue-eyed bird, wanting with all her might to slap him off his perch by the wooden door.

The *wooden* door? Leah's heart skipped a beat as she saw the outline of an entrance cut into the dark, wood wall. The owl sat on the doorknob, tilting its head, staring at Leah as if he was wondering why on earth she was so blind.

She sighed. "I'm tired," she grumbled.

The owl moved so that Leah could pull down on the ancient handle. The door gave under the pressure of her sweaty hand, and creaked open. Stepping over the threshold into the tiny room Leah was reminded of a confessional; inside sat a medium-sized effigy and a small bench covered in red velvet.

Trying to make out her dark surroundings became difficult, when the owl landed on the effigy and its eyes turned black; the helpful blue glow was extinguished like a match.

Leah gave a heavy sigh. "Great. Now what?"

A bright light came from behind her and she turned around quickly, staring into what looked like a policeman's flashlight searching for her bloodshot eyes. She turned quickly back around and ended up slamming her knees into the small bench. "Look, I'm sorry," she began. "I didn't mean to break your roof."

Gareth's familiar laugh came out loud and strong inside the room as he aimed his flashlight at the ground.

"How did you—?"

Offering a sympathetic and somewhat guilty look, Gareth pointed at the back wall of the wooden well. A door stood open directly across from her and Leah could see a set of stairs leading up and out.

"You have *got* to be kidding!"

"The line of gray tiles on the porch was actually a trap door. It was hollow so I pried it open and, 'poof!' stairs." Gareth placed his hand on her shoulder. "But, lady, you did great! You were so brave and—"

Leah put her hand in the air. "Stop, or I'll 'poof' you into next year." She stared at Anippe. "Say anything and I'll bury you right where you stand."

Anippe nodded, apparently not interested in angering Leah's green-eyed hero again. "What was in there?"

Leah shrugged. Turning back to the confessional, she stole the flashlight from Gareth and placed it on the floor, allowing the strong beam to illuminate the contents of the room. The breath caught in her throat when she recognized the statue's determined eyes staring back at her. "She flew from the temple to the 'wooden wall' of Athens," Leah repeated the guide's story that was now running through her mind.

"What?" Gareth asked.

"This was the original statue of Athena. It's made of wood, and came long before the fancy ivory and gold icon that stood inside the Parthenon. People say it was this statue that fell from the sky to protect their city, but it disappeared after the Persians lost."

"Taking with it the magic olive that'd been protected in this temple?" Anippe wondered aloud.

Leah nodded. "That's the story, anyway. Chances are some nice believer knew the Persians were coming and hustled this artifact underground. This temple has more than one layer, remember? She's probably been sitting here since around 400 B.C." Leah stared down at the small bench. "Someone sat with her . . . watched out for her."

Garth reached out and touched the statue. Running his fingers lightly across the dusty wood, he carefully brushed the cobwebs off the six-foot warrior. "She looks just like I thought she would," he whispered. "The helmet, the spear, the shield—her snake curled up beside her—just like they said it was."

Leah heard the faith swell in his voice as he, too, stared at the wooden figure, wishing that the statue could somehow talk and tell them stories about the original Athens. What it was like . . . who the people were . . . if the other mythological creatures of Greece were once actually real?

Leah felt a twinge of regret flow through her soul, knowing that she'd been born way after her time. Like H.G. Wells, Leah had spent her life wishing for a time machine. Perhaps, she thought, staring up at Gareth Lowery, her wish had been granted. Ever since their first meeting she'd seen things that she never thought were real. By his side, Leah knew that she'd experienced some true historical miracles.

"Oh, poor owl." Anippe's sad voice cut through her thoughts.

Raising her gaze, Leah stared into the now wooden eyes of the tiny owl perched on Athena's shoulder; the feathers were no longer white and gone was the bright blue glow of its miraculous life. Now he was simply a piece of wood, an inanimate carving forever watching out for his goddess.

Leah reached out and touched his small head. As she drew back, her hand thumped against Athena's helmet, causing a strange sound to echo inside the small chamber. "Wait a minute," she whispered.

Picking the flashlight off the floor, Leah illuminated the head of the very determined looking goddess which caused her wooden helmet to somehow shimmer.

Reaching out, Leah tapped the warrior's headdress. "This is metal, not wood."

Gareth reached up and brushed his hands along the famous helmet that made its wearer undetectable. His fingers ran across the front, tracing the indentation of a crescent moon turned upside down. He looked at Leah. "A horseshoe?"

Anippe spoke behind them, "An olive wreath."

Leah stared over her shoulder as Anippe pulled the metal olive wreath from her coat and stared down at the strange relic that'd held Plato's mysterious words.

Moving aside, Leah watched Anippe's hand shake as she took the wreath and moved it toward Athena's helmet. She held her breath as the olive wreath settled into the carved cutout with a sharp click.

Sounds like a deadbolt, thought Leah. Or, more accurately, the sound a bullet makes when it enters the pistol's chamber.

The whirring sound was distant at first, like a ceiling fan had been switched on somewhere nearby. But soon the eerie sound intensified and the trio stepped back from the ominous statue and watched Athena's metallic and ivory figure emerge from inside her wooden coffin.

In rapid succession the wood splintered, freeing the Goddess's ivory hand that held her sword in front of her. The large shield came next; the gold weapon of protection fell forward from the statue's grip, as if she was offering it as a gift to the people who'd set her free.

Leah gasped when she watched the gold serpent sitting by Athena's side open its mouth, exposing a large black olive resting on its shimmering forked tongue. Unlike the rest of the inanimate object, the owl suddenly came back to life and flew from Athena's shoulder, racing out the open door and up the waiting staircase.

Leah said her goodbye. Perhaps the small protector had taken the Goddess' soul from her shell and was right now flying her back home to sit atop Mount Olympus.

Reaching her hand toward the snake, Leah stared at the so-called enlightener of mankind as she took the olive it offered, knowing that this was the 'seed' that would lead her to an unknown place where her father was struggling to survive.

The ancient olive was petrified; it resembled a black, oval stone. But according to myth, it possessed the powers of a true warrior; it made magic spring from the earth and, hopefully, was part of the miracle that would bring everyone Leah loved home safely.

She stepped back and stared at Gareth, holding the olive in the palm of her hand. "I don't want to break it."

Anippe reached out and tugged on the chain around Leah's neck. "Carry it in your pendant."

"You broke that, remember?"

She could have slapped the girl's face when Anippe delivered a big sigh into the room. "Look at it, Leah. It's still connected at the bottom like two, well . . . olive leaves."

Leah stared down at the gift of luck and love that Gareth had bought for her in Whitechapel.

He shrugged. "It is from Athens originally, so maybe she's right?"

She sighed. "There's a first time for everything, I suppose." Ignoring the exasperated huff that came from Anippe, Leah placed the olive between the two leaves of her pendant.

Like magic, the halves closed around it, sealing it inside. Instead of a teardrop, the pendant seemed to grow into a large emerald circle, like a priceless saucer hanging around her neck. With the olive safely inside, it looked like a big black eye was staring out at the world, as if hexing anyone that crossed in its path. *Hopefully,* Leah thought, *Athena's traveling with us now; she can offer protection from any of those unseen foes.*

Leah stared back at the golden and ivory statue that was still offering the shield and spear to the people who'd freed her. "Think we need those?"

"I wouldn't turn them down," Gareth replied.

As Leah reached out, she could feel the spear begin to shake, as if the warrior's power was still pumping through the metal like a lightning rod.

Feeling a shiver of fear run down her spine, Leah remembered the emotional weight of the famous staff she'd once carried and turned, patting Gareth on the chest. "Here you go. I'll take the olive." Moving quickly, she marched to the staircase.

"After all," she shouted back over her shoulder, "I'm just the companion on this one, pal. You're the hero!"

Gareth's relieved laughter filled her ears as she ran up the steps and out into the cool evening air that blew gently across the Acropolis.

CHAPTER 13

As dawn broke, the light burrowed under Leah's eyelids, forcing her to wake up and greet the new day.

The math went through Leah's mind like a bullet; a full day was now behind them. If the clock truly started when Leah had walked through the door of the Connecticut mansion, then they were already into their second day. Only five would be left when the sun closed its eye once again. In other words, she groaned, it was time to wake up.

Leah took a deep breath, trying to calm the panic that flooded her body. She was lying on the stage of the Theatre of Dionysius staring up into a bright red and orange sky. The clean, spicy scent of the olive trees and citrus groves laced the air and her stomach responded with an angry growl.

Garth turned his head away from the gold weapons that he'd been studying, and gave her a smile. "Hungry, dear?"

"Food. Now. Please . . ."

"Where do we go from here?" Anippe's increasingly annoying voice made her headache even worse.

Leah sighed heavily and placed her head back on the stage floor and allowed the pictures from her father's map to race through her mind. The owl had flown from a small clump of silver and green trees. *Olive trees*, thought Leah. Inside the grove there'd been a painted cross, which apparently stood for a place somehow involved in Christianity. Beside it, Leah remembered, there'd been a drawing of what looked like a torture device; a large block or club being smashed down on a figure that was lying on a circular table of death. She remembered the streak that'd been added, like a river of blood was flowing from a crushed head.

In addition to that horrible image, the giant skull drawn on the mountain was just as frightening. Leah had no idea what kind of sicko place they'd have to travel to next, or what god-awful monster would be greeting them when they arrived.

She touched the bandage on her cheek where Gareth had nursed her cuts and bruises. "I have no idea where we're going, Anippe."

"The only Skull Mountain I've ever heard of was in Scooby-Doo," Gareth said with an exhausted smirk.

Leah snickered, as Anippe immediately stood up and stalked off the stage, like a disgruntled actress who'd been denied roses during her precious curtain call.

"She's a real pain in the ass," Leah grunted.

Gareth nodded. "You two certainly rub each other the wrong way." Leaning over, he kissed her lips; his eyes were filled with worry. "She's right, though. Time's ticking away and I have no idea where to go next."

"Any sign of Athena's owl?"

"Not a hoot . . . no pun intended."

"Well," Leah sighed, taking a last look around at the remarkable venue. "We followed Plato here. He stood here. Maybe he has something more to say."

"You think there's something buried here?" Gareth looked around at the endless ring of stone seating. "It would take forever to find."

Leah shook her head, breathing in the olive-scented air. "No. I was thinking about his Academy—his garden. The men who took my father had the red tattoo on their hands."

"But where is The Academy? Does it still stand?

Leah sat up beside him. "It was just a garden, remember? It was a garden of olive trees enclosed by a stone wall that held the statues of the great philosophers."

Gareth looked up at the ruins of the Acropolis and the tree-covered landscape that surrounded them on all sides. "A stone wall around an olive grove. Yup, that should be easy enough to find . . . in Greece."

Leah smiled. "I'm sure there's someone who can help. The locals would certainly know where the great Plato used to teach."

Gareth stood. The sword and shield were in his hands, making him look like a golden-haired warrior ready to take on an army.

Leah snorted. "I think we should hide those until we're ready to leave. Something tells me that people would become suspicious if you carried them through downtown Athens."

Anippe shouted from her perch on the circular stone seats, "Can we *please* go now?"

Leah cringed. "If we get through this alive, remind me to slap her."

Gareth grinned.

"Really hard."

———

The rich Greek pastry filled with cheese made Leah's stomach dance with delight. She ate two, watching through the bakery window as Gareth spoke to the locals inside. He had a way about him, attracting men and women alike with his honest, soothing voice and brilliant green eyes. She watched him laugh heartily, as he slapped his new friends on the back and walked briskly out the door.

Leah smiled. "How can you look so good after no sleep whatsoever?"

He winked. "I don't know, but it's a good thing those men in there liked me. They saw all your cuts and bruises and thought I knocked you around."

"How did you convince them otherwise?"

"I told them how mean you are and that you like to pick fights with people," he said, with a smile. "For some reason they believed me. Must be the red hair; they think you're some kind of evil spirit or something and feel bad for me."

Punching him in the shoulder, giving Gareth's new friends something to talk about, they walked away from the bakery.

Anippe flowed behind. Her head kept snapping around as she continued to stare over her shoulder, as if some dark and sinister being was following them through the streets of Athens.

"Well?" Leah spoke, finishing her luscious breakfast. "Did they know where to find Plato?"

He nodded. "It's in a suburb of Athens called Academos."

"Of course it is."

———

Leah stared at the almost haunting site. Among the grassy areas were huge foundations left over from when The Academy was running at full steam—now abandoned and alone. Gareth pointed out the large stone rectangle that'd once been a gymnasium where their athletes practiced to be the best they could be.

The remnants of a stone wall did indeed enclose the site, and only one house was still standing. Leah walked through the structure, which was comprised of seven rectangular rooms on either side of a long corridor and looked at Gareth. "This is where the students lived?"

Anippe's voice immediately entered the conversation, "This is called a 'sacred house.' There were sacrificial remains found here when the site was excavated, which means the house was most likely used for religious practices."

Leah stared at the young woman. "Good to know."

Anippe attempted a smile and Leah immediately felt guilty, knowing that the Egyptian woman was happy when she could help, happy to know something that could possibly be of use to save her uncle.

Leah walked toward her. "Look, Anippe. I'm sorry about my attitude. You have to understand that I'm just as worried and scared as you are, but I can't let it get to me."

"It's okay." She nodded. "Gareth told me your attempts at humor are how you get through pain."

"Attempts?" Leah turned to her love. "I'll have you know that I'm *very* funny."

Gareth pointed at the wall. "Look! Is that an olive grove I see before me?" He quickly walked away. "By God . . . it *is*!"

Leah felt the smile on her face as she turned to follow him. "Smart ass."

Anippe fell into step beside her. "Like I said, you two make a good team."

"Uh, huh," Leah replied. "When this is all over, remind me to slap him upside the head."

Anippe giggled.

"Really, *really* hard."

The breeze whistled softly through the grove, as the ladies followed behind Gareth. The grassy path wound its way through the clusters of trees; the silvery-green leaves offered a breathtaking canopy for the weary adventures. As the path split, the trio went their separate ways, each enjoying their own peaceful slice of the warm morning.

Leah stepped over a stone wall and continued forward, unconsciously staring at the ground for any clue that the great Plato might have left behind.

"You look like crap."

Her head popped up and Leah found herself staring at Khait. The once helpful guide now sat on a large, flat rock underneath an olive tree.

Leah smiled. "Crap? That must be Greek for . . . what? Beautiful, lovely, charming?"

"Nope." Khait laughed. "Even in Greece, crap means crap."

"You should see the other guy."

Her lips drew into a smile, as her straight hair moved like black waves in the breeze. "Did you find what you were looking for?"

Hearing the slightly odd tone in her voice, Leah took a step back from the woman and sat down on the stone wall. "What was I looking for?"

"I'm not one of the bad guys, Leah."

"Then who are you?" Leah glanced at the woman's hands, but they were clean. There were no markings of any group she may or may not be working for.

"Just a friend," Khait responded.

"And what do you, as my friend, of course, want to tell me?"

"I want you to stop what you're doing. I want you to go home and forget about anything you think you know." Khait sighed. "I also want you to consider the ramifications of what you've done—what you're thinking of taking out of Athens."

Leah felt the emerald pendant underneath her jacket, hidden from the woman's eyes by the soft leather. "What am I taking out of Athens?"

Khait stood up and began to pace. "Athena was the most powerful being here; maybe in the whole world. She possessed things that protected full armies. In the wrong hands, these things could be used to annihilate races of people."

Leah felt her eyes grow wider, but she remained silent.

Khait turned around to face her. "If you need the seed to continue on, then take it. But leave the rest. It can protect you along the way, but in the end—if you have to give it up to save yourself— you could end up killing millions of innocents."

"Explain," Leah said, barely breathing.

"Plato believed in shadows, Leah. There are shadows all around you. Just because you're sure of something standing right in front of you, you could very well be wrong."

"I'm a very cautious woman."

"I'm sure you are," Khait shot back. "There is, however, a faith in you that is undeniable; maybe not faith for gods and goddesses, but certainly for the people closest to you. Just because someone . . . uncovers something that they think is one thing, it could very well be something completely different. Then, when the truth is laid out in front of them it is usually too late to back out."

Leah sighed. "Look. I don't want to uncover anything, unveil anything, find anything—none of that." She stopped, recognizing the knowledge that this woman somehow owned. "I just want my father back. I could care less what this whole thing is about. If someone wants a dead, smelly olive that's their own business. I think it's pretty dumb, actually. Money, I get. But a relic that was basically Jack's magic bean? It's like Atlantis—a complete and utter fairytale."

"Atlantis may be a fairytale, Leah," Khait's voice grew loud, "But there are other things that are most assuredly not."

"They have my father."

"Remember what I said," Khait calmed her voice, taking a moment to back down. "Please leave with only what you need and do not get drawn into something that will make you do the opposite of what you believe. There is a very thin line between what is real and what is fake, much like the line between good and evil. Be careful which side you end up standing on. Because even if you do something for all the right reasons, your actions could do harm to the people you love."

Leah shivered as the memory of Heaven's Gate loomed before her. Which side had she been standing on then? If they'd crossed over, Gareth's actions would have killed millions. He had chosen correctly. And now Leah wondered . . . would she? Yes, she had done her good deed not so long ago, but that particular moment had nothing to do with having to sacrifice her own flesh and blood to see the right thing done

"Leah? Where are you? Come here!" Gareth's deep voice flowed through the garden like a savior's call.

Leah stood from the stone wall, shaking the horrific thoughts from her mind. As she moved forward, she turned around and stared into the woman's troubled gaze. "I just want my father back."

Khait nodded. "Good luck then. But please remember what I said."

"I will."

"By the way," Khait continued; her eyes turned to cold, gray steel, "You should know that The Academy was shut down because a king thought that Plato's teachings went against Christianity. They were scared of him, you see, just like they were scared of others who preached of a higher power. Plato was declared a heretic . . . by a King. There have been many of those."

Stopping, she stared up at the lovely silver canopy. "Many have sat in these mystical olive gardens and prayed for things to get better. Whether they prayed to Athena or to some other entity, doesn't really matter. Plato was still taken from this garden." She leveled her gaze at Leah as the brilliant sun beamed down on the duo. "It was as if he was cast out of paradise."

Offering a slight nod, Leah turned away from the strange words and stepped over the stone wall. She marched quickly to Gareth as he knelt on the ground in front of a crescent-shaped rock; large Greek letters were carved into the rough surface. He looked up as Leah approached, with a stunning smile etched on his face.

Leah stared down at the stone. "What's it say?"

"The Cradle of Civilization."

"Is under that rock?" Leah asked.

Anippe chimed in, "Actually, most believe that the Cradle of Civilization is located in the Fertile Crescent. The region that includes Egypt, Israel, Jordan—"

Leah raised her hand. "I know where the Fertile Crescent is. My dad was an Egyptian nut, too."

"Sorry, I forgot."

Leah shook her head, waving away the apology. "I thought that Africa was the Cradle of Civilization."

"Actually," Gareth chimed in, "you're both right. Many countries and regions have claimed the title due to archaeological finds of literate societies, writing tablets, etc. But Mesopotamia is actually where we first found a developed society that dates back to around the fourth millennium B.C."

"Okay," Leah said, accepting the brilliance that flowed from his lips. Her insides felt like a tightened bow, waiting for an arrow to be loaded and shot out of her chest "So . . . we're going to Mesopotamia?" She thought of the map and sighed deeply. "Is there a big mountain with a skull staring out? Olive trees? A man taken out of a garden?" Her voice dropped to a whisper, "How do we know we're going in the right direction?"

Gareth's face suddenly went white and Leah immediately reached out and touched his cold cheek, leaving all other thoughts behind. "Gareth, are you okay?"

Grabbing her elbow, Gareth marched her out of Plato's garden. Without a word, Anippe followed along behind—her face was once again a mask of confusion.

Leah's voice was filled with worry. "What's wrong? What did I say? Where are we going?"

For reasons unbeknownst to her, Leah's flesh began to crawl. She could even swear that she heard a surprised gasp come from behind the olive trees when Gareth finally answered her question.

"Jerusalem."

CHAPTER 14

The Rolls Royce engines on Lowery's Concorde offered a relaxing purr; a hum that seemed to cool Leah's temper and allow her to close her eyes and dream only good dreams.

But her mind would just not let go. She'd remained silent the entire walk back, watching Gareth's determined face. His jaw was clenched tight and the vein in his forehead throbbed beneath the blond veil of hair.

Racing them back to the Theatre of Dionysius, he'd pulled the golden spear and shield from their hiding place in the ancient trees, but had remained silent ever since his announcement.

Leah felt like screaming at him. Maybe they should've left Athena's powerful weapons behind—let the Athenians keep the artifacts safe as they had done for centuries. But when Gareth was determined, he was determined. Like a bull on a rampage, there was nothing—no blockade—that could be thrown in front of him to stop his progress. Therefore, the weapons left Athens by his side.

Sitting on the plane, he stared down at the map unfolded in his lap. Anippe looked out the small window as Leah sipped another cup of the wonderful coffee. She wondered briefly why the attendants didn't comment on the strange gold relics that were sitting in the seat beside Gareth. But perhaps the billionaire, Lowery, had paid them extra for their silence.

Reaching out, she touched the shimmering metal shield. Leah

had a hard time believing the mythical stories, but as her finger traced the Medusa's snarling head etched in the gold, it was hard to deny that the ancient Greeks had to have known something.

Touching Gareth on the shoulder, she increased the pressure until his handsome face turned in her direction. She smiled. "Are you going to tell me what you know, or is this going to be another surprise? Before you answer," she said quickly, holding up her hand, "You should know that I don't think my heart can take any more surprises."

"When you were talking back there," his voice cracked. "The olive trees, the garden, a big mountain with a skull . . . it all of a sudden made sense."

Leah waited, staring at the place Gareth was pointing at on the map. She read, "The seed of the one who'll bind all wounds and lead you to Temptation."

Gareth nodded. "Except, I think your father really meant *through* temptation."

"And?"

He took a deep breath as a shadow moved across his face. "Please don't get upset."

"Why would I get upset?" All of a sudden Leah felt like she was about to go into the history books as the very first person to ever jump from a plane while it was in flight.

"Well," he began slowly, "It looks like we're embroiled in something . . . slightly religious again."

Leah threw her hands in the air. "Are you kidding? I thought we were on an Ancient Greek treasure hunt."

"That makes it better?"

Leah shifted in her seat, suddenly uncomfortable with what she was about to hear. "You know that I have a hard time accepting some of this stuff."

"Even after all you've seen?"

Leah thought about the image of the Son and how He'd spoken to her inside the famous room where the final supper had been eaten. Her mind went over the private words that the Son had left behind and she remembered how the feeling of peace had flowed through her, yet the nagging doubts still lived inside her librarian's realistic mind. Yes, she'd been given all the proof a person could possibly hope for, yet the analytical woman that lived inside her brain made it hard for her to accept the whole thing as pure, undeniable fact. "Well . . . I'm okay with the Son," she said.

Gareth smiled. "Good. Okay. Then you should be just fine with this."

"Why?" she whined.

Gareth put his head back on the rich, luxurious leather. "Have you ever heard of the Garden of Gethsemane?"

The card catalogue opened slowly on its hinges inside Leah's weary mind, and produced a cloud of dust. "Nope."

Ignoring Anippe's audible gasp, Leah waved Gareth on, begging him to speak before she had to reach over and slap the girl.

Gareth smiled. "The Garden of Gethsemane is where Jesus was when they came to take Him away. He was praying with His disciples when the soldiers entered and dragged Him out to be crucified."

"How do you know that's the garden we're looking for?" she asked

"Everything points to that spot, Leah. For one, the location corresponds with the map." He pointed at the small cluster of trees where a cross was enveloped by the silvery-green leaves. "The Garden of Gethsemane is also referred to as the Garden of Olives. It's also set at the foot of the Mount of Olives, which is the site where God is supposed to redeem the dead."

Leah shivered as Khait's words suddenly struck a nerve. She wondered, if she made a mistake on this journey would she even be offered redemption? Or, would she be cast into the pit with all the others who'd supposedly wronged the world?

Gareth continued, "Jesus and His disciples went to the garden after the Last Supper the night before he was crucified. It's also said that Judas betrayed Him in that garden."

Gareth closed his eyes and began to conjure up the faith that always rested inside of his soul. "They went to a place called Gethsemane and Jesus said to His disciples, 'sit here while I pray.' Jesus was deeply distressed. He said, 'my soul is overwhelmed with sorrow to the point of death. Stay with me and keep watch.'

His disciples kept falling asleep and Jesus said to them, 'watch and pray so that you will not fall into temptation. The spirit is willing but the body is weak.' " Gareth opened his eyes that were now filled with tears. "The disciples fell asleep again and Jesus told them that, 'the hour had come, and that the Son of Man was betrayed into the hands of sinners.' "

"I don't mean to be a jerk here, but what does this have to do with a great big skull?" Leah interrupted, pointing to the large black drawing beside the cluster of olive trees.

"Carrying His own cross, Jesus went out to the place of the Skull . . . Golgotha. At this place, it was stated that a tomb sat inside a small garden and that's where He was buried."

"Until he rose again," Anippe added.

Leah stared over her shoulder at Anippe. "I knew that one."

Gareth smiled. "Joseph of Arimathea persuaded Pontius Pilate to release Jesus' body to him for burial, and he buried the body in the Garden Tomb."

"The Grail guy."

"Yeah, the Grail guy," Gareth snorted.

"And this stuff has all been found?"

"All of these places are there, yes. But there are some who believe that Jesus' tomb is in the Church of the Holy Sepulchre which Constantine built. However, the church was supposedly within city limits at that time."

"So?"

"Jewish customs required executions and burials of the so-called 'condemned' to be held outside the city walls, which would make the Garden Tomb a better bet as to where Jesus was laid to rest."

"Okay," Leah took a deep breath, "I get the garden . . . that makes sense. Certainly fits a pattern that we're following. The olive trees, too. But . . ." Leah stopped as Khait's words once again filled her mind. She obviously had wanted to make sure that Leah knew there were many people who'd been ripped from their gardens of paradise and declared heretics.

She shook her head, trying to erase the mental picture of a being so wise, so peaceful, that the only way a king could take care of Him was to flay the skin from His bones. "But . . . did Jesus have an olive? A magic seed like Athena's that could be planted in the earth to grow a tree?" Leah pointed at the large olive tree in the center of the map.

Gareth shook his head. "Never heard of that, but the garden was filled with olive trees and the name, Gethsemane, actually means 'oil' or 'oil press.'"

Leah could feel the plane dropping from the sky, like a bullet that was lining itself up to hit flesh and bone. Noticing her finger shaking, she pointed at the big black device of torture that'd been drawn near the skull. "He was on a cross. What is this thing supposed to be?"

Gareth shook his head. "I have absolutely no idea. But whatever it is, I sure as hell hope we don't run into it."

As the landing gear squealed across the tarmac, Leah's stomach was suddenly debating whether or not to digest the rich Greek pastries she'd had for breakfast.

———

The rented limo came to a stop beside the beautiful church. Leah was always astonished at the sight of tourists with cameras. Some visitors, of course, were true pilgrims, but most just snapped away so they could host a slide show with their friends and neighbors when they returned home.

She looked at the ground, avoiding the gaze of one true believer who seemed to be glaring at her. Leah wondered if they would know on sight that there was a total hypocrite like her in their midst.

Gareth pointed all around and told Leah how much the Kidron Valley had changed since ancient times. The world had moved on. Roads had been widened to accommodate the motorists, and hotels had been erected near the ancient site that'd birthed the true tourist attraction they were now staring at.

Leah simply nodded as Gareth and Anippe walked ahead of her, sharing their knowledge of the ancient wonder like two Sunday school students who'd finished at the top of their class.

There were people walking by, babbling about the cave where their disciples had stayed while waiting for their destroyers to come. Others talked wearily about things like, if there was a McDonald's somewhere in the area where they could feel more at home. Leah smiled. No matter what the location, culture, or background—McDonald's would always be the same.

The deep voice startled her from her thoughts, and Leah turned around to find herself staring at a man with the kindest face she'd ever seen. His skin was tanned within an inch of its life, as if he'd spent every minute of every day boiling under the hot sunshine. The glasses he wore had turned amber underneath the rays of sunlight, and his smile was so sweet that Leah felt like she'd known him all her life.

"Excuse me?" she asked.

"I asked if you were lost?" he replied.

"You're American."

He winked. "Well . . . don't hold that against me. So are you, after all."

Comfort flowed through Leah's troubled heart from his fun voice and happy demeanor. Reaching down, she watched him pull a small weed from a cluster of flowers that sat her feet. "Are you the gardener here?"

"Caretaker." He smiled wide and put out his hand. "Call me Robert."

"Okay. Robert. Can you point me in the general direction of the garden?"

"I can do even better than that. Follow me." His voice was low, but Leah could hear the constant stream of happiness that ran though his tone. He reminded her of someone who was completely at peace—someone who knew exactly where they were going and enjoyed immensely where they had been.

She listened carefully, letting his serene voice envelop her like a father's arms around his frightened child.

"This is the path that takes you up the mountain, but we won't need to go that far." Turning to his right, he walked toward an iron fence.

Leah could see the large cluster of lovely foliage and took a deep breath. Robert opened the gate and ushered her inside.

"If these trees could talk, huh?" he laughed, tapping one of the gnarled, hollow trunks of an olive tree.

"These were here when . . . it happened?"

He nodded. "Well . . . as with everything else, there are those experts out there who say no. However, believers say yes."

"And you say?"

"They were here," he stated in a positive voice, "Just as sure as you and I are standing here now."

"Were these the first olive trees ever?"

Tilting his head to the side, he seemed to be searching his memory banks, "I think the first olive tree sprang from Jericho," he stated, as they continued their trek around the church. "Actually, this old path leads right to Jericho if you keep following it."

Pointing up at the lovely building, he smiled. "They call this the Basilica of the Agony. Understatement, huh? What happened to Him was way worse than agony. Heck, its agony nowadays just to drive your car on the highway."

Leah couldn't stop herself from laughing at Robert's brutally honest words. The people praying at the religious site shot her disgusted looks. "Sorry," she mumbled.

As the breeze tickled the branches of the olive trees, Leah could smell the scent of apple pipe tobacco coming from Robert's clothes. For some reason, it made her feel even more comfortable.

"There's no reason to apologize," Robert said. "Jesus appreciates a sense of humor."

Leah stared up at the heavenly canopy above. "I can't imagine Him kneeling here that night, praying for comfort, peace and solace. Frightened for His own life, or worried about how the world would turn out after He was taken?"

"I'm glad you said that," Robert stated. "No one ever thinks about stuff like that." Putting his hand on her back, he led her along the path. "I would have to say He was very frightened. No one wants their lives ended that way. Even when He did come back, it still had to hurt. Kings," Robert said, spitting on the ground. "Look back in history and you'll see we haven't had many good ones around the globe."

"I thought Pontius Pilate was a governor?"

"Governor, King—same difference to me. People with too much power always think they're better than everyone else. They tramp over the land killing people, building their palaces and then burying their crimes. Make me sick . . . all of them. With gold and silver and an army behind them, one person can be unstoppable. Frightening when you think about it."

They came around the corner and Leah felt her heart nearly explode inside her chest. Large, dark holes in a huge skull stared down on her. "Skull Hill? This is where they . . . did it?"

Robert nodded. "It has eroded badly. I am surprised you can still see the form at all?"

Keeping silent as they walked up the slope of the hill, Leah stared at the ground. She didn't know if it was to pray or to grieve.

"Here we are then," Robert's soft voice blew the horrible thoughts from her mind. "Much better place to visit, if you ask me. No one's here right now; closed it up myself about an hour ago."

Leah raised her gaze and stared at the small iron gate. Inside was a tiny garden filled with flowers of every shape, size and color. "What is this?"

"This is the Garden Tomb. This is where Joseph brought the Son to be buried until, of course, He rose into Heaven."

Leah smiled, grateful that some parts of the story never changed.

Robert waved her in. "Come and sit a spell. Nobody'll be around to bother you." Once she entered, he turned to walk back out of the gate, stopping briefly to pluck a bright green weed from a perfect bed of flowers. "That's better," he mumbled.

"Aren't you going to stay?" Leah asked.

The small frown turned into a truly stunning smile. "No need. Unlike others who have passed through this gate, you'll be trusted with the truth."

CHAPTER 15

Leah clasped her hands behind her back and walked forward. In front of her sat a strange sort of archway carved into the stone. On the right hand side was a small window supported underneath by a large cluster of stones. One section looked like a small brick wall had jutted out from the flat rock, offering a ledge where someone could sit peacefully and let the sun stream down their face. On each side of the tomb was a flat wall where flowerboxes of beautiful blossoms had been placed, welcoming the visitor with their spectacular colors.

Leah took note of the window that was located high up on the left-hand side of the façade, and almost passed out cold. Nestled in the dark alcove was a small owl; its feathers were as white as newly-fallen snow, and a pair of bright blue eyes stared down on her.

Flying from his perch and through the iron bars that were guarding the tomb's entrance; Leah saw the small security system to stop overzealous tourists and believers from entering the space that may have once held the body of their beloved Son.

Leah stepped forward. The owl let out a screech that echoed through the window. His small body hopped up and down on the ledge and then soared back through the bars. Back and forth it went, its tiny wings slapping against the iron as it passed by.

Leah wondered if the owl was back because it had delivered the Goddess Athena safely to her home, and had now come to Leah's aid to help find the next mysterious seed.

One more screech rattled the bars, and the small gate suddenly opened, allowing Leah access to the Garden Tomb.

She didn't know what to do. Looking left and right, she wondered how angry Robert would be if he saw her entering the reverent building. Wanting to turn around and shout for Gareth, needing a friendly face who'd act as a lookout for her, Leah continued to search her surroundings. But the little bird had other ideas as it raced through the bars directly at her surprised face. He screeched loudly as he circled her once again, before taking his place in the tiny alcove located at the side of the door,

Leah stared up at the demanding blue eyes. "Okay! I'm going."

The owl hooted.

"Don't rush me," Leah said. Swallowing her slight fear, she carefully stepped into the empty tomb. Looking around quickly, Leah searched for any sign of an olive tree or some miracle seed that might be waiting for her.

The afternoon sun was so warm that Leah felt like a pile of dough being heated to a golden brown inside the oven of rock. And when the first wave of dizziness hit her squarely between the eyes, Leah sat down on the floor willing herself not to pass out.

Taking deep breaths, she stared at the long rectangle that'd been carved into the floor. Someone's expert hand had smoothed the rough stone, rendering the strange looking bed smooth as silk.

Leah closed her eyes and put her head between her knees. The pressure on her chest felt like it was going to explode as cold sweat saturated the back of her neck, making the soft auburn curls feel like a hundred pounds of brick had been glued to her head. The ringing in her ears grew louder and the black spots burst like flashbulbs before her eyes.

It wasn't until the screech of the owl echoed in her ears, that Leah raised her chin. She turned her neck and stared at the small bird now perched on her shoulder, shrieking at her to wake up.

Leah looked back at the rectangular bed carved into the floor and the room suddenly filled with soft, blue light from the eyes of the all-seeing owl.

Her breath eased and the black spots disappeared . . . all except for two. One that seemed to hover in her field of vision expanded, turning into a man, dressed in tailored purple robes His head was bowed and he held an object in his hands.

Leah's gaze was drawn to the other black spot that seemed to expand over the place of rest. And soon a tall figure stood in the center of the warm bed.

Her eyes focused on the familiar image. His robes were crème in color, and His hands were raised in front of Him as if He was calling to Leah to come and give her old friend a hug. His eyes were the brightest blue she'd ever seen. Brighter than her own brilliant sapphires and the owl's wisdom-filled orbs. In His, Leah could see the most spectacular sky and the crystalline waters of a perfect sea that was refreshed from a powerful storm that'd just passed by. His were . . . beautiful.

She stood up warily, trying not to disturb the man on the floor who was deep in prayer.

The Son stepped forward and took Leah's hands. "How are you?"

She swallowed hard, as the overwhelming tears of regret and happiness seemed to run through her like a raging river. Finding no words, she simply nodded.

The Son touched her bruised cheek, her swollen eyes, and the cuts above her brow.

She whispered, "The seed of the One who will bind our wounds and lead you to Temptation."

Staring into the face of the most wonderful being she'd ever met, Leah was overcome by the magnitude of the Son's smile and the warmth that radiated from His eyes.

She felt a tear slide down her cheek. "I'm sorry for what happened to you here."

He smiled. "Everyone's always so sad about endings. I think beginnings are much harder."

"But you're going to a nice place, aren't you? I mean . . . didn't you?"

"Still don't believe the stories?" His smile remained in place.

Leah felt a bit of guilt as the answer she knew she should give got stuck in her throat.

He continued, "You are the one who read my words."

She nodded.

"And?"

"I believe in you." The truth shot like gunfire from her lips.

"A lot of proof you held in your hands."

"Proof of you."

"And others."

Leah sighed. "I'm sorry. It's just really hard to believe in . . . everything."

"God?"

Leah thought. "Well . . . not Him, specifically. I've seen strange power and, like You said, held it in my hands. But I look around at all the agony people are going through and I just . . ."

"Have a hard time believing that a savior exists when people keep feeling so much pain."

Leah could feel the fear course through her veins wondering what her punishment would be for her disbelief. But when she gazed up at Jesus, He was still smiling; still offering the comfort that warmed her heart.

"It is all right. I told you that before. Here," He waved his hand in the air of the tomb. "Here was an end. But the beginning, any beginning, is much more frightening."

"What do you mean?"

"Leah, you are on a journey that is leading you to many beginnings." Reaching up, He set a hand on the small owl whose eyes bathed the Son's face in a soft blue glow. "Ancient worlds, ancient people—you will find that some beginnings did not go very well for some. That has not changed since my time here. There are many people who began one way and changed over time. It happens more often than you think."

"I feel like I'm changing all the time," she whispered.

"For the good." He smiled. "You were told that you and Gareth would find many things and go on many adventures. No one told you how hard they would be, or how mixed up they might become. But I ask you to hold on to what little trust you're building inside yourself. You need to make sure that you see the truth. Not know it, Leah. Not believe it, because that's what you were educated to do. But actually see the truth."

"There are lots of shadows in this world."

He nodded. "Sometimes the truth is hidden so deep that it is almost impossible to find. But whatever you find, whatever you hear, I'll be with you."

"You're not going to tell me what's going on, are you?"

"It all depends on what you and Gareth choose to do."

"That free will thing again?" Her lips curved into a smile before she could stop them.

The sparkle in His eyes was like the sun rising into a bright, blue sky. "Keeping your sense of humor helps, too." He took Leah's hand. "There are always forces at work. There are beginnings buried all over this land. Maybe they should stay buried. You and Gareth have had to make choices before. I am sure you will make the right one this time. And, if not? We will figure it out . . . together."

"I hope so."

He placed His hands on her shoulders. "There is a lot of pressure on you, Leah. Sometimes it will feel like you are being crushed. There may come a time when you will have to walk through the pit to save other innocents like yourself."

Leah tried not to laugh.

"In some matters you are extremely innocent, child. Now, I think it is time for you to step back out into the sunshine and go find your hero."

Frustration mounted, knowing that she couldn't complete her horrible task if she left this tomb without the magical piece of the puzzle. "Um?"

He waited, as Leah searched for the right words. How exactly does someone ask the Son of God for an olive? Leah stared down at the man who was still praying quietly by the empty bed. "Who is he?"

"That's my friend Joseph."

"Of Arimathea?" she asked quickly. "The grail guy," she whispered into the wind.

A sound like wind chimes swaying in a soft breeze came from the Son's mouth. The burst of happiness made Leah's troubled soul feel better. "I think he is traditionally referred to as a knight. I call him Joseph," He said.

Leah felt the blood rise in her cheeks, as the Son happily continued, "He brought me here. He prayed over me."

Leah pointed at the object in his hands "Is that . . . is that it?"

He nodded. "The cup will give him life and sustain him for what he will need to accomplish."

Leah studied the cup. "You know . . . you see so many movies, read so many books—"

"Hear so many theories?" He added.

"The Grail is the cup that held your blood."

"It is whatever you believe it to be."

Leah sighed.

"The frustrated librarian wishes to hear facts and not tales."

She bowed her head immediately. "I'm sorry."

"No apologies. That is how He made you. There is nothing wrong with wanting to know the truth. You saw this particular cup in the cave in Glastonbury."

She couldn't stop the slight smile that appeared on her face. "It was darker in there."

The Son nodded. "Some say I made it with my own two hands. Others believe it came from a crown." Reaching down, He pat Joseph on the shoulder.

The man raised himself off the floor, clutching the cup in his hands. He bowed to his Savior as a tear rolled down his cheek, and Jesus hugged him, sending him out the door without a word.

The owl flew first, as if he was the front flank of a remarkable army.

He turned his attention back to her. "Good luck to you and your friends."

Bowing, Leah stepped into the sunlight and saw that the iron gate which had blocked the doorway was now gone. In its place, a large stone had been rolled away from the opening. The bright flash of light felt like a warm blanket had been tossed over her, enveloping her in peace and protecting her from the cold drafts of reality. "Amen."

She shook her head and opened her eyes, but the knight was still standing in front of her. Leah knew he couldn't see her; it was if Leah was privy to an ancient miracle, watching it unfold from the seat of her time machine.

Joseph bowed his head; his tears fell into the cup that held liquid life.

The screech echoed as the owl suddenly raced past the knight's head; it shook the man's body with such force that Leah wondered if a falcon's soul was somehow trapped inside the little bird's body.

As Leah watched the small drop of blood wash over the rim of the cup and fall onto the earth in front of her, Joseph of Arimathea disappeared into a white cloud of smoke, taking the mystical owl with him.

CHAPTER 16

Reality came out of nowhere. Leah could once again hear the wind caressing the olive leaves, inhale the spicy, flowery scent and feel the weight of the world come back full force.

The iron gate creaked behind her and Leah stared down at her feet. After all she'd been through, she actually felt no surprise to find that the illuminating drop of blood had turned into a glistening olive.

Reaching down, she picked it up, listening to the small click underneath her shirt. As if this was still part of the dream, Leah slowly lifted the pendant with Athena's large black olive eye staring out and placed the Son's silver-green seed beside it. Leah watched as the emerald pendant grew, re-configuring its mass to allow room for the second precious object.

Leah snapped the clasp back into place and stared at the emerald. She turned it over in her hands. Once a delicate teardrop, the mysterious stone from Athens had grown into a large disk. With the two olives sitting side by side, it now looked like a strange little face was staring out at the very strange world.

Robert's voice startled her. Dropping the pendant down into the neckline of her blouse, Leah turned and offered the pleasant man a smile.

He placed a hand on her cheek. "I see all your bruises are gone. Must have been the magic of the garden, hmmm?" He said, knowingly.

Leah nodded. "Those olive trees must really have healing powers."

"I've heard that." He winked. "Your friends have been looking for you. I'll take you to them."

"Thank you," Leah sighed. She wanted nothing more than company right now, as her analytical brain went to mush. Leah couldn't hear sane wisdom; all she felt was a happiness deep inside her and knew that eventually her soul would win out over the all-knowing librarian.

"Where to next, young lady?"

Leah stared over at Robert's profile. His head was constantly moving—eyes to the ground—apparently searching for any weeds that had the gall to hide in the garden. Small gray and white hairs intermingled with the black sheen, showing the signs of passing youth, and Leah felt a sudden burst of déjà vu. He reminded her of someone; another man who was also kind and gentle. Someone who—"

"Heading back home now? Find all that you came to seek?"

Leah shook her head, losing the image that'd begun to form inside her mind. "Yes. I mean . . . no. I think I have to go to temptation."

"You mean, through." He stared at her strangely. "Don't you?"

"Um . . . yeah." Leah's head was spinning, as she made her way carefully down the rocky slope toward the sound of Gareth's voice.

Robert touched her arm, stopping her from running to the one person that still made sense in her world. "This is as far as I go." Robert looked up at the waning sun as it dipped lower in the sky. "You take care of yourself, young woman. Get what you really need and then go home. Leave the unnecessary things behind." He cupped her chin in his hands. "You have more power and more protection than anyone could ever hope to have."

Leah thought of Gareth, her hero, and her heart shouted at her to go to him. Being without his power and his protection was draining her energy. "Thank you, Robert."

Bowing, the man reached down to pull at a menacing green stalk jutting out from the raspberry-colored flowers. "I don't want weeds in paradise," he remarked. Walking away, he waved his hand above his head and was soon swallowed up by a cluster of olive trees.

Leah continued on the path, walking quickly toward Gareth. As she turned the corner and exited the overhang of the lush canopy, the calm feeling of friendship and love evaporated like the morning dew on a hot summer meadow.

The terrifying black device loomed before her, and a scream flew from her lips.

Gareth turned and marched quickly to Leah's side taking her into his arms. "Are you all right? You *can't* disappear like that! You had me scared to death."

"Disappear?"

"I've been looking everywhere for you. Then I saw this . . . thing from a distance and I thought maybe you had been put in here . . . fell into it . . . I didn't know what to think!"

"I was in the Garden . . . in the Tomb."

Gareth's eyes filled with confusion. "We were at the Tomb. The gate was locked; no one was in there."

Leah tilted her head, staring into the befuddled face of her hero. "I was just there. Robert, the caretaker, left me there to commune."

"Who?"

"The guy walking around; sixty, salt and pepper hair, amber sunglasses? He's going up and down the path pulling out weeds from all the flowerbeds. You must have passed him."

Gareth's bright green eyes stared over Leah's shoulder, scanning the grove of trees behind her. "I didn't see anybody. Anippe and I were together the whole time searching for you. Then we found this. We haven't seen anybody else."

Leah once again felt the twinge of jealousy as she stared at the lovely, lithe Egyptian standing in the setting sun. Leah couldn't understand why the dark circles of exhaustion hadn't formed beneath her glowing eyes like the rest of the weary adventurers. Her clothes were never dirty, her delicate hands were always manicured, and her tanned skin always shone like silk. Leah tried her best to ignore her as she let Gareth lead her to the large, black object. A huge stone was sitting on top of the round base—a base that looked like a gigantic wheel; so mammoth, that it probably once fit on Zeus' chariot. "What is it?"

Gareth opened his mouth, but Anippe's voice came out first. She stopped and smiled at Gareth, as he gallantly bowed his head to let her tell the tale.

Leah felt another wave of anger run through her veins at their polite exchange.

"This is an olive crusher," Anippe explained. "I know it looked like someone's bleeding head on the map, but this stone crushes olives . . . not people. The line drawn on your father's map wasn't blood, it was olive oil. You see," she continued.

Leah watched Anippe walk around the object like a museum guide. The woman used small words as if she was explaining the ancient contraption to a pack of grade-schoolers.

"They placed the olives in the basin at the center of this millstone, and then used a donkey to pull this big bar attached to the stone slab. The donkey's movements would roll the huge stone and crush the olives into pulp."

"I know what an olive crusher is." The statement seethed through Leah's teeth at the tone of condescension in Anippe's voice.

But the oblivious woman simply continued, "The olive oil was squeezed into a pit and put into clay jars." She raised her finger to her lips. "Strange that it's up here, though."

"Why strange?"

"Because they always kept olive crushers *inside* a pit. They needed the cooler temperatures to make sure the oil production remained steady. Heat has a nasty effect on olive oil."

"This one kind of makes sense, though," Gareth said. "I mean, being here, where Jesus was the night before His horrible death."

Leah stared up at his handsome face. "Why's that?"

"Well," he began, "Luke said that 'Jesus' sweat was like drops of blood falling to the ground.' It supposedly ran from Him like olive oil . . . into the pit."

The card catalogue flew open inside Leah's mind so fast that it startled her. "The pit of despair," she whispered.

"What?" Gareth asked.

Leah's voice seemed to come from miles away as it echoed in her own ears. "It's like a metaphor. My dad likes metaphors. The weight of the world was pressing down on Jesus like the rock that presses down on the olives. The pressure is . . . unbearable sometimes." The face of the Son rose in Leah's mind as the pieces, His words, started clicking together inside her head.

Her eyes traveled back and forth between Gareth and Anippe. "Is there an olive pit around here somewhere?"

"Why? Did . . . wait, someone told you something?" Gareth stared down at her and a smile came to his lips. "I didn't even notice, love. Forgive me?" Stepping back, he gazed at her. "Your bruises, your cuts . . . they're all gone. I'm going to assume that the second olive was found?" He grinned.

Leah nodded. Lifting her pendant from beneath her shirt, she showed Gareth the brilliant green olive that now rested beside Athena's.

His eyes grew wide, but filled with happiness and not fear. "And how is our Friend?"

"Fine." Leah smiled.

Gareth laughed and pulled her into his arms. "I love you, lady. You are truly amazing."

"You brought us here. You were the one who knew where to go," Leah reminded him.

"Anippe's right. We make a very good team." He lifted her chin and Leah felt the kiss down to her toes. It reminded her that of all the shadows and falsehoods that may exist in her world, Gareth Lowery would always be the one constant truth.

She heard the slight stutter behind Gareth's back, like a small child who wanted to be included in the special moment between Mom and Dad. "There's a huge olive pit that was found in Qumran, but I'm not sure it was ever called the 'pit of despair.' The monks used it when they were there."

"Qumran . . . of course," Gareth said, slapping himself on the forehead.

Leah shuffled through the data in her brain. "They found the Dead Sea Scrolls at Qumran."

Anippe's face turned from tan to red before Leah's eyes, as the woman stepped forward and suddenly ripped the map out of Gareth's hand.

Leah stared down at where she was looking. Beside Skull Mountain, and the now innocent torture device, the owl's path went to the top right hand corner of the paper and hovered over a large, black hole. Leah's heart thumped hard in her chest as she stared at the small 'X' and her father's ominous words, *Is it still there?*

But Anippe didn't point at the troublesome notion, or even the dark pit that may house something infinitely worse than anything Athena or Plato could have envisioned. Instead, she pointed to the number '64' painted on the steps in the trunk of the large olive tree sitting dead center on the map. "It's the Copper Scroll. It has to be!"

"No one has ever found that stuff," Leah said. You didn't have to be a Head Librarian or a scholar to know of the mysterious document that Anippe spoke about; the odd scroll that'd been found with the others inside the ancient cave. The Copper Scroll had differed from the rest. Not only was it quite obviously made of copper and not the parchment used by the learned monks for the rest of their works, but it also held no literary or historical value whatsoever. It was basically just a laundry list of hiding places for fictitious treasures.

There were sixty-four locations etched on the scroll, offering completely ambiguous directions, like 'forty pounds of silver can be found in an opening at the edge of a canal on its northern side.' There was no map however—no directions on where to begin the search—which means the so-called treasure could be found near any canal across the globe. As with anything, without a place to begin there would be no hope of finding the actual location where these various gold and silver treasures were supposedly buried.

"People have looked for that stuff forever," Leah snorted. "It's some kind of joke; like the monks just wanted to teach greedy people a lesson."

Gareth, the avid adventurer, put his hands on his hips. "Leah, that is so wrong. Of course the treasures exist. And when someone finds number sixty-four on that list, they'll have five hundred times my own wealth . . . at least that."

Leah watched, amused, as his eyes glittered. She knew the spark had had nothing to do with money. After all, a man who could reinvent the Concorde didn't trouble himself with looking for more. And Leah knew that there wasn't a greedy bone in the man's amazing body. It was, and always would be, the challenge, the puzzle, the mystery that drew Gareth in and made him sound like an excited boy on Christmas morning.

He sat down on the olive crusher. "Not only does the Copper Scroll talk about silver and gold, but it talks about coins, vessels, religious artifacts . . . can you just imagine?"

Anippe sat down beside him, but kept her eyes affixed on Leah. "Some say the starting point is here in Jerusalem because it referred to the wealth of the Second Temple."

Leah shook her head. "If I remember correctly, the Copper Scroll was written in Hebrew like the rest of the documents. But the others were religious. The Scroll was written using a very simple vocabulary."

"But it was written in Hebrew," Gareth reminded her.

Another sigh escaped her. "I know that. But it was extremely different from the others, as if that one was written by someone else's hand. The chosen scribe for the Copper Scroll made a ton of errors in the text, errors that someone familiar with the language wouldn't have made. Anyway," she said, waving her hand in the air. "Most all of the locations refer to canals, cisterns, reservoirs . . . with our luck what we're looking for is buried in Venice."

Anippe's voice grew louder, "I know that's what the '64' on the map stands for, Leah. It's the only thing that makes sense."

Leah tried to hold her anger in check. "We're nowhere near the *end* of that map, Anippe. I wouldn't jump to any conclusions if I were you. Remember, Plato warned us that there are a great many shadows."

Taking a deep breath and closing her eyes, Anippe looked as if she was desperately trying to calm herself before trying once again to make her case with a bull-headed librarian. "Number sixty-four on the Copper Scroll refers to a location where, if found, is another scroll that gives the exact starting point; the exact locations of all the buried treasure that was listed. They say that the second scroll has detailed instructions etched into it, and it's made of pure silver."

Leah couldn't help herself; she laughed at the truly wistful tone. "Buried treasure? A scroll of silver? You sound like a Spielberg movie. Snap out of it, will ya'?" She caught sight of Gareth's sheepish grin. "What?"

He smiled wide and flicked a fake tear from his eye. "You know who Spielberg is. I've never been more proud."

Leah shook her head. Frustration ran through her veins, as she ripped the map from Anippe's hands. Holding it up, she pointed at the pictures, following the owl's directions. "Look at this! This is already a movie without you adding to it. Not only that, but this movie will end in a whole lot of death if we don't focus."

Anippe's eyes filled with tears, thinking about her beloved uncle.

Leah quickly continued, "The olive pit is up next. And right now we don't know what it is, what will be in it, or where we go to get this lovely showplace of pain that's drawn down here." She jabbed her finger at the mansion on the map that apparently held a hidden cache of bodies inside it. "I'm already not looking forward to that one. We can't even *get* to this big, old olive tree and the number '64' until we figure out what that grotesque picture is all about. So, please! Focus!"

Throwing the map at Gareth, Leah stalked back up the slope. She hurried underneath the eerie gaze of the skull and down the path toward the parking lot. Muttering loudly as she went, Leah caused more than a few tourists to keep their distance.

Reaching the car, she threw herself inside, reveling briefly in the fact that, wherever Gareth Lowery was, an air-conditioned limo was never far behind. The driver remained silent, obviously waiting for orders from the man who hired him.

Leah kept her eyes closed, as the leather seat moved and Gareth's voice filled the interior. "How far away is Qumran?"

"About fourteen miles, Sir," came the efficient reply.

Gareth sighed. "Take us there."

"Absolutely."

"Is there a hotel in that area?"

"The InterContinental Jericho is open for business, Mr. Lowery. It's a beautiful place that looks out over the old city."

"Fine . . . go."

Anippe's voice seemed as small and weak as a mewing kitten in Leah's ears, "We're going to stay at a hotel? We're starting on our third day."

"I am aware of that, Anippe," Gareth growled. "But if we don't get some sort of rest soon and something to eat, none of us are going to be left alive to find anything or anyone."

Leah felt his hand on her knee. She opened her tired eyes and stared into the second kindest face she'd ever seen. The words of truth flowed from her lips, "I love you."

He tilted his head to the side. "You do?"

"Of course I do," she said, slapping his hand. "I would think you already know that considering the fact I yell at all the people I truly love. That is their gift from me."

Anippe let out a soft giggle. "I guess I should be very pleased, then. Considering how much you yell at me, we must have an incredibly strong bond."

Tallent and Lowery stared over at her, and Leah let out a chuckle. "Well, would you look at that . . . she's funny!"

"Who knew?" Gareth smiled.

For the first time, the trio of weary souls enjoyed a moment of peace in the middle of their nightmare.

CHAPTER 17

David Tallent stared out at the landscape. It was still so hard to fathom the panorama that included such ancient sites now seemingly 'plunked down' in the middle of a bustling twenty-first century city. Once an oasis in the desert for weary travelers marching across the hot sand, this area of Jericho was now filled with businessmen dining at five-star restaurants, gambling at casinos and working out in the deluxe fitness centers that the elite hotels provided.

He stifled a laugh as another long, black limo entered the driveway ten floors below.

"I met Leah, you know."

David turned away from the window and walked to the overstuffed chair. He stared across the table at Aaron. "When?"

"She came to Petra right before Christmas. She was looking for Emmanuel."

"The fiancé," David whispered. "She and Lowery were at our home in Connecticut for a pre-holiday dinner when Gareth's sister, Kathryn, called and said her fiancé was missing."

"That's the guy." Aaron nodded.

"He was in Petra?"

Aaron's gaze felt as if it was boring through David's soul like a drill gone out of control. "There were a lot of things in Petra."

David sighed deeply. Leaning forward, he planted his elbows

132

firmly on his knees. "Why don't you tell me what happened?"

"You know about Leah's first adventure . . . with Lowery?" Aaron asked.

David nodded, remembering her outrageously unbelievable story about thirteen orbs that'd led her to the cave in Glastonbury. "She told me."

Aaron leaned forward. To any outside observer staring through the balcony windows, David Tallent and Aaron Cain would look like ferocious lions thrown into the arena, sizing each other up before the first one chose to attack. "I assume you do not know that you're related to Moses?"

———

The feelings went back and forth in David Tallent's mind; first fear turned to confusion then to incredible glee, on to anger before the final feeling of acceptance flowed through his veins, as he sat and listened to the story of the Sapphire Staff being relayed to him word for word by a man he'd long ago sworn to never see again.

When Aaron finished he sat back on the couch and sipped the rich, olive tea from the sterling cup. "So . . . there you are. Now you are up to speed with your daughter's life. Or, at least the part I know of."

"So Leah and Anippe have met each other?"

Aaron nodded.

"Did they get along well?" David swallowed, feeling yet another card fall from the base of his trembling house of lies.

"Not at all," Aaron replied immediately. "From what I could tell, Leah couldn't stand her. Found her very annoying."

David felt the regret well in his soul. "Oh."

"Anippe's a very quiet woman. She's been used badly," Aaron practically yelled the latter, as if wanting David to feel pain deep inside his heart. "William Knight certainly wasn't kind. I think Anippe has spent most of her life searching for someone to love."

"She has you," David interrupted. "Knowing you, you've shown her more love than . . . anyone else could have."

"I do love her." Aaron nodded. "We've gone everywhere together, although Anippe mostly likes to stay in the Coptic Museum. That building is her little paradise on earth."

David chuckled, thinking of his firstborn. "Leah feels the same about her library. If they'd let her I think she'd live in the basement and never come out."

"I guess paradise is different for everyone."

David swallowed hard. He felt the color rise in his cheeks, as the fear grew in his soul.

Aaron spoke. His voice remained calm but there was an undercurrent of frustration building in his tone. "I've stepped up. Now it's your turn."

He tried to avoid his uneasy glare.

"What the hell is going on, David?"

Along with the deep sigh that came from his lips, David offered Aaron the truth. He told the story of his find; the pages he'd stumbled across in old books; piecing together a trail that seemed, at first, just like pure entertainment. It started out like a *Times* crossword puzzle, something that would keep his mind occupied in the evenings after he'd come home from yet another boring day at the office.

He told Aaron that he'd forgotten who he used to be. The fire that had once roared inside his belly as a young man had died long ago. David Tallent had worked his fingers to the bone building an empire that could support his wife and children after he was gone, and had left his adventurer's fedora behind after one horrible night to embark on a life that he'd chosen. He had intended to make up for all his lies by being the best father and husband he could possibly be. Perhaps he'd even hoped that by becoming a perfect dad . . . a perfect husband . . . that his past mistakes would somehow be forgiven.

He couldn't even hate Gareth Lowery, the man who embodied everything that David Tallent used to be. David had already figured out most of the puzzle by the time the billionaire had walked through his door on the arm of his beloved daughter. But when Leah had started telling her tale of the thirteen orbs—the fire that David had tried so hard to forget had sprung to life once again inside his soul. It had begged him to go back to his roots; throw caution to the wind and become the type of man he used to be . . . the type of man his daughter now had by her side.

As he told his story to Aaron, he left nothing out. No emotion was held in check, as David found himself crying before the wide-eyed man. He begged his forgiveness; he prayed Aaron would understand that he had no choice in the matter. The young man from long ago—the wild, passionate man who'd cared about nothing but his true love and their next adventure—had come back to life inside his aging body. He wanted to go back and try to understand what had gone wrong—mend old wounds and begin again.

When the speech concluded, Aaron sighed. "So all this crap is just about some silver and gold? Are you kidding me? That scroll was just an ancient cosmic joke played on greedy fools who dreamed of nothing but wealth and power!"

David shook his head, violently denying the simple answer. "No, Aaron. It's about way more than buried treasure. That's the problem. When I found out what was really down there . . . I had to stop. I couldn't let anyone find out what the real treasure is. Not to mention the tools needed in order to unearth it. If those tools fall into the wrong hands, the bearer will become . . . invincible."

Aaron let out a sarcastic snort and stood from his place on the couch. "Anippe has been put in danger over *this*? I don't care what the truth is. I don't care what could happen if these so-called 'tools' fall into the wrong hands. For god's sake, David, you may have just signed the death warrants of the people you supposedly love because of some ridiculous need to feel young again."

"That's not what this is!"

"Then what the hell is it?" Aaron grabbed him by the shirt. "Correct me if I'm wrong, but you have more money than most small countries. You live in a huge mansion, you're adored by everyone—who don't really know you, of course—you have wonderful children, a goddess wife who—" Aaron immediately stopped talking and took a step back. "Wait a minute . . . Tell me this isn't about . . . her!"

David hung his head.

"It's about her?!"

David marched away from the bright red face and stared out at the pink neon lights below. The long, black limo had disappeared—no doubt having delivered its occupants to the gaming tables to try their luck. God, how he wished the strangers had a good night, because luck always ran out.

"Jesus, David," Aaron's punishing voice came from behind. "She's gone. She's been gone since 1972. It's not like you can come back and find her."

David's throat closed. "I haven't. I love my wife."

"You should."

"I do. Mary has been a wonderful gift."

"More than you deserve." Aaron's statement sliced through the air like the jagged edge of a knife.

David nodded. "Once is a miracle . . . but twice?" He turned to face the angry man. "I don't deserve her. I agree. I don't deserve the wonderful relationship I have with Leah either, and I deserve no words of kindness from you."

"Oh, I wouldn't worry, Mr. Tallent," Max's loud voice made the panes of glass shudder. "By the time this is over, you will get *exactly* what you deserve."

Max held the door open, as one of his grimy goons lugged in a dinner tray and then left the room. He smiled at his captives. "It's a shame that you're not free to roam this lovely hotel. We have a fantastic restaurant downstairs called, 'The Olive Tree.' You can smell those dishes on the table from a mile away." He grinned. "Greek, Italian, Spanish—every food that makes the palette dance with joy. Of course, you're going to enjoy it right now," he said, pointing to the platters that had been placed on the table. "But it's just not the same without the blissful atmosphere of the restaurant itself—the beautiful women, the spectacular view of the Dead Sea through the windows. That's what I told him . . . it's all about location."

"Him, who?" Aaron asked.

David took note of the strange look that crossed Max's face and a thought popped into his head. "You're not in charge."

Max offered an evil smile from across the room. "I am in charge of you, Mr. Tallent."

"All this," David continued, pointing out the glass doors, "is not your idea. In fact, you probably don't even know what's out there. You're just a stooge following orders."

Although anger flashed in the predator's eyes, Max simply turned and took a step into the hallway. "Don't you worry about me, Mr. Tallent. When the end comes for you and your family, I'll be on the front lines. It doesn't matter who the host is as long as you're invited to the party. Now, if you'll excuse me, I think I'll go down to that restaurant and enjoy all those beautiful women." He winked. "Don't wait up . . . Dad."

CHAPTER 18

Leah stared out at the endless landscape. The scene of the ancient city with the Dead Sea hovering in the background was truly a breathtaking sight. The clump of dirt located dead center seemed to rise from the earth like a huge pitcher's mound just waiting for the Yankees to arrive. She chuckled at the image.

"What?" Anippe asked.

"I'm losin' it. I swear to God, I think my so-called brilliant mind has dried up. Probably looks like Athena's olive by now."

"I hope not." Anippe smiled. "We still have a long way to go."

"And a short time to get there," Gareth added.

Leah snorted at yet another movie reference from her beloved, as the waitress silently walked forward and delivered their dinners. Leah felt the drool collect inside her mouth, like a stray cur watching the hot dog vendor in Central Park—just waiting for him to slip and drop one of his tasty treats on the ground. She looked at Gareth. "Thank you."

"Oh my God!" Gareth announced with a loud laugh, scaring the diners at the surrounding tables with his sudden outburst.

Anippe dropped her fork on the plush carpet and Leah let out a little yelp, jumping back in her chair. "What?" she asked.

"I just remembered the dinner we had in London."

The picture of Gareth dressed to the nines floated in front of Leah's eyes.

"You were wearing that emerald dress that Trish—the happy shopkeeper—had picked out for you." His voice slowly turned into a sexy whisper that made Leah's skin burn.

She swallowed, briefly noting Anippe's forlorn gaze. "I also remember the food was so bad we wouldn't eat it."

"And you thought coffee and desert would be the way to go," he grinned.

"Yeah, spotted dick was on the menu, if I recall."

Anippe smiled wide, enjoying their memory. "Exactly what does that look like?"

"Don't know," Leah squeezed Gareth's hand. "We were your typical rude Americans—just stuck to the coffee to be on the safe side."

Anippe grinned. "You *see*? That's what I want."

Gareth raised an eyebrow. "Spotted dick?"

"No," she said, reaching out and slapping him on the arm "What you two have. The stories, the adventures—you've actually been through things together."

"Not all the things were good," Leah reminded her.

"It doesn't matter," Anippe remarked. "You did them together. You made it through . . . together. You're very lucky."

"That we are," Gareth agreed, leaning over and kissing Leah on the lips.

She loved this kind of kiss. There were many that Gareth Lowery offered: The passionate kiss of intense love-making; the hurried peck on the cheek or forehead as they raced around the world and held each other up in order to survive; the one he placed on her lips fast, right after he said something sarcastic and was moving quickly to get away from any barb she shot back—but this one was Leah's favorite. This was the one that was pure possession—hard and long. This was the one that stopped her brain from working; it was as if he was putting his stamp on her, making sure that anyone watching would not be confused for a second as to who Leah would be sleeping with when the moon rose high in the sky.

Remembering their guest, she pushed against his chest, breaking the connection. "Location, location, dear heart. We're in a highly public place."

"So?"

Leah sighed. She didn't know why she wanted to erase the sad look off Anippe's face considering how much she detested her presence so far on this trip, but she wanted to. Her heart actually felt like it was breaking when she watched the beautiful woman's face fall. "So . . . I'm hungry," Leah announced.

"Me, too," Gareth whispered provocatively.

"For my Greek salad." She pointed at the overflowing plate.

"I'm part Greek." He winked.

"Mmm, hmm . . . and you'll be the buffet for later." Leah slapped his hand and began shoveling food into her mouth. The steaming bowl of linguine beside it made Leah's head spin with happiness and her empty stomach sighed with relief. The table turned quiet, as all the weary travelers attacked their plates like a pack of starving wolves.

Anippe was the first to speak. "Do we go to Qumran later tonight . . . after we get some sleep?"

Gareth shook his head. "No way, we'll never be able to see anything out there."

"It's a pit. We won't be able to see anything during the day either," Leah reminded him.

"I know that, O' Exalted One," he snorted. "But at least during the daylight hours we won't actually fall into the pit and break our necks."

"Good call," she replied, washing down the amazing dinner with a glass of bright red wine.

Anippe stared out at the old city bathed in the pink light coming from the Oasis Casino next door. "It's been more than forty-eight hours." Her voice came out as a frightened whisper, barely audible above the cacophony of clinking glasses and shuffling silverware.

"We've accomplished a great deal in just forty-eight hours," Gareth remarked.

Anippe nodded. "I hope it will be enough." She gazed at Leah. "Do you think they're still okay? I mean, do you think your father and my uncle are being treated . . . okay?"

Leah's throat constricted, as a picture of her father chained to the wall of a cave suddenly appeared in her mind. "Well, they're probably not living in the lap of luxury like this," she said, with a forced smile. "But I'm sure they're okay. We have the full seven days, supposedly, and I'm sure they're fine, Anippe."

"Until the time is up," she whispered.

Leah took a deep breath and nodded. "Until the time is up."

———

The meal was complete and the room was heaven—pure heaven.

There was never a time when Leah felt more serene, more sated, than after Gareth had filled her with every part of him. His body, his touch, the words of passion that he whispered in her ear—the whole package made her soul sing and her body ache with excitement. Every time their bodies met, the world simply disappeared. Pain, fear and heartache were simply taken away on the wings of some kind of angel, leaving Tallent and Lowery with the power of a love that was impossible to explain.

When she could catch her breath, Leah curled up beside him and laid her head on his warm chest. The exhaustion was overwhelming, but the feeling that ran through her limbs was sheer bliss. With the endearing words of true love ringing in her ears, Leah fell into a deep—well protected—sleep.

———

"For the love of God it's *January*! Why is it so bloody hot?!" Leah's voice made the limo driver twitch slightly in his seat.

"We're actually expecting a heat wave that's supposed to last here through next week, Miss. It's not usually this hot this time of year," the driver remarked.

Leah grimaced at his words. "Well . . . we have good luck."

Gareth laughed. "I think my companion wanted to enjoy a swim in the pool and grab a tan instead of going out and exploring a bunch of rocks."

He nodded. "Perfectly understandable, Miss. I'd rather do that myself," the driver agreed, clearing his throat. "If I may say so, all of our tourist spots will be a trial today in this heat. Perhaps the lady has the right idea, Sir."

"What else is around here?" Leah asked.

Anippe whispered beside her, "Ignorant American."

Leah slapped her on the arm, as the driver flashed a truly

beautiful smile in the rearview mirror. "The Tel es-Sultan, of course, which is the ancient city of Jerusalem, is the most famous."

"The first recorded settlement in the world, right?"

"Yes, Ma'am. Some believe that it's even much older than Mesopotamia. There's also the Masada site, which is where the first-century Jewish revolt against the Romans occurred. There's the Dead Sea . . . beautiful sight that is. There are even old palaces here."

Leah's ears perked up at the word, remembering the frightening picture on the map. "Whose palaces are they?"

"Let's see," the driver began, tapping his leather gloves against the steering wheel. "There's Herodium, which was King Herod's palace that he carved out of a hilltop. There is also Hisham's Palace, which has an incredible mosque, ancient fountain . . . it's actually a lot more impressive than the Herod excavation."

"What's that up there?" Anippe pointed out the window at the bright red cable car that was climbing up the mountain west of Jericho.

Leah raised her eyebrows. "Ignorant Egyptian. Shouldn't *you* know all this stuff?"

"Do you have any idea how many excavated sites there are in this area? *Everything* happened here," Anippe replied with a smile.

"The Yankees never won the Series here," Gareth added, with a grin.

Anippe bowed her head. "Of course, I meant that all the *interesting* things happened here."

Gareth winced and turned to Leah. "There's just no place like home, is there?"

"Not when you're a snotty American playboy," Leah answered, patting him on the shoulder.

"I'm very misunderstood," Gareth said, staring out the window at the cable car in the distance.

The driver smiled at the happy banter coming from the back seat, as he answered Anippe's question, "That's Mount Temptation, Miss."

Leah leaned forward immediately. "What did you just say?"

The car came from out of nowhere and the limo driver swerved to the side of the road to avoid the manic sedan. Leah could hear the strange new accent, as anger filled the driver's voice.

Crossing himself, the driver stared into the mirror and lifted his arm in the air. "Cell phones! Going to kill everybody someday. Worst things on the planet so far."

"Actually," Leah said with a smile. "The worst ones play, 'Here Comes the Bride.' "

The man lifted an eyebrow above his elegant sunglasses. His small black mustache curved into a smile above his lips, as his occupants burst into laughter at the obviously private joke.

The long car pulled off the road into a fairly empty spot of land. There were signs pointing the way to an amazing site, but Leah couldn't read most of them. Instead, she followed Gareth's lead.

Her hero spoke to the man at the gate, and then turned back to her. "I told him we won't be needing a guide considering we're all archaeologists who have been here before."

Leah plastered a fake smile quickly on her face and nodded at the older man, trying to communicate the fact that they would rather die than disturb anything in the ancient site. *Are there any three faces in the world you could trust more?* Leah thought.

. . . Apparently not. The man waved them through without question and pointed toward a rocky ledge in the near distance. Leah and Anippe walked silently beside Gareth, already missing the cool refreshing air of the limousine.

Looking back over her shoulder, Leah noticed the driver standing by the side of the grand car. He was saluting her and smiling.

Puzzled, Leah turned away from the strange sight and marched across the already burning hot sand, praying they would find what they needed quickly and exit the desolate, eerie land in one piece.

CHAPTER 19

Gareth felt the lines of sweat run down his back like miniature waterfalls. They'd only been here a few minutes and already the rising sun had saturated his clothing, creating a second slimy skin. He felt a slight shot of panic, remembering that he'd left behind the spear and shield in the trunk of the luxury vehicle. But, Gareth waved away the anxiety, knowing that the dutiful driver—like all of his other well-paid employees—would sit and wait for them to reappear and claim the items. He just prayed that they wouldn't need Athena's ultimate protection to get through the pit.

He followed his beloved librarian through the doorway of the rock enclosure and into the empty room.

"You know what's funny?" he said.

"What?"

"Everywhere we've gone, no one has even asked about Athena's stuff. I mean . . . wouldn't someone wonder?"

Leah shrugged. "Probably think we're ignorant tourists who just spent all their money on fake artifacts." She turned around and kissed him on the cheek. "They're probably laughing their asses off at you right now, Lowery."

He pulled her close, willing to accept the burden of even more heat as long as she was the reward.

Leah pushed him away. "Way too hot in here for that, cowboy."

Gareth felt a twinge of worry and passed her another water

bottle. "Keep drinking. Won't help if we get dehydrated."

"You know what else is weird?" Anippe's head materialized in the small window.

Leah jumped back. "Jesus!"

"What?" Her eyes were wide.

"You have a gift for appearing out of nowhere. It's creepy." Leah turned away from her. "Cough or something when you're around."

Gareth stopped his smile from appearing at Leah's frustrated voice. He looked up at Anippe. "What's weird?"

She smiled. "Athena's stuff, there were strange markings on the inside of the shield. On her helmet too, come to think of it."

Gareth watched Leah walk back to the door, exiting the hot, steamy cave. He followed her into the stifling sunshine.

"You mean the swastika?" asked Leah.

Anippe nodded.

Gareth watched the woman who was everything his heart begged for, lift her hand up and shield her eyes. She stared across the strange landscape, searching for anything that might point her in the right direction. "That's not really weird," Leah began. "Before old Hitler got going and decided to use it as a logo for the massacre of innocent people, the meaning of the ancient symbol was luck and prosperity."

"She's right." Gareth nodded.

Leah turned and stared at him.

He added quickly, "As always." He winked. "The Ancient Greeks and other warriors used it on the uniforms of their armies for luck. Even the Boy Scouts used it around the turn of the century."

Leah chuckled. "Were you a scout, Lowery?"

"I am always prepared, love."

Leah snorted and Anippe sent a smile in his direction.

Garth stepped forward toward the rim of rock and looked down at the large hole. "Is that the olive pit?"

Leah shook her head. "Nope, looks like a well." She pointed at the other ditches and cracks dug into the ground. "It reminds me of Petra. Those are the aqueducts that carried the water into the well. That big dam over there must've diverted the water into this center area, where it then ran into the smaller cisterns over there."

Gareth followed her finger, like a map being laid out before him. He recognized the round, smooth spots in the dry earth that used to be pools for the monks who'd lived here. "Makes sense," he said, over Leah's shoulder. "The Dead Sea Sect was known for their daily purification rites. They were pretty rigid with their rules."

Leah started to walk down the rocky slope toward the foundations that clearly marked the land. "The Dead Sea Sect, huh?" she said, lightly. "Okay, Mr. Professor. Tell us what you know."

Anippe smiled, as she walked beside the hero and his companion.

Gareth's deep voice rang out through the oppressive heat. "This place was once referred to as the City of Salt."

"Makes sense," Leah nodded.

"According to the documents that were found here, the Sect was made up of celibate males."

"Too damn hot out here to fornicate anyway," she grunted.

Gareth poked her in the ribs. "There's some dissent in the archaeological community about them, however."

"What a shocker."

Anippe chuckled at Leah's sarcastic tone.

"You wanna' hear this or not?"

Leah put her hands in the air. "Yes, Mr. Lowery, Sir. Sorry, Mr. Lowery, Sir."

"Good." He continued, "Two documents were found out here. One was called the Manual of Discipline, which stated that the people here lived a communal life. They ate communally, were blessed communally . . . you get the picture. In fact," Gareth added, pointing to the large rectangular pathway, walled in by ancient stones. "That's the dining hall. There were three rows of tables found inside where, according to their documents, they all came together and ate in silence."

"Like monks," Anippe added.

Gareth shook his head. "Sort of, but not exactly. You see, the Dead Sea Sect, per their own documents, were kind of an extremist off-shoot. Their biggest belief was in the apocalypse. The basic papers that they left behind talked of their expectations of death. They believed that mankind would be divided between the 'sons of light' and the 'sons of darkness.' Now, the sons of light would be led by the 'prince of light' and—"

Leah raised her hand. "And the 'sons of darkness' would be led by the 'prince of darkness'?"

Gareth smiled. "Actually, Miss I-Know-Everything, they would be led by the 'Angel of Darkness.'"

"To-may-to . . . To-mah-to."

He smiled. "They knew that the wicked would be destroyed and perversion would be eliminated."

"Good for you that the second part hasn't happened yet."

"Very funny." Gareth stared up at the caves that'd been carved into the rock, where the occupants used to sleep. "There were so many places that could possibly lead into a pit, and time was ticking away. Before the end of days came, of course, they believed that God would pick a community of elite who were destined to be saved and would be the nucleus of a new, devout society on earth."

"And they would be called?" Leah asked.

"The 'sons of the spirit of truth.'"

Leah rolled her eyes. "Whew. That's a mouthful."

"Indeed."

Anippe stared at the mounds to the north and south that had to have been used as the Sect's cemeteries. "I remember reading that there were women found buried out here." She turned to Gareth. "I thought they were celibate males."

Gareth shrugged. "Therein lies the problem with history. Too many questions . . . not enough answers. Their second document was called the Damascus Document, which told of a completely different existence. This was a part of the Sect that also existed at one time where the men were allowed private property—children, women."

Gareth smiled. "Maybe that just didn't work out, so they changed their thinking."

"Washer dryer," Leah said.

"Women were communal property," Anippe spat. "Men! Some things never change."

Gareth didn't fight the angry tone, considering he knew what tricks William Knight had played on her. "Some men," he corrected.

Anippe's head shot up. "Sorry. Some men."

Leah laughed. "Yeah, others are simply humble, non-assuming souls who build their own Concorde. Gareth, how's that vow of poverty coming?"

"I rented that thing for you, lady. Not to mention, do you know how hard it was finding those male models to attend to your needs?" He turned to Anippe. "Leah doesn't like stewardesses."

"Flight attendants," Leah muttered.

He continued, "So, I scoured the countryside looking for young, handsome, virile men to mill about the cabin. I even got a veritable Don Juan to be the pilot."

Leah pouted. "I didn't get to see him."

Gareth shrugged. "He had a hat on and dark glasses, but I'm sure he would've passed muster."

"To be honest," Leah smiled. "The only thing I want from my pilot is to arrive safely." She stared at the barren landscape, apparently searching for anything that might have changed in the last few minutes. "So . . . these guys just sat around in this heat, day after day in caves, eating, washing and waiting for the end of the world."

The voice of his angel flowed through Gareth's ears, and he grinned at the sunburned face that almost matched the dark auburn hair stuck to her forehead. "No dear. In fact, two and three story buildings were uncovered where they found pottery kilns, mill, an old stable, and even a laundry."

"Told ya. Washer dryer."

"These . . . guys . . . were very self sufficient and made a working, blossoming community in the desert."

"Yeah, I've heard of those," Leah snorted. "David Koresh had one in Waco, Texas, if I remember correctly. Did they serve Kool-Aid here, too?"

Gareth sighed. "The people who came here were volunteers who joined the Sect of their own free will."

"Uh-huh."

"They were obedient to the rules, however. If not, the form of punishment was exclusion from the group." Gareth leaned toward her. "By the way . . . they had a heck of a library."

Leah tilted her head. "So they weren't all bad." She continued,

"I suppose that's where all the scrolls were found?"

Gareth pointed up at the caves in the surrounding hills. "Nope. The scrolls were found in the caves. The Scriptorium they uncovered was empty. All they found were writing benches and parchment— probably where they wrote and kept the scrolls until the armies came and they had to hide them away."

"What happened to the Sect?"

Gareth shrugged. "Don't know. Maybe they ran when the Temple fell. Maybe they got tired of waiting for the end of the world and went somewhere else. I did hear that King Herod set fire to Qumran. Maybe that got them all."

"So much for the sons of whatever."

Gareth nodded. "Yeah, old Herod was the King from Hell, if you ask me."

Wiping the sweat from her brow, Anippe lifted the mass of black hair off her neck and twisted it into a bun on top of her head.

Leah sighed. "If I tried to do that I'd look like Little Orphan Annie on speed."

Anippe's brows furrowed on her forehead as Gareth laughed out loud. "I'm still getting used to your sense of humor."

"Like I said, it's an acquired taste," Leah mumbled. "Well!" The sweaty librarian slapped her knees. "Now that the history lesson is over with, Herr Professor, where's this pit? Let's get whatever little nugget we need and get back to the world of air-conditioning."

Gareth stared at Anippe. "Please tell me that you know."

Smiling, Anippe stepped forward and marched toward an embankment that rose above the ancient well. Without a word, she walked past them; her lithe body sauntering through the desert heat like a mirage.

Gareth stared into the sapphire eyes that knew him better than he knew himself. "Should I take that as a yes?"

Leah grunted and followed the woman's path. "You know . . . she's strange. Sometimes I like her bur most of the time I want to—"

"Beat the crap out of her?"

"Is that wrong?"

He smiled, poking Leah in the ribs. "I don't know. You should ask yourself, what would Jesus do?"

Leah muttered, remembering the words she'd read not so long ago. "He didn't mention beating the crap out of people."

"Maybe the situation never came up."

"Alas." Leah smiled. "Another mystery."

"Let's solve this one first, shall we?"

Anippe waved frantically at them. "By George, I think she's found it."

They walked up the slope to join the other sapphire-eyed lady. "Who's George?" Leah grinned.

Feeling the banter coming to a close, Gareth already missed the light-hearted humor that he and his ladylove used to get through times like these. He closed his eyes again, thanking anyone who was listening for the companion who stood by his side.

CHAPTER 20

Leah stared into the black hole that'd been planted in the middle of the desert. She looked over at Anippe, standing on the opposite side of the pit. "How did you know this was here?"

She shrugged. "I assumed it would be near the water receptacle. They needed the cool conditions to keep the oil safe so they would've done the pressing of the olives near the coolest place they could find."

Anippe threw herself over the edge and began to step carefully down the ladder of rock that'd been carved into one side.

Staring up at Gareth's deep green eyes, Leah smiled. "See . . . she's annoying."

Worry clouded his features. "I should've gone in first."

"Not an issue. If she screams, we'll find another way in."

"You're mean, Madame Librarian."

She put her foot on the ladder and began climbing down. "Too late for me to be reborn, you think?"

He laughed. "I think so."

Leah wanted to stop breathing. A wretched stench invaded her nostrils, and she suddenly wished that oxygen wasn't a necessity. "God Almighty, what is that?" She stepped down on the floor of the cave.

Anippe stood still, her silk scarf covered her nose, and salty tears filled her eyes. Her voice was muffled through the fabric. "Olives."

151

Leah choked. "But I like olives."

"Yes, well, these are rotted. Makes a difference."

Gareth jumped down beside them, turning the large flashlight on and sending its beam down the pitch-black tunnel. "They probably used this for ages. The wet stone acted like a sponge and trapped the odor in here. When it heats up, it's like the past comes back to life."

"Ugh," Leah snorted. "Too bad they didn't make perfume instead of olive oil."

The trio walked forward, away from the brilliant sunshine and into the dark recesses of a forgotten time. Because of the horrible stench, the cooler air no longer seemed like a gift.

"The pit of despair, huh?" Gareth remarked. "The only desperate part in here is the smell." He waved the flashlight around, illuminating the flat, undecorated walls. "Pretty boring place, if you ask me."

"Just keep walkin," Leah said.

"You okay?" Gareth asked, as the sound of sheer panic flowed through her voice.

"Fine." Leah swallowed. "I can't remember a time when my life was boring since I met you."

"Sure," Gareth huffed. "Blame me."

Anippe sighed. "So, what exactly are we looking for in here, anyway?"

"This was on the map, Anippe. I suppose it leads to the mansion of some freak, according to the pictures."

"Where the last seed resides," Gareth added, quietly.

"Oh, right. So maybe nothing's supposed to happen here," Anippe said, lightheartedly. "If the seed's in the mansion, this is just a tunnel. Maybe your dad just wanted to show us a way to get there that was out of the hot sun."

Leah remained quiet, remembering the strange phrase—*Is it still there?*—written in her father's hand. Her eyes searched the dimly-lit enclosure, following Gareth's flashlight like a hawk follows its prey. She didn't know if there would actually be an 'X' that marked the spot, but if there was, she wasn't going to miss it.

"What is that?" Gareth's hushed words sounded creepy in the

dark cave.

Leah stared over his shoulder. She took a deep breath, focusing on where the bright beam was aimed. The group's quickened gait diminished to the tiny, careful footsteps of a frightened crew about to come upon a vicious killer.

Leah leaned forward and whispered in Gareth's ear. "Is that . . . gold?"

Before he could answer, Anippe crossed in front of Gareth's flashlight. She stepped forward and reached up, touching the border of the door. She ran her fingers across the strange etchings that someone had made in the gold-plating. "It's Egyptian," she announced. "An Egyptian mine."

Leah turned to Gareth. "The members of the Dead Sea Sect were Egyptian miners? I thought they pressed olives, wrote scrolls, and waited for the end of the world."

Gareth nodded. "I never heard of mines being in this area. This place has been excavated to death. No mines were ever found."

Leah stared at the tiles decorating the entrance. There were people carrying bricks, lugging heavy objects on their backs and kneeling down before another shirtless figure, holding a whip high in the air. "Maybe we should go back and find another way through."

Her stomach clenched, as a sound echoed behind them. The resounding crash was excruciatingly loud, making the rock walls shudder around them. It sounded like the door of a vault swinging shut, closing them in for all time. She swallowed. "Maybe not."

Anippe's frightened voice filled the space, "I guess we're on the right track."

Gareth nodded. "Someone wants us to go through here."

Leah looked around. "Walking into a dark, abandoned mine. So much for the dream of boredom."

Anippe suddenly lunged for the flashlight and ripped it from Gareth's grip. She ducked her head and entered the dark tunnel.

Gareth shouted, "What the hell are you doing?" He grabbed Leah and followed the light.

"Maybe my uncle's in here." She turned to Leah. "Your father?"

Leah shook her head. "Anippe, according to the map, we're not done yet."

Her face fell as Leah's words echoed in the smaller tunnel. "But look, we found something new and it must lead to the final picture on the map. We're close . . . real close."

"Anippe," Gareth interrupted. "Give me the flashlight. Look at this."

Anippe handed him the bright beam and Gareth aimed it at a strange map that seemed to be written on the walls. Big black and green lines crisscrossed each other, looking like a million little rivers were snaking through the rock.

"Hieroglyphs?" Anippe mumbled

"No," replied Gareth. "They're veins."

Leah's stomach revolted. "Veins?"

"You know . . . mountain veins; the veins of ore or iron that combine to produce gems—rubies, sapphires, things like that. These look like mica. Might even be quartz."

Leah released the breath from her burning lungs as the science teacher in Gareth took over and began to ramble.

Anippe smiled at her. "He knows a great deal."

"Yup, when it comes to gemstones, Lowery really knows his stuff."

Without warning, Gareth suddenly stepped back, falling over Leah's foot. Anippe yelped in surprise when he fell to the floor.

The flashlight rolled around on the hard surface as Leah fell to her knees to search for any wounds in her hero's skin. "What! What is it?"

Gareth pointed at the wall. Leah could barely make out the strange outline that seemed to be etched into the rock. She reached over and grabbed the flashlight, shining the beam on the figure.

"My God," she whispered.

"It's a mummy," Anippe breathed.

It was a frightening image. Leah stared at the threads of rotted, dirty cloth peeking out of its coffin of rock and mud.

"Obviously not a Pharaoh," Anippe said, quietly. "No markings, no ornamentation . . . he must've been a slave who worked the mines."

"And they just left him here?" Leah's high-pitched voice echoed off the walls.

Anippe stared down at the floor littered with broken slabs of rock. "Maybe there was a collapse and his fellow miners had to bury him here. There are probably more of them in these walls."

Leah swallowed the nausea back down and offered Gareth a hand off the floor. She pulled him into a hug. "Don't worry. You're still the strong, macho hero you've always been. Just you forget about that mean old mummy."

Gareth took a deep breath. "Yeah . . . thanks."

Leah pointed the flashlight down the dark corridor and urged the others to walk forward, trying to escape the hideous place of death as fast as she could.

As time passed, the exhaustion rolled in and all Leah wanted to do was sleep. The lack of oxygen was overwhelming as they moved further into what felt like the center of the earth. "God, I hope there's a way out of here."

Anippe let out a yelp behind her and Leah turned quickly, pointing the flashlight in the woman's face.

"Sorry," Anippe sighed. "It surprised me."

The beam of light came in contact with a large scorpion. Leah watched its mighty tail rise in the air, readying itself to jump from the wall and stab its first victim.

"That's a big guy," Gareth said. Placing an arm around each of the women, he pulled them down the tunnel. "Let's just get the hell away from it, shall we?"

Leah nodded, keeping her eye on the creature as they worked their way down the passage. "Maybe it'll just stay where it is."

Being a die-hard New Yorker, the desert parasite was not exactly something she wanted to be in close quarters with. Trying to regain her composure, Leah watched as the scorpion did, in fact, stay completely still on the wall. But . . . he wasn't alone.

As they rounded a corner in the rock, the temperature immediately changed; it felt like it was over a million degrees. Leah pulled against the now itchy fabric of her silk shirt, undoing the buttons on top to relieve her skin of the extra pressure.

"Jesus," she breathed, staring at the wall. All she wanted to do was scream, but the fear literally choked her throat. "It's moving."

It was almost as if the trio went into shock, watching the wall shift back and forth before their eyes. What seemed like millions of small, black scorpions raced across the rock, maneuvering over bumps that protruded from the stone like large welts that blossomed from abused skin.

Leah tried to steady the quivering flashlight in her hand as she illuminated the horrible sight.

"The walls are green," Gareth whispered. His voice sounded hollow, as he took a step back from the scorpion brigade.

"Emeralds," Anippe added in a quivering voice. Even the native seemed frightened of the sight.

"Okay," Leah said, trying to summon the strength that she hoped was somewhere inside her "Let's walk slowly. No need to disturb them."

"Emeralds?" Gareth mumbled, "Oh, my God."

"What now?" Leah felt anger rise up in her soul, taking over the fear. She couldn't stand any more bad news.

"Leah . . . I think we're in the ancient mines of Cleopatra."

"Cleopatra?"

"Uh-huh. You know . . . the Queen."

"Sweetheart," Leah began. "I don't care if they belong to the Queen of Sheba. I have a slight aversion to scorpions and I really don't want a history lesson right now."

She could almost hear Anippe's body quivering beside her.

"Leah," Gareth continued quietly, "The mines of Cleopatra were said to be a palace of demons . . . inhabited by snakes, scorpions, wolves—beasts of prey that became very unhappy when anyone intruded into their world."

Leah thought back to the mummy near the entrance. She wondered if a cave-in wasn't the reason his body had been enveloped in the rock. Perhaps the slave had met up with the demons of Hell as he went about his work; a job that was focused on making sure a Queen could decorate her body with jewels. "Okay. Well, I say we don't intrude any longer."

Leah inched forward, staying in the center of the passage so as not to disturb the bevy of scorpion soldiers guarding the Queen's emeralds.

She held her breath, as the sound of Gareth's growl filled her ears. She stared up at him. "What?"

His eyes were focused on the walls of death.

Leah shook her head. "Great . . . now I'm hearing things."

The sound of pure agony tore from Anippe's throat. Leah tried to turn her head to see if one of the horrible things had jumped on her, but it was too late. Leah fell. Her body was pulled forward, away from the other two. The strange, monstrous form dragged her by the ankle across the hard floor.

Leah couldn't find her scream. She couldn't even conjure up a prayer as the wolf suddenly placed his front paws on her chest and stared down into her face. Its breath was hot and rancid. What looked like pieces of bloody flesh hung from his glistening teeth like red chandelier earrings.

Leah slammed her elbow against the immovable chest of matted fur and tried to push it away, but it was no use. The wild wolf didn't budge. Leah could almost feel her soul begin to pack its bags inside her, waiting to take the flight to Heaven. Gareth's shouts and Anippe's weeping grew distant, as she stared into the dark gray eyes that seemed to see into her soul.

Its face lowered to her neck, and he sniffed his frightened prey. But the jaws suddenly slammed shut. Leah stared at the eyes and could swear she saw the menacing look of evil disappear, as the wild dog stepped quickly off her chest and sat back on its haunches. Breathing heavily, it stared at Leah as she slowly sat back up, not wanting to scare the wolf with any sudden movements.

The wolf twitched its ears and stared at Leah's exposed neck. Raising its head, it sent out a howl that echoed so violently within the small area, that it made the walls of the mine tremble under its power. Leah looked down at her shattered ankle. The blood dried up before her eyes and the puncture holes seemed to disappear. Leah moved her gaze to the shaking walls. The scorpions fell to the ground like a deadly hail storm. Leah's limbs began to tingle and suddenly she knew . . .

Ignoring the frightened wolf, Leah threw herself backwards. Snatching Gareth's hand, she grabbed Anippe with the other hand just as the venomous scorpions lashed out, brutally stabbing the flesh of the trio with their tails.

Leah looked down at the disgusting creatures as they tried with all their might to poison their victims, but she felt nothing. She turned around and raced down the passage. As they ran past the howling wolf, the scorpions fell from their bodies as if their victims were suddenly enclosed inside a glass bubble. Black bodies slid from her skin and hit the floor as Leah continued to run, pulling Gareth and Anippe behind her.

As they rounded another corner, the air became cooler. The path widened and a huge opening appeared before them. A golden frame hung above the door. The border was covered with emeralds. Leah took in the large, sparkling gemstones that looked like a crown above the exit. She wondered who could've stolen the huge, round emerald from the empty saucer-shaped hole in the center.

Breathing a sigh of relief, Leah threw herself over the threshold and into the cool night air.

Anippe yelled and tumbled to the ground. Gareth landed beside Leah on the hard stone and let out a gasp of air.

Lying still, Leah pressed her flushed skin against the nice cool rock. Taking a deep breath, she tried to calm her racing heart.

Gareth's hand pressed against her back. "Leah? Leah, can you hear me? Are you all right?" The fear was evident in his panic-filled voice. "Please talk to me, sweetheart."

Leah raised her head a fraction of an inch and opened her eyes. "Really, I wouldn't mind being a little bored once in a while. In fact, I think it would be good for our relationship."

He reached under her and cradled her in his arms. "Jesus, I thought I'd lost you. That wolf . . . how?"

Leah buried her head in his chest. "The seeds."

"What?"

She reached down and raised the emerald saucer from around her neck. She whispered, "The protection of the warrior . . . the protection of the Son."

"A shield," Gareth realized.

Leah nodded. "The wolf backed off as soon as he saw it. The power that they hold made me—"

"Indestructible."

"That's why I grabbed you, and Anippe. I figured that whatever

I was touching would be protected too."

Anippe cried out. Coming out of the cave, sauntering slowly like it owned the place, was an impossible creation of nature. The large, black scorpion could only exist in myth and legend. Yet there it was, stinger raised high in the air as if preening for the captive audience.

The air crackled with electricity and a sonic boom pierced the sky. The scorpion exploded in a burst of reddish-brown goo. Leah's instincts took over as she looked around for remnants of the live mine that the creature must've tripped when it exited Cleopatra's domain; but all she saw was the pistol in Gareth's hand.

Her words came out slowly, "Since when do you have a gun?"

Gareth pulled his gaze away from the scorpion's mutilated body and placed the weapon in his belt. "Since we finished up in France," he smiled. "Remember in Petra when you said that one of us should 'pack heat' just in case, because we keep getting into situations like this?"

"You were a boy scout."

He held her tight. "Always prepared."

Anippe moved closer to the loving pair. Leah wanted to hold it together, but the power of the moment and all they'd been through was too great. The backlash of what could've happened resonated through her head as she stared at the mangled body of the deadly scorpion.

As God's paintbrush created the magnificent dawn, Leah knew the clock was ticking. When the sun fell, the fifth day would begin, and they were no closer to finding her father. Letting the exhaustion overtake her, Leah melted into Gareth's arms.

CHAPTER 21

Max twirled his cane like a baton, as he smiled at the two angry men perched on the sofa. "You should be very proud. Leah's quite smart. She's right where we need her to be now. All that's left is for her to find the last one and show us where to plant them."

David sucked in his breath, visualizing the map in his mind. "She made it through the mine?"

Max tilted his head. "What mine?"

David grimaced.

"You *see*? If you had just told us where everything was, we would've just got them ourselves and wouldn't have put your daughter through all this. What a bad father you are."

Staring at the floor, David remained silent.

Max offered an evil smile. "Not a very good father, are you Mr. Tallent?"

He placed his head in his hands.

"Of course, you never really were."

"What?" Aaron said. "What could you possibly know about—?"

"About?" Max raised an eyebrow.

David lifted his head and stared at the goons by the door.

"Don't worry yourselves," Max smiled widely. "Soon all this will be over. He is sure that your lovely Leah will find the last one and figure out the location."

David snorted. "If it even exists."

"Why would you say that?" Max walked forward. Raising his cane in the air, he poked David's shoulder. "You're the one who worked out the clues."

"Just because someone thinks there's a pot of gold at the end of a rainbow doesn't mean it's actually there. My theories were just theories."

"Yes . . . but your theories have been right on the money so far. And, well, Leah Tallent has become the bearer of more than even you bargained for."

David stood up quickly, causing Max's protectors to raise their guns. "What's that supposed to mean?"

"It means your daughter has stumbled across something far more powerful than she knows . . . more powerful than you ever imagined it to be. You should be happy about that. With the power she holds, she no longer rates as 'expendable' on our little list. I can assure you that Leah will live a long time after this is all over. I think she's already found a special place in his life."

"Are you talking about Gareth Lowery?" Max took a step back and tilted his head to the side, like a tourist studying a priceless artifact in a museum. "Now, why would you think of him, I wonder?"

David reached down, picked up the large vase of flowers and threw it across the room. "I've had enough of this! If you find your gold—fine. Take it and leave us alone. But if you dare try to take my daughter like you took my—"

"Stop talking," Aaron mumbled beside him. "Stop talking now."

A demonic gleam flashed in Max's black eyes. "Figuring it out, are we? Good," he laughed. "Very good." Placing his hat on his head, he pulled the leather gloves out of his pocket, covering the red and black tattoo on the back of his hand. "That's the beauty of philosophers; they never stop hunting for the truth."

He walked to the door and bowed to the angry men. "The shadows are lifting like a veil of fog that disappears in the morning sun. I like that. Perhaps I, too, am a philosopher at heart."

David sent a snarl across the room. "You're no philosopher. You're the Devil."

The bald man produced an evil-looking smile, as if he was the sly wolf staring at a buck that had no idea it was about to become dinner. "What makes you think the Devil isn't a philosopher?"

CHAPTER 22

Leah didn't want to listen to the voices. She wanted nothing more than to take Gareth by the hand, get back on the remarkable plane, dump Anippe in Egypt and go back to work. She could almost smell the heavenly scent of paper and ink that lived inside the New York Public Library.

She even missed the obnoxious tone of Skylar's voice, the assistant librarian who was much more interested in handsome patrons than her job. Leah also missed her twitchy little boss who constantly barked orders, trying with all his might to make up for his five-foot nothing frame by asserting his authority. She desired the old, clanging pipes that attempted to heat the always-chilly basement. She yearned to go home—back to her paradise. But the voices wouldn't stop. The pressure in her head wouldn't go away, and the clock kept ticking down to what she assumed would be the last day of her beloved father's life.

"Leah, we really have to get going," Gareth whispered. He brushed the hair away from her cheek.

The cool morning air caressed her face. Leah took a deep breath and opened her eyes. Gareth was smiling down at her. "We're almost done."

"We are?"

Gareth laughed. "No idea. But we're still alive and we're still together . . . that's gotta' count for something."

Leah nodded. She stood up and stared at the broken slabs of rock that surrounded them. "Where are we?"

Anippe appeared over the slight incline. "We're at Herodium." She pointed to the west, at a huge mound of earth that rose like a truncated cone out of the desert floor.

Leah gazed up at the monumental flight of stairs that led to a mass of broken turrets and stone slabs. "Wow," she whispered.

"The seed of Hell's King that will show you the innocent reality of who will come again," Gareth read from the map in his hands.

"Herod was Hell's King? He was the Devil?"

Gareth shook his head. "Nope. Just a jerk, really; a puppet of the Romans," he pointed at the cone. "What you're looking at was Herod's own Acropolis. At the base of the hill were small houses where slaves lived. They were the ones who lugged the water and filled the huge cisterns underneath the palace. They would also walk up the stairs to the large cistern at the top of the hill. It had to be kept full because Herod had pools for bathing."

"Sounds like a great job to run up and down a staircase in the hot sun to make a moron happy," she sighed. "I suppose we have to climb that thing, right?"

"No escalators back then." Gareth smiled.

They began their short trek across the smooth rock. Leah stared over at Gareth's wide eyes. He was already reveling in the thought of what he would fine when they reached the top. She could tell. His eyes always glittered with the flame of adventure when he walked through history. She cleared her throat. "Was he into scorpions and wolves?"

"No," Anippe replied. "He mostly just killed children."

Leah's head snapped around and stared into the serious sapphire eyes. "Excuse me?"

"Oh, come on! You *have* to know who King Herod was."

"Characters in the Bible for two hundred, Alex?" Leah snapped. "What?"

She sighed and punched Gareth in the shoulder. "Tell her."

He smiled. "Leah wasn't raised in a religious household, Anippe. She knows almost everything, but when it comes to characters in the Bible, she only knows the real 'stars' of the show."

Leah nodded. "There you go."

"Strange," Anippe muttered.

"What is?"

"That you two make such a good team. I mean, Gareth's parents were part of the Nag Hammadi dig in 1945. You're a descendant of Moses—you've stood in front of Heaven, for goodness sake—yet, you know almost nothing about the Bible."

"Do you have a point?"

Anippe shook her head. "It is just strange. You've said that you have a hard time believing in this stuff. Yet, you're *that* hero's companion." She pointed at Gareth.

"God works in mysterious ways." Sarcasm flowed through Leah's voice. "Good thing I am his companion . . . considering."

" . . . Considering?"

"If I hadn't been, you would've been stung to death by millions of scorpions."

A shudder raced through Anippe's body as Leah continued, "Now . . . don't you want to get on with telling me about all this so I might be prepared to save your skinny ass again? Or, would you rather just keep poking me with a stick and see how that works out for you?"

Anippe swallowed hard. "King Herod was visited by the Magi. They're the three wise men."

"Got it." Leah raised her hand in the air. "Them, I know."

Gareth chuckled.

"Yes. Well, they visited Herod and asked him if he knew the location where Jesus could be found. They told him the King of the Jews was being born and they were on their way to offer Him gifts. Herod, who was the Roman King of Judea at the time, thought his throne would be taken away from him by this so-called Savior . . . this new King. So, he told the Magi to find Jesus and bring Him back to the palace so that Herod could also worship him.

"The Magi were visited, in their dreams, and were told of Herod's plan so the Magi avoided Herodium completely. When the Magi failed to come back, Herod ordered the slaughter of all male children—two years old and under."

"But," Gareth interrupted. "Mary, Joseph and Jesus had already fled Egypt."

"How many children were killed?" Leah looked up at him.

"Depends on what version you believe, I suppose."

"Like the Holocaust?"

"Exactly like that. You see, the Massacre of the Innocents is only mentioned by Matthew in the Bible, and people believe it was to simply show that Jesus was the next great leader of the Jewish people—taking the place of Moses. Some have said that it never happened—that it was simply a metaphor for the great 'King' Jesus became." His voice turned sad, "Others say that anywhere from fourteen thousand to sixty-four thousand innocents were actually killed by Herod's army. There are even more who say, considering the size of the villages at that time, only about twenty children were killed."

"One would've been too many," Anippe said.

Leah's stomach lurched, visualizing the map with the secret panel that'd been pasted over the palace. The stick figure bodies that'd been drawn underneath made Leah physically sick. She didn't want to think that she was standing in a place where a man had destroyed innocent children.

As if reading her thoughts, Gareth spoke, "People believed that the children were killed in Bethlehem, not at the palace."

"But there were some recorded killings of children at this palace."

Leah's head pounded.

"Who?" Gareth asked.

"His sons," Anippe replied. "Herod was so worried his precious kingdom would be taken from him that he killed two of his own sons and a wife, supposedly burying them in a staircase inside the palace."

"What a great guy," Leah snapped.

Gareth shouted. "That's it! That's what happened to Qumran. I remember now. At the end of Herod's reign, two teachers and a bunch of 'pupils' from Qumran were going to come and tear down the Roman statues—eagles or something—from the entrance to this palace. They thought it was a sin to make idols. Herod's army found out about their plan, used the mine that we just went through to sneak in and burned them all."

"What's his thing with Cleopatra?" Leah asked, trying with all her might to steer the subject away from the gruesome killings. "She liked him."

"Actually," Gareth began. "Mark Antony was the one who recognized Herod as the national leader of the small Jewish region. Cleopatra leased this land to him for his palace. Probably, considering how paranoid everyone was back then, she had her slaves watch him from that lovely mine of hers, keeping tabs on him and making sure he didn't decide to take more than he was entitled to. They kept him on a short leash, making Herod look like a friend and ally of Rome. They had more land and money. He probably thought he was hedging his bets—joining the winning team."

Leah nodded. "Yeah, who cares about religion, morals or beliefs when the one with the most money always wins anyway, right?"

Patting her on the shoulder, Gareth smiled. "Actually, Mark Antony and Cleopatra lost—big time."

"Of course." The card catalogue in her mind pulled out the wealth of Egyptian data from its files. "When they lost, Herod gave his loyalty to Octavian when he became the first Emperor."

Gareth nodded. "Who called himself Augustus. Herod was rewarded and received, for his loyalty, Jericho and Gaza. He is still remembered for the extensive building he began in this country— the walls of Jerusalem, the citadel and the Temple, to name a few. In fact, after an earthquake destroyed thousands of people and buildings during his reign, he made all kinds of changes to Jerusalem. He built a theatre and a market . . . lots of things for the Jewish people to enjoy."

"Unfortunately, for him, he went too far. He built, from scratch, a very snazzy city called Caesarea, in honor of the Emperor. But, it wasn't like Jerusalem. It was laid out like a grand Greek city—almost a carbon copy of Alexandria. And, of course, had pagan temples built dedicated to the Emperor. Gareth pointed up at the large mound. His palaces were also Greek. He installed baths, villas and towers. Some of the Jewish people even believed that Herod stole objects from the tombs of David and Solomon to add to his own personal collection."

Leah sighed. "Please tell me there's a happy ending to all this. Like the Romans said . . . this guy sucks! Then they pummeled him to death. Or, the people of Jerusalem set fire to his feet."

"Unfortunately, no. He died of a cancer-type illness safely in his bed."

"That's too bad."

As they reached the foot of the cone, Leah gazed up the never-ending staircase. She took a deep breath and began to climb, wishing with all her heart that a stray rain cloud would come along and cool the anger inside her soul.

———

As her foot hit the top step, Leah let out a sigh of relief. "Thank God."

The stone breaking in two was like a whisper in the still air. The stair shuddered beneath her feet and she felt herself falling over backwards. Leah tried to stop herself but it was too late.

Gareth let out a yell and ran the last ten steps to save her from a neck-breaking fall.

But, before he could reach her, Leah felt a strong arm grab her around her waist and pull her forward. A pair of golden-brown eyes, like those of a loveable pet, stared into her soul.

His accent was slow and sexy. His smile was slightly crooked, as if his lips were a bit too large or his teeth were a bit small. The stubble that covered his chin was soft and delicate as it brushed against Leah's cheek.

"Hello there," he said.

The deep roar of a lion came from behind her and Gareth appeared. He untangled Leah from the man's grip. "Hello back."

CHAPTER 23

The stranger stepped back from Gareth, as Anippe appeared over the rim of the staircase. He smiled wide. He tipped his hat to the new arrivals. Taking off his dirt-stained glove, the stranger extended his hand to Gareth, offering a pleasant greeting to diffuse the fire that gleamed in his emerald eyes. "Welcome to my dig."

Gareth ignored the olive branch and walked past the tall, well-built man. Leah tried not to chuckle when Gareth's hand tightened around her waist.

Anippe's strangely flirtatious voice entered the hot dry day. "*Your dig?* And, you are?"

"Daniel Bauer," he replied. "And, who are you, my lovely?"

Leah forced Gareth to turn around. She heard the slight snarl of his words when he spoke over Anippe. "I'm Gareth Lowery . . . sweetheart."

Leah choked down her laugh, determined to show her loyalty. "Leah Tallent. I am Mr. Lowery's companion."

The deep brown eyes twinkled with mischief. "He looks a little young to need a nurse."

"Companion, as in fiancée, Mr. Bauer."

"Ah . . . I see." He looked around at the broken stones and toppled towers of the ancient monument. "Strange place to hold a wedding."

"My name is Anippe. And we're not here for a wedding. We're

here to find out—"

Leah's heart leapt into her throat. "More information about King Herod."

He placed a small stick of wood into his mouth and rolled it around his tongue like a toothpick. "Really?" Daniel Bauer asked. "Are you archaeologists? Scientists, perhaps?"

"Way better than that." Leah smiled. "I'm a librarian."

The man's tanned face broke into a wide grin. "I'm not sure if Herod was a big reader, Ms. Tallent. Perhaps you should explore Qumran. The Dead Sea Scrolls were found there . . . probably much more interesting for you."

"Already been there," she said.

He pulled his gaze from her and stared at the others. "You are librarians, as well?"

"No," Gareth stated. "And it's really none of your business who we are, is it? You may be running a dig, but you certainly don't own Herodium."

Leah jabbed Gareth in the stomach. "We'll just look around. We won't touch anything or bother your people."

His smile returned. "I sent my people back to the hotel for some much needed rest. We've had a very good week, so I gave them all today off."

"Nice boss," Anippe said, softly.

Without moving his gaze off Leah, Daniel Bauer offered his arm to the beautiful black-haired woman. "I would be more than happy to show you around the site. Perhaps you'll find what you're looking for."

Gareth mumbled, "Or, perhaps I'll rip your arm off and beat you over the head with it."

Leah snorted, as Anippe and Daniel walked arm in arm away from them. She turned around and kissed Gareth hard on the lips. "Maybe it's not such a good idea for you to carry a gun."

His eyes took a break from shooting poisonous darts into the back of Daniel Bauer's head and looked down at Leah.

"I don't like him."

"You don't know him."

"I don't like him," Gareth repeated.

"Then I don't like him either," Leah said, with a smile. She reached up and captured Gareth's face in her hands. "But I definitely want to know what the hell he's doing out here all by himself."

"Don't believe the 'boss of the year' story?"

Leah waved her hand around the broken palace. "No tools, no trucks, no tire tracks, no leftover sweat cloths of brushes—not one empty beer can in sight. There's no *way* that a bunch of diggers have been working here for the past week."

Gareth's eyes twinkled. "I love you."

"Now, *that* I believe."

———

Leah had to admit that Daniel Bauer's accent was intoxicating. Like the Irish, his Australian tone was like a tonic that washed over her. It was almost as if a soothing narrator was telling her a story and she clung to every word.

At times, he spoke like a realtor, hell-bent on selling an amazing 'fixer-upper' opportunity to the newly-arrived fish he'd caught on his line. "The foundations we've just unearthed are beyond exhilarating. Vaulted ceilings were used to strengthen each floor above them. We believe now that there must've been at least five stories on this mound at one time that towered over the courtyard. These levels were probably used for the soldier of the fortress and armories for their weapons."

Leah interrupted, "I thought this was a fancy palace."

The tall, handsome man turned around. He was as graceful as a ballet dancer, avoiding every overturned stone that could trip-up his elegant carriage. "It was, Ms. Tallent. It was a combination of fortress *and* palace. We've found the remnants of at least four towers that protruded from each of the palace walls. They sat on massive round bases and the decorations we've found show that the rooms were very elaborate. We can surmise that these were used for the King's royal entourage."

"The Roman-appointed King," added Gareth.

Daniel stepped back and stared at the huge man with the deep voice. "King, nonetheless."

Gareth snorted, "King of Judea? Not according to the people who lived here . . . who still live here. The man was a farce. Kissed

Cleopatra's ass, sucked-up to Mark Antony, and then when that didn't work out, he switched sides and puckered up to Augustus—just to be on the safe side."

Daniel laughed. "Not a fan, aye?" He shrugged, taking Anippe's arm once again and leading her up another small slope. "Let me show you Herod's private quarters."

Leah rolled her eyes behind the couple and stared up at Gareth. "With all the towers, soldiers and weapons, I don't see why he had to build the monumental staircase to keep people out. Talk about paranoid."

Daniel Bauer whipped his head around, making the dark sheen of hair blow around his face like a crown of silk. "Actually, Ms. Tallent—"

"Cut the 'Ms.' crap," she mumbled. "It's annoying. Leah is not a hard name to say."

He raised a perfectly curved eyebrow. "My apologies. Of course, you're soon to be a Mrs. anyway, right . . . Leah?"

She folded her arms in front of her. His charming voice was now filled with challenge, like he was daring Leah to contradict him with Gareth standing right beside her. "Point taken, Mr. Bauer; perhaps I should enjoy being a 'Ms.' while I still can."

To Leah's surprise, his bedroom brown eyes filled with what could only be called an open invitation. "*I* certainly think you should."

She swallowed. "I'm sure *your* wife did before you marched her down the aisle."

Gareth wrapped his arm tighter around Leah's waist.

Daniel's face remained passive. "If you wanted to know if I was available, Leah, all you had to do was ask."

Leah felt Gareth turning to the dark side; his hand held her waist like a vise.

Daniel's smile was innocent once again. "Unfortunately, I have yet to take a wife." He stared down at the work gloves covering his hands; his chiseled jaw twitched. "But, as I've been presented with two such beautiful ladies today, I think God's telling me to just play the field a bit more before settling down."

"I'm sure all woman-kind will be extremely grateful to hear

that," Leah deadpanned.

The excavator bowed his head at the sarcasm that flowed through her lips. "Of that, I have no doubt." He cleared his throat. "As I was saying, that monumental staircase was constructed for the funeral procession of the great King. You see, Herodium is where King Herod chose to be buried. The name alone is a memorial to the fallen man."

Leah watched Anippe subtly let down her hair. She felt her stomach turn as she studied the familiar look that appeared in the woman's sapphire eyes—the look of a woman caught completely off-guard by the 'special something' that the stranger emitted.

Leah had felt that just once in her life. As she looked up into Gareth's great green eyes, Leah was still truly amazed at what that feeling could do to an otherwise intelligent woman; how it could inject into their veins so much emotion that they were willing to walk through fire for the person who inspired it. As she turned her gaze back to Daniel Bauer, Leah knew beyond a shadow of a doubt that he would definitely not be a candidate to walk through fire for.

Leah dropped her eyes to the ground when she realized that she was standing still studying the stranger with her intense gaze.

"You seem flustered, Ms. . . . Leah." He winked. "Heat getting to you?"

She could feel Gareth's questioning stare. Leah straightened her spine and summoned the stoic librarian who rested inside her for just such an occasion. "Actually, Mr. Bauer, I'm becoming rather bored with your transparent line of bullshit."

His grin was inviting. "On we go then. I wouldn't want you to waste any more . . . precious time." He bowed, holding her gaze with his own. "The entrance to Herod's private quarters is right around the corner."

Daniel turned and led Anippe around the corner, past a large, excavated pool. Leah felt a shiver run down her spine as she listened to his voice fade away, "This was Herod's private bath. An extraordinary achievement . . . found a way to put holes in the floor to allow steam to rise up and heat the water . . . first steam bath . . ."

Gareth took Leah by the hand and turned her to face him. "What was that all about?"

Leah shook her head. She'd no idea what it was about Daniel Bauer that infuriated her so. It was as if she were somehow caught inside the man, like she could hear the intimate thoughts that raced through his head. Perhaps it was the violin-like voice that blatantly flirted with her right in front of Gareth. The audacity of his actions made her heart race for no reason. "The heat, I guess."

Gareth handed her another bottle of water that had been securely fastened to his belt.

Leah could barely meet his eyes. The emerald gaze was steady, causing Leah's throat to close around the cold water. She immediately began to choke. The water went down the wrong pipe and Leah began to cough uncontrollably, sending the water bottle flying from her hands to the center of the pool.

Gareth slapped her on the back . . . hard.

Leah stood up quickly and wiped the tears from her eyes. "Ouch. Hello? Not so rough."

Gareth turned away from her and began walking around the corner of the large stone wall. "Whatever."

Leah followed quickly, pulling on the back of his sweat-soaked shirt. "What's wrong with you?"

Gareth wheeled around. "Me? What's wrong with you?"

"What?"

"You've been staring at that moron with some kind of dreamy look in your eyes, like a high school girl who just ran into Johnny 'friggin' Depp."

"You have *got* to be kidding me. Are you . . .? You're not jealous?" Leah sighed. She wasn't sure who she was angrier at; Gareth, for sounding like a jerk; or . . . Gareth, for being right. "Maybe you're correct," she shot back. "After all, with the way you're acting, I sure feel like I'm back in high school right now. Considering all we've been through together I would think that this conversation is *more* than a little ridiculous . . . wouldn't you agree?"

Gareth shut his angry green eyes and took a deep breath. When they re-opened, the Gareth she'd known for the last two years appeared before her. "I'm sorry," he said, shaking his head. "This place is just getting to me."

"Maybe it's the heat." She stared at the strange swimming pool, listening to the water flow into the small open holes. It was almost like the last droplets of hope were draining away. "No," she sighed, "*I'm* sorry, I just . . ."

She could feel the swelling behind her eyes and she began to cry.

Gareth pulled her into a protective hug. "I know, beautiful. We'll find your father, I promise. Let's get this seed from Hell's King and get the hell out of here."

She stared up at him.

"Aye?" He grinned

"Aye."

———

When they rounded the corner, Leah gasped. Before her was a huge sarcophagus. The stone ornament had been torn to bits, like angry men with jackhammers had decided to turn the ancient artifact into a pile of dust.

"What in the world?" Gareth's voice came out like an angry father, completely livid with his child for breaking such a valuable item. He turned his gaze on the dark-haired mystery man. "What did you and your men *do* to this? This is an archaeological site and you've . . . you destroyed it!"

"I'm like you, Mr. Lowery. I would never harm a priceless treasure."

Gareth snarled, "You're *nothing* like me, Bauer."

"Truer words have never been spoken," Leah whispered.

Anippe walked quickly to Gareth. "He *found* it this way."

Leah felt her heart freeze at the sound of protection flowing through Anippe's words. It was like she'd already taken a step away from them and joined Daniel Bauer's camp. "Anippe," Leah began.

Anippe reached out and took Leah's hand. "No. Really. My uncle told me about this dig. People have been searching for Herod's body forever. I'd heard that the mausoleum had just been discovered, but no body."

Leah heard the anger in her own voice. "Maybe we should concentrate on that uncle of yours, Anippe. And *not* on this guy."

Shoving the comment aside, Anippe whispered, "Our grapevine knows all about this discovery, Leah."

The reminder that the two women were somehow joined by

the 'all-seeing eye' tattoos that marked their hands, made Leah shiver. She wondered how many eye bearers were hearing about this journey right now. Would they care? Would they appear to help Leah bring her father home? Or, were they upset with her for stealing sacred objects to save one of her own family members. "I wouldn't recommend talking about this in front of him," Leah whispered back, nodding at the archaeologist.

Daniel's lilting laughter flowed through Leah's ears. "Don't be silly. I already know about you all. I saw the tattoo on your hand when you jumped into my arms."

"Fell," Leah reminded him. "It's called gravity. I would think a scientist would know that."

"Whatever makes you feel better," he said, with a wink. Daniel removed one of his gloves and held his hand in the air.

Leah recognized the familiar Ark image. A picture of the kind monk from long ago, marked with the same tattoo—who'd risked his life to protect Noah's ship—appeared in Leah's mind. She wished with all her might that Gregory was with her. "Why didn't you just say you were one of them in the first place?" she snapped.

Daniel leaned his handsome head to one side and put the glove back on. "I noticed that yours is a bright sapphire eye, not the familiar green that's on so many other beautiful hands." He winked at Anippe.

Leah's stomach roiled when she heard Anippe's schoolgirl giggle.

Daniel moved his gaze back to Leah and Gareth. "I also noticed that Mr. Lowery was free of any such mark. I wanted to make sure that you all were . . . safe to talk to."

Gareth growled, "If *you* are who you say *you* are then you should've *known* we were friends. We've met the men who wear the same marking that you do. I would think your 'Circle of Friends' would've told you about our last little adventure with them."

He shrugged. "The grapevine is larger than you think. That information hasn't trickled down to everyone yet."

Leah snorted. Gareth didn't move. She could feel the anger burning in his soul. Stepping forward, Leah was consumed with the fact that she was running out of time. "Why don't you just tell us where Herod is? Okay . . . Daniel?"

He swept his black hair off his forehead and looked up at the sky. "Of course; the shadows will be on us soon and we'll lose the light."

Leah listened to the warning bells that suddenly filled her brain.

CHAPTER 24

"There have been quite a lot of searches here, as Anippe told you; not only for Herod, but also for any sign of John the Baptist who was beheaded in this palace."

Gareth stared at the broken mosaic tiles that made a path beneath his feet. "John the Baptist was found a long time ago. His head is in a church."

Daniel offered a condescending smile. "True, but there must be something of his presence left here. After all, his body had to have been buried in consecrated ground. Herod killed the man because of his daughter, Salome's wishes. He didn't want to. He would've built some kind of shrine or monument to the man."

"Hedging his bets to get into Heaven?" Leah snorted.

"Maybe," Daniel replied stoically. "Who knows?"

"I think a king, who beheaded a religious man and tried to kill Jesus, would not be on the short list for Paradise. Just a guess, of course," Leah sneered.

"I heard some say that Herod buried bodies inside this palace," Anippe added, with a whisper. "I know that he buried his two sons at the bottom of one of these palace towers, in the stairs."

Leah's revulsion returned.

Daniel bounced happily at her words. "You know of the Massacre of the Innocents?"

Leah flicked her gaze at Gareth and smiled. "*Everyone* knows about that."

Garth burst into laughter.

Daniel waved his hand in the air, like he was familiar with their private jokes. He focused his attention on Anippe, and continued his lecture, "Herod's sarcophagus was most likely decorated with precious stones. The base would've been solid gold. He sounded like a man stuck inside a wonderful dream. The famous historian, Josephus Flavius, said that Herod wore a purple robe. A diadem of gold and stones was wrapped around his head and, next to his hand, was a golden scepter. The funeral procession marched up the staircase. Herod's body would've been surrounded by his family—"

"The ones he didn't murder," Gareth cut in.

"Followed by the guard," Daniel continued loudly. "Next, came the remainder of the troops in full dress uniform, with the free men and servants carrying spices and gifts at the back of the line. A lot like the processions held for the ancient gods and goddesses of Athens and Rome, if I remember my history correctly. According to Herod's directions, he was interred here . . . in this very room." His voice lowered and his hands caressed the broken pieces of the sarcophagus. "Now we have a place to start."

Leah held her breath. It was as if the narrator had once again taken over her mind. He was like the Pied Piper, buried inside her head, telling her where to go and what to believe—controlling her completely with his magic flute.

She tore her gaze from the bedroom eyes that were now locked on her face and shook the vile thoughts from her brain. "Yeah . . . so? Where is he?"

Daniel looked down at the casket; his face flushed with color. "This damage was deliberate; some Jews, no doubt, who hated him so much that they took it upon themselves to desecrate his grave."

Leah shuddered at the bigotry and hate that flowed through his words.

"During the Jewish revolt against the Romans, they referred to Herod as the 'puppet-ruler' with the emperor pulling his strings." He turned back to Leah and Gareth; the soft brown eyes were filled with the light of adventure. "Can you imagine that? A great ruler like Herod being called a puppet?" He gave a snort, as if the tale was nothing more than a ridiculous falsehood. "Herod was the one who rebuilt everything after the earthquake hit and robbed Jerusalem of its buildings."

"And raised taxes to pay for them so that most of his people starved to death," Gareth snapped.

Daniel's full lips pursed together. "He was a great King of Judea."

The image of her friend at Gethsemane appeared in Leah's mind. "There was only one true King," she said.

Daniel smiled. "On that, I must agree. And it wasn't Herod."

Anippe cleared her throat. Her voice was high as if trying, with all her might, to break any and all connection between the two of them. She stepped in front of Leah, shifting Daniel's attention back to her. "So the grave-robbers took Herod's body?"

"Grave-robbers?" Gareth shouted.

Leah pat him on the chest. "Never fight with an idiot, dear. Let's just get through this, shall we?"

He nodded, but remained focused on the insolent man. Leah could almost feel the wind against her face as the daggers flew from Gareth's cold, green eyes.

"Possibly." Daniel smiled at Anippe, as she sauntered towards him. "I hope not, though. It took us a long time to find this place. I don't want to go home without the big prize."

Anippe released another girlish chuckle into the air, reminding Leah of her three silly sisters back home in Connecticut. God, how she missed them right now. It would be so nice to swap this ugly place for their sheer moronic conversations about the Club and what dress they'd just purchased from Macy's. She whispered in Gareth's ear, "How exactly are we supposed to find the seed of Hell's King when there's no King?"

"I have *no* idea." Gareth kneeled down and traced a pipe with his fingertips. "You know what would really be funny?"

"Picking up one of those big stones and beating this guy over the head until he screams like a little girl?"

Gareth grinned. "Yeah! But also . . . what if—with all these cisterns and pipes, old towers, aqueducts and channels—what if this is the place that the Copper Scroll describes?"

Leah let out a roar of laughter, disturbing Anippe and Daniel as they huddled close together. "Yeah, and Bigfoot is walking across the desert as we speak."

He grunted, "No. He likes woodsy areas."

"Gareth," Leah sighed. "We came to the conclusion that the scroll was a fake. It was just something the monks left behind as a joke; they wanted to toy with the greedy humans who wouldn't be saved at the 'end of days.'"

Gareth stared up at her. "No. *You* decided that it was a fake. *I* believe that the Scroll is real."

"Okay, fine. But you don't need gold. So, can we just worry about the thing we're actually here for? Please?"

"It's not about gold and silver, Leah," Gareth remarked calmly, as he stood up. "It's history. We're standing smack dab in the middle of history, Leah. Aren't you at all amazed by these things?"

"You betcha. A guy who kills his sons and maybe tons more children and buries them under the floors and towers of his house? Amazing . . . right? Where's the gift shop so I can buy a poster of him for my room?" Leah deadpanned.

Gareth shook his head and walked toward Anippe, abandoning Leah to her sarcastic thoughts. "What do you think?"

Her sapphire eyes glowed with happiness, like she was the geek in the corner who'd just been asked to the homecoming dance by the quarterback. "This could very well be what the monks were talking about. I mean, Qumran's only a stone's throw away and Herod was here during the fall of the Temple, which is where the gold and silver was before it was moved to an unknown location. I wish we had the Scroll so we could find out."

Leah was astonished when Daniel Bauer joined the conversation, "You know, you're right. I studied that text quite a bit in college. With over sixty-three locations, if we started digging near the cisterns and other prominent places, we *could* start finding some really fantastic things out here."

Completely dumbfounded by the strange new threesome jabbering away about the mysteries that may sit inside the private palace, Leah stayed silent as a stream of information flowed from Daniel's lips. Leah found herself frozen in surprise when Gareth pulled out a pad of paper from the pocket of his faded jeans and began taking notes.

"The eastern part of the palace had a garden. I believe it measured exactly forty-one by eighteen meters," Daniel said, pointing his hands at the buildings and monuments around them. "There were porticos on all sides. There's one visible right there. And you see that strange piece of circular stone with the holes in it? That was a domed roof that allowed the sun to shine through into Herod's bedchamber. Now . . . over here, there was a hallway exactly sixty-eight feet away from the cistern. Over there . . ."

Leah shook her head as she watched them walk through the far entrance and disappear into an underground chamber. She stood still, trying to understand the strange turn of events. Had Gareth really just abandoned her father for a chance at a new discovery? Had the gaze of the hunky archaeologist in their midst blown the image of her missing uncle right out of Anippe's head? Leah stared up at the darkening sky, searching for any answer that the 'big guy' might want to shout down to her. "What am I? Stuck in a cartoon?" she whispered to the silent heavens.

Staring out across the desert, her question remained unanswered. She half-expected a big purple roadrunner to appear on the horizon, being chased by a coyote carrying a bomb that read ACME on its side.

Turning away from the ridiculous group, Leah walked around the corner of the stone tower and stared across the expanse at her water bottle. The bright, blue label looked so silly against the deep red color of the ancient pool. She wondered if the spilled liquid would produce steam through the holes carved into the pool's floor. Perhaps puffs of smoke would rise up through the tiny openings like little mushroom clouds and destroy the mutineers walking in the chamber below her.

She whispered to the wind, "I can't believe it! They're really interested in hanging out with a guy who killed his own sons and beheaded the guy who baptized Jesus to solve an ancient farce of a puzzle?" Once again, she stared up at the sky. "Seriously . . . why am I here?"

The breeze was silent. Leah closed her eyes and heard the faint dripping coming from the pool. She laughed. "Geez, where does the water go? Hell?"

Her heart jumped into her throat. Like a theater curtain rising from the floor, the lights came on inside Leah's brain. Jesus. She stared across the huge monument and marched quickly to the edge of the pool. Placing her foot on top of the man-made structure, Leah pressed down. The stone was solid. Kneeling, she stared through the small holes that'd been carved into the floor and rapped her fist against the screen. Solid.

Working her way across the wide expanse, Leah stopped every foot or so and repeated the same strange movements. As the moon appeared above her, sending its silver light streaming down, Leah reached the middle of the structure and knocked her bloody, aching fist against the unyielding rock. A hollow echo met her ears; there was a cave, a passage of some kind, underneath the center of the pool.

A line of sweat appeared on her upper lip as she poked her finger through one of the small holes and pulled hard. She heard the crack and a thin layer of stone gave way, shattering in the palm of her hand. Working quickly, Leah thrust her hand inside the new opening, pulling chunks of stone from the immaculate surface of the pool. Wider and wider, her circle grew with each handful of stone ripped from the ornate frame.

As she uncovered the cave, a bright ray of silver moonlight illuminated the dark space; Leah's eyes caught sight of the small pale skeleton and her shriek blasted across the desert, shaking the gates of Hell.

CHAPTER 25

Not knowing why, Leah covered her mouth and forced the scream back into her throat. Her limbs were shaking uncontrollably as she looked away from the tiny skeleton with hollow eyes. The small arm bones were bent sideways, as if they were reaching up for her, begging her from beyond the grave to bring its killer to justice.

Revulsion churned her stomach. Leah aimed her chin at the sky and took a deep breath, needing the fresh night air in her lungs before entering the cramped cave. She thanked God that she'd kept Gareth's flashlight, as she clicked on the bright beam and illuminated the frightening interior.

Stepping down into the disgusting space, she was truly sick at the sight. Below this section of the pool was a small cemetery. Body after body, adult and child had been placed side by side. Barring the invention of gas chambers, it seemed that the King had simply disposed of his victims beneath his private quarters. Leah couldn't imagine the smell that'd risen around him during his daily bath. The man had obviously been a pig. She wondered if the scum had enjoyed the scent of flesh burning below him while he took his steam baths. Or, worse, had he listened to the cry of his victims, burying them while they were still alive? Had their fingers poked through the holes trying to claw their way out?

Leah shook the twisted images from her brain. The air was cool inside the space; the tiny holes acted as an ancient ventilation system. The smell of rotted flesh had dissipated over the centuries but Leah still kept her mouth covered, trying to stop herself from shouting at the hideous disrespect for human life.

Crouching down, Leah worked her way through the narrow pathways that led between the bodies. Sweeping the flashlight around the dark stone walls, the bright ray suddenly beamed back at her. It was as if the light had hit a mirror, illuminating the cave like a flaming comet.

Lowering the flashlight, she crept unsteadily toward the source. Her breath came in gasps, as she stared down at the broken limbs of a full-grown man. Leah's eyes stung with salty tears when she took in the mammoth scepter at the skeleton's right hand. The diadem that crowned his head was broken in two, like a huge stone club had come smashing down on his misshapen skull.

"Good," she stated loudly, hoping the souls of the victims around her would hear. She knocked her fist against the scepter. She hoped this was the weapon that'd come crashing down on the man's head. There had been no grave-robbers. The people who'd accomplished this had come for retribution . . . not gold. They'd left the priceless scepter and crown behind. All they'd wanted was for the great King to be treated with the same respect that he'd shown to his people.

Leah stared down at the large, empty sockets in the damaged skull. "An eye for an eye, right, Herod? You deserved it, pal. You should have suffered more."

The skin around her neck suddenly burned as if her blouse had caught fire. Leah reached down and lifted the hot pendant off her skin. The bright green olive inside had turned silver. The seed of the Son had come alive. Perhaps He was telling Leah to forgive the trespasses of others. But she couldn't. She stared down at the silver olive beaming through the emerald-green pendant. "Sorry, but I'm only human. Forgiveness is your job."

The object continued to glow, sending a beam of light onto the diadem. Leah moved forward on her hands and knees, staring at the round gem that was set in the band of gold. Her hand shook when she reached out and plucked the strange looking object from the broken crown.

Her head swam with emotion, knowing that she was one large step closer to finding her father alive. She held the bright red stone in her hand. It looked like a thin olive with a lush, red pimento inside its almost transparent case. The click of the clasp was all Leah could hear, as the pendant opened like a book and accepted the seed of Hell's King.

Leah could feel the emerald grow against her flesh. From a flat emerald disk, it now resembled a saucer dangling from the golden chain. The bright silver glow still came from the necklace. The seed of the Son lit the cave with His spectacular light, releasing the souls of the victims—the innocents—up through the floor of the pool and into the arms of Heaven.

CHAPTER 26

Tripping over a piece of the broken sarcophagus, Leah fell headfirst into one of the giant towers.

Holding in her cuss words, knowing that the Son was traveling with her, Leah stood back up. She aimed the flashlight forward and walked through another door into yet another empty chamber. She searched for any sign of Gareth—any sound of the calming voice that would lead her back to his side.

She turned corner after corner, entered room after room of the palace of death until finally, Anippe's strange sobbing voice led her in the right direction. Leah tripped again and again over the fallen monument, aching to call out to Gareth and bring him to her side. She could see the faint light flickering ahead of her and walked through the small, dimly lit doorway.

Her flashlight fell to the floor and her heart plummeted in her chest. The card catalogue in her brain opened with a shriek. This time it wasn't data that it offered up, but a wealth of emotions. She didn't know what to do. Should she scream? Should she pick up the flashlight and bludgeon the people standing in front of her? Were tears the way to go?

Anippe dropped her arms from around Gareth's waist when the flashlight slammed solidly against the rock floor.

The green-eyed hero's hands were flat against Anippe's shoulders, pushing her away from his body, as he untangled her lips from his own.

Leah tried to understand the scene. Her eyes wanted to see the truth—to draw any conclusion other than the one that'd instantly formed inside her brain.

Gareth raised his hands in the air, "This is so *not* what it looks like."

With all the emotions burning in her heart, Leah could think of only one she felt comfortable with. "Heat get to you again, did it? Aye?"

She stared at Anippe's guild-ridden face. "You really suck at picking men, you know that? First, a homicidal maniac and now mine. You know, I just met a man out in the pool who would've been perfect for you."

Anippe shook her head and stepped towards her. "I'm sorry, I didn't—"

Leah raised her hand. "Stay away from me." Her voice came out calm and cool, "I thought you both might want to know that I found the seed of Hell's King." She could feel the flame of disgust shoot from her eyes as she stared at Anippe's surprised face, "And the seed of Hell, itself, apparently."

"Leah, be reasonable. You know better than that."

Leah turned her gaze on her illustrious hero, a man she'd fought beside for the last two years. Her stomach flipped and she bent over at the waist and retched into the dirt, holding up her hand to stop anyone from coming near her. A stream of hot water fell from her mouth, the only thing that's entered her empty stomach in the past twenty-four hours. "I always told you that you made me sick," she gasped. "Now, I've finally proven it . . . Professor."

She stood up and, wiped her mouth with the back of her hand. Turning around, she walked out of the chamber. "I've had enough."

She heard Gareth's footsteps behind her as she quickly made her way out into the cool night air. He pulled on her elbow but Leah ripped his hand away. Turning, she glared at her once perfect idol under the silver moon.

He stepped back immediately. "Leah, you can't honestly believe that I was . . ."

"Looking for a stray eyelash that was blinding the poor girl?"

Gareth sighed heavily. "She was just upset when that Bauer guy disappeared into another chamber. He was talking about the Scroll, and she said something about maybe a starting point where we could begin to look, and the guy just freaked out on her."

Leah remained silent.

"Bauer started yelling at her and said she was not the right one to help him and called her a fool."

"And you defended her maidenly virtue."

"I called him an asshole and he walked out."

"A hero to the very end."

Gareth took a step forward, but Leah retreated. He stopped and stared at the ground. "She started crying and saying what bad luck she had with men and that no one would ever love her. She hoped she would fine someone as nice and caring as—"

"You?" Leah snorted. "That's rich. I guess loyalty isn't one of her requirements."

His broad shoulders dipped further toward the ground, as the weight of her words and his actions pressed down on him.

"Let me guess? She was so heartbroken that she threw herself into your arms and kissed you. *You,* of course, were pushing her away as I walked in, ready to tell her that you were so much in love with another fair maiden that you simply couldn't be the man of her dreams."

He shouted, "As a matter of fact, that's *exactly* what I was doing when you walked in! Jesus, Leah, do you actually believe for one second that I could even *think* about being with another woman? I'm so head over heels for you, its sick."

"Well," Leah began, her sarcasm burying her tears. "Thank goodness there's a cure for your sickness." She turned around and walked away.

Gareth's boot came down hard on the rocky terrain.

Her voice drifted over her shoulder. "I need to be away from you right now."

Leah followed the light of the moon, away from the man who she'd always thought was the one who held her future in his hands.

———

Passing by the pool of death, Leah continued around the corner of the tower and tripped over the figure that was kneeling on the rocks.

Daniel Bauer reached up and caught Leah's falling body in his arms. "We have to stop meeting like this, luv."

Leah pushed against his chest. Freeing herself, she stood up. "Cut it out! Read my lips—Not Interested! Just save all that Aussie charm crap for some bimbo who won't see through it."

Daniel stood up and stepped back from her. He leaned against the huge stone wall and aimed his flashlight on a small mound of rock at Leah's feet. "See that?" The flirtatious tone disappeared from his calm voice.

Leah peered down at the markings etched into the slab. She wiped the tears from her eyes and ignored the sound of her heart breaking in two. "What is it?"

"It's Hebrew . . . a place of rest for John the Baptist."

Leah raised her head. "I thought Gareth said . . ." She stopped; her brain commanded her to go back and listen to the man she truly loved. "I thought that he'd been found and was in a church somewhere."

"This stone is a monument to his life. Probably the same people who robbed Herod's tomb put this here to remember the man—a place for believers to pray for his soul."

Leah shuddered, knowing that behind her lay a hundred souls who had no place to be remembered. "This *palace* is disgusting."

"You don't care for John the Baptist?" His beautiful smile beamed in the silver moonlight.

Leah sighed. "I mean, Herod is disgusting. This place, what happened here, is sick." She stared down at what she knew was an empty grave underneath the memorial. "Judas betrayed Jesus."

"Well . . ."

Leah raised her hand. "Yeah . . . I know. But before all those 'papers' were found, he was one of the bad guys. Lucifer betrayed Heaven."

"In all fairness . . ."

"Stop," Leah ordered. "I'm not getting into a religious debate with you. I'm just saying that all these good people were betrayed." She pointed at John's tiny temple and the stray bodies underneath the pool. "A man beheaded. Children massacred. Betrayers live all around us and yet *I'm* supposed to believe!"

"You don't?"

A wave of sadness entered her soul. The faith that'd grown inside her over the past two years was constantly at war with the librarian who lived for proof—trusting only the facts. "You can't believe anything," she sneered, thinking of all those 'truthful' documents that'd been proven false over time.

"I'm sorry," Daniel said, stepping close to her. "Are you okay?"

"Just . . . extremely tired."

"Have you been betrayed, Leah?"

Her head popped up at his strange question. "Excuse me?"

"You seem very upset tonight," he shrugged. "Is there anything I can do for you?"

She shook her head, releasing the anger in her soul and letting it fill to the brim with despair. "I just want to get out of here."

"What about the Silver Scroll?"

"Oh, please!"

His voice sounded worried, "Did you get everything you came for then?"

"Yes."

"There's nothing else you have to do?" Daniel's voice was deep and strong, like a magnet that was attempting to extract information from her brain.

But she was so tired, she simply didn't care. "No, there's nothing else here."

"You're sure?"

She nodded again. "This is the home of Hell's King—a place of death. There's no way anything—any life at all—would grow out of a place like this."

Leah didn't even flinch when Daniel Bauer reached out and took her hand. His soft, suede gloves caressed her skin. "They say the trials and tribulations of life are the lessons God teaches us in order to build our character."

She let out a burst of laughter. "Sweetheart, if I become any more of a character, they're gonna' have to build a ride for me at Disney World."

Daniel offered a sly grin. "You're something else, you know

that?"

She took back her hand. "Can I borrow your flashlight?"

"Why?"

"Falling down a flight of two hundred stone steps, while a fitting end to this crappy night, isn't something I want to try."

"You're leaving?"

"I think I should go before God decides to give me another character lesson."

"You're gonna' just walk across the desert in the middle of the night, aye?"

"Oh . . . right, it's night," Leah mumbled. The clock inside her head let her know that she had less than seventy-two hours left to save her beloved father. Warmth filled her when she thought of him. With all her heart, she longed to speak to the only man left in her world who'd never lied to her or let her down.

CHAPTER 27

Going down was far easier than climbing up, Leah thought, as she stepped back onto the hard-packed dirt road that circled Herod's mighty palace.

It was so cool and quiet that Leah wanted nothing more than to lie down at the base of the ancient monument and go to sleep. Her stomach was empty, her head swam with painful images and her throat still burned from retching. Her body was so empty, in fact, that she thought she was going to die. If it wasn't for her father, Leah could see herself going back into Cleopatra's mine, throwing away the weighty pendant and letting the wolf devour her. Then, at least one of them would be satisfied.

She shook the stupid thought from her head, and continued down the vacant road, angry with herself for thinking such ridiculous nonsense. The last thing in the world Leah was, was a quitter. She thought about the promise she'd made to her mother back in Connecticut. Even though Mary Tallent had looked at her like she was the Devil personified, Leah had told her she would bring her father back home. And that was a promise Leah fully intended to keep.

Twin beams of light danced in the distance growing bigger and bigger as she trudged away from the palace. "Great," she whispered. "Now I'm hallucinating."

But as the strange lights grew brighter, Leah extinguished the small flashlight she'd taken from the Australian stranger and her heart leapt with glee, as the big, black limo pulled to a stop in front of her.

The tall man, still adorned with sunglasses and a big, black cap, jumped from the car. "Are you all right, Miss?" His accent was so strong that the question came out muddled.

Leah was never happier to see a stranger in her life. She could almost kiss the thin mustache dancing on top of the man's upper lip. "Thank God."

"I received a call on that horrible phone from Mr. Lowery. I was so worried. I've sat at Qumran all night and all this day waiting for you to come back."

Leah pat him on the shoulder, watching the small particles of sand rise into the air. "It's okay, um . . ."

"My name is David, Miss."

"Leah," she said, "David? Really? That's my father's name."

"Good, solid name." He laughed. "Some fathers are great . . . others, not so much. But at least we, as the children, are offered a chance to make up for their mistakes."

"Could you please take me back to the hotel?"

The chauffer stared up at the huge, dark mound behind Leah's shoulder. "But where's Mr. Lowery? And your friend?"

Anger swelled in her chest, but she continued to smile. "They're still up there. They'll be digging for a while yet, so Gareth—Mr. Lowery—wants you to come back for him at dawn. I was done first so he called you to come get me. I need some sleep." The lies flowed from her lips as easily as water from a faucet. She wished he would take off his glasses so she could see if he believed her or not.

"Well," he began. "I can certainly do that for you, Miss. The hotel isn't far."

"Great." Leah nodded.

The man raced around the side of the limo and opened the door. The interior light beamed onto the sand and the driver stepped away quickly to allow Leah to climb in and rest her weary bones.

The young man then raced around the back of the car to take his place behind the wheel. As he set his gloves on the leather, he flashed a slightly worried smile in the rearview mirror. "Are you certain they'll be all right up there?"

Leah nodded. "Don't you worry, David. They have each other."

Whether choosing to ignore the snarl that came from Leah's lips, or just intent on doing his job correctly, without question David raced across the desert to the highway.

———

"I hope you get to see other things while you're here, Miss."

"Leah," she corrected.

"Yes . . . Leah." David continued, "As I said yesterday, there are many places you could enjoy. The old city—the Tel es-Sultan is quite remarkable."

"I don't think I want to be climbing any more mounds of dirt while I'm here, David. Thanks anyway."

"I understand," he said quickly. "But the monastery is beautiful, though; the one located at the top of Mount Temptation. And the cable car will deliver you right to it, remember? So there's no dirt required." David pointed out the window at the mountain sitting right behind the historical city of Jericho.

Leah watched as the small red transport moved slowly down the mountain toward the street. Up above, lights could be seen flickering through a line of tiny windows carved into the rock face. "Then...I guess you should take me to Temptation," she whispered.

The map floated inside her head. The palace, the bodies beneath the hidden floor, the seed that would show her the innocent reality of who would come again, and the path she had to walk led right *to* Temptation. But who would come again? The Father . . . Son? Or, would Hell's King rise up from the sand? Leah pushed the horrible thought from her mind. "Is anyone up there?"

David nodded. "Monks live up there, Miss. I mean . . . Leah. There are also hermits who live in the caves in the mountain, but they are not harmful. They live there because they believe. They wish to be closer to that place, and what Jesus did there."

Leah tilted her head. She wanted desperately to ask, but there was no way she wanted to sound like a fool to the local who'd been so kind to her. He would probably think of her as just another one of those American morons if she dared to question what it was that Jesus had to do with the monastery. Heck, even she would call herself an infidel for such a dumb question spoken aloud in the ancient city that had hosted famous moments in Jesus' life.

She leaned forward in her seat. "You know, David," she began. "It'll be dawn soon and I may have to leave tomorrow, so I think I'll just pop up there and look at the Mount right now."

"But, it's the middle of the night. You would be all by yourself on the journey." His voice filled with worry, "I could take you, I suppose. I'll just call Mr. Lowery and see if it's okay that I wait a little longer to go get him."

Leah took the phone out of his hand. "David, these things are bad for you, remember? They're gonna kill someone someday."

He stopped the limo in the parking lot beside the red cable car that'd come to a stop. The dimly-lit box was empty.

"Who came down?" Leah asked.

David shook his head. "The car goes back and forth every ten minutes. In the evening it's set up to do this so no one needs to stay up all night to watch over it, just in case a believer needs help quickly."

"Great," she replied, jumping out of the limo.

"But, Miss?" David followed her; his anxiety made the veins on his forehead throb.

Leah took him by the arms. She was slightly amused when he bowed his head to the ground like a mischievous child who was about to be yelled at. She stared at the top of his glossy, black cap. "I'll be absolutely fine, David. And I'm going to let Mr. Lowery know what an excellent job you've been doing for him. Now, go back to Herodium and wait for him there. I'll meet them at the hotel when I'm finished."

The young man turned away and walked back to the open car door; his stare remained fixed on the rocky ground.

Leah stepped into the metal rig just as the motor hummed to life. She stepped back from the double doors, letting them close her into the slightly shaky-looking box.

Waving from the small window, Leah cast a glance at the big, black car—the chariot that'd saved her in the desert—and smiled. "You're a good man, David," she whispered. "But I need to go to Temptation alone."

Laughter bubbled up inside her as the white glove saluted from the car window. As the brake lights turned onto the highway back toward Herodium, Leah sighed. She didn't know how long she had before Gareth came after her but she wanted to enjoy at least a few hours of peace. Perhaps the driver would keep her secret, although she doubted it. People named David just didn't seem to have the ability to lie.

CHAPTER 28

David Tallent woke with a start, as the nightmarish image of his dead daughter floated inside his mind. His heart beat wildly, and he tried with all his might to catch his breath. For the last five days, all he'd done was have nightmares.

"There's no rest for the wicked, aye?" Aaron spoke from his place on the couch.

Walking to the balcony doors, David wiped the sweat from his forehead and stared out at the small car once again climbing the famous mountain. Tears slid down his cheeks at the thought of the man who'd gone against all odds, starving Himself for days and nights up there, yet never succumbing to the temptations of the Devil

How he wished he was that strong. How he wished the character that he'd shown to the world all these years was really who he was deep down inside. But now, because of his innocent journey through books and maps, piecing together a puzzle that he thought would simply be a fun journey for he and his wife to take, he'd unearthed not only the most amazing discovery of his lifetime, but also resurrected the secrets and lies he'd tried his whole life to bury.

He thought back to Max's lunchtime visit. "That son-of-a-bitch," David whispered. "If Leah gets hurt, I'll find a way to kill him."

"At least she's got Gareth Lowery by her side," Aaron said. "When I met him in Petra, they seemed like a good team; he'll protect her. But, Anippe? Who'll hold *her* hand through this, David? Who does *she* have?"

All David wanted to do was throw open the locked doors and scream into the night. He tried so long ago to follow the words that'd been left for him. His heart had burned when he walked away, leaving two pieces of his soul behind in this desert.

David took a deep breath. Anippe and Leah couldn't be harmed. There was no way he would allow his sins to lead to someone else's destruction. . . . Not again. "Aaron . . . I *am* sorry."

"Too late for sorry. You heard Max. They walked through the pit and God knows what happened . . . what they had to survive in there."

Heart thumping, bones trembling, David returned his gaze to the small cable car climbing up the mountain. Leah couldn't possibly know what was in that cave. He'd explicitly raised her away from religion, only touching on the subject of Mary and the old French church that'd been dedicated to her. Of course, he knew from Aaron that Leah had now found about Moses . . . Noah . . . Saint Gregory—and he could barely believe that his own daughter had held the Son's words in her very own hands.

But he'd never taught Leah the evil parts. He'd been so scared when Leah had spoken of her first adventure with Lowery—how she'd stared into the face of the Devil, himself. But she'd come away unharmed. Perhaps, thought David, she was saved *because* Leah didn't believe everything that the books had said. Perhaps her questioning mind had helped her to look pure evil in the face and not believe. For *nothing* could harm a person, David knew, if they simply refused to let it.

There was no way Leah could've known what was attached to Cleopatra's evil mine. And there was simply no chance it could still be in there. Even if it were, he thought quickly, there was no way Leah could possibly know that it'd fallen from the sky and that others were killing people to find it.

"Do you think they're all right?" Aaron asked. "Do you think Leah will find a king that's been missing for centuries? Do you *honestly* believe that what you found out about this place is even correct?

"It has to be, Aaron. If it wasn't, we'd be dead by now."

He could hear the quick intake of breath from across the room. "Is the gold and silver there . . . in the palace? You never told me."

"In order to find the treasure of the Temple," he replied. "Number sixty-four has to be found first. The Silver Scroll was buried away from everything else and tells the exact locations of the million-dollar treasure. But it also gives the *exact* starting point. Without it, the Copper Scroll is useless. That was just a map to the real map."

"Like the one you drew?" asked the exasperated man.

"I drew what I thought to be correct, Aaron. I can honestly tell you that I have no idea what's under there. I just . . . believe."

Aaron sighed heavily. "For the Lord's sake, David, searching for a mythical place that some philosopher used in a play is one of the most ridiculous things I've ever heard. I can't believe that my wonderful Anippe is in danger over such a fairytale."

David shook his head. "I'm not talking about Atlantis, Aaron. That's just a shadow; a name someone used long ago to cover up the truth."

"Do you want to know what the truth is?" Aaron lowered his voice. "The truth is that you're an idiot. You dredged up the past, put all our lives in danger—and just because you were a bored billionaire with nothing else to do." His eyes grew wide. "God help, Leah. She's hooked up with someone just like her father."

"Lowery is a good man. You said so yourself. He'll protect her," David answered back. "He made the right decision when it counted the most."

"*After* he put everyone in danger." Aaron put his head in his hands. "Yeah . . . some hero."

"He was right," David said softly.

"You're not. In fact, you never were."

Anger swelled in David's chest "I did the only thing I could do at the time."

"You could've stayed and looked for her. I would've helped you."

"You know who we were up against. We had no chance," David yelled back.

"Yeah. The same people we're up against now! The names and uniforms may have changed, David, but don't kid yourself. We're all in this for a reason. They think you had something back then and hid it. They've probably been watching you forever, waiting to see if you would slip-up."

"I never had the stone. I saw it . . . but I never had it."

Aaron's eyes glittered. David knew that all he wanted was to stand up and slam him in the face with his fist.

"What makes you think they're not going to wait and see if you do have it?" Aaron began pacing the room.

"Did it ever occur to you that if they didn't find the stone at the end of this little treasure hunt that they might just take Leah and hide her in the same place as Neith until you finally give up?!"

Hope appeared in David's soul. "You think she's still alive?"

Aaron sighed, turning away from the man who very obviously was not listening.

"Jesus . . . maybe they *did* keep her for a bargaining chip," David whispered. "Maybe we could still save her."

"In less than two days *we'll* be dead," Aaron stated, staring at David in complete frustration. "So will the girls. I wonder, would she be proud of what you've done to them?"

David stared out at the cable car. It stopped its ascent and unloaded a small, dark figure at the monastery's doors. He found himself suddenly praying for the tiny silhouette—hoping beyond hope they would find the answers they'd gone there to seek.

CHAPTER 29

As the sun opened its lazy eye on Leah's fifth day, she exited the cable car and stared out at the breathtaking panoramic view of the Jordanian Valley. There was only one other location in her whole life where she'd felt her heart fall in love with such a magnificent scene. And that, of course, was her beloved New York City; when she'd stood on top of the Empire State Building for the first time and reveled in the feeling of being an 'unknown fish in a gigantic pond.'

Here, in Jericho, she felt closer to Jesus; there, she felt closer to herself. Here, she was walking in the footsteps of the Son; there, she had made her own path—set up her own life—as she wiled away peaceful, perfect hours in the basement of her magnificent library.

Leah sighed. She was standing in a place that'd been marred by war and destruction for hundreds of years in the name of a higher power.

For someone so cynical, so filled with realism about the darkness of mankind, Leah still had a hard time understanding bigotry. After all, if all people truly believed they were created in 'somebody's image'—no matter who that somebody might be—then why would there have to be any fighting at all?

Catching a glimpse of the casino that towered over the landscape, she muttered, "Money and power. That's what it always comes down to."

"True." A voice suddenly spoke behind her. "Temptation has

always been Man's biggest downfall."

Swinging her body around with such force that she practically tumbled over the side of the cliff, Leah shouted, "Jesus!"

The white-haired monk smiled; his face lit up with the comfort and peace that only came from a happy soul. "Not exactly."

The familiar grin struck a direct hit to Leah's heart and she flung herself around the old man's neck. "Gregory! My god, you're here!" she yelled into his ear, and the old monk began to laugh.

"Goodness," he said. "If I'd known I would have received such a wonderful greeting, I would've surprised you earlier."

Stepping back, Leah's happy tears rolled down her cheeks. "You're here." Confusion appeared in her mind. "Wait. Why are you here?"

Gregory brushed a curl of bright, white hair away from his face. "I wanted to be here for you when you arrived."

"How did you know I would come *here*?'

He raised a teasing eyebrow.

"Let me guess . . . a vision?" Leah grinned.

"No," he smiled wide. "But don't knock visions, young lady. If I have to be honest . . ."

Leah pointed at the cross around his neck. "You do."

What sounded like a small child's giggle erupted from his mouth. "Obviously. A friend of mine—another Good Samaritan who meets people all across the world—told me he ran into a beautiful lost soul on the road to Jericho."

Leah remained silent.

"His name's Robert. You met him, I believe in the great Garden of Gethsemane."

Leah's eyes grew wide. "Bob, the caretaker? He was a monk?"

He chuckled. "No. The caretaker is a caretaker. But he's part of the grapevine that lets us know if a friend is in need."

Leah sighed. "Well, you are certainly my friend, Gregory. It is so wonderful to see you again."

Images floated through Leah's mind as she remembered their first meeting. Gregory had been the one to show them around another monastery a short time ago; one that ended up leading she and Gareth to solve their second adventure and view the most awesome boat in all the world. It had been he, and he alone, who had sheltered them from the demons who were coming to abduct Leah and the power she had carried in her hand. Gregory, and the rest of his brothers, had pledged their lives to continue to protect the secret of St. Gregory and the power of the Son's words.

Leah took a step backward, forgetting that she was standing on the rim of a deadly precipice.

Immediately, Gregory reached out and grabbed her by the arm, pulling her forward.

She held the savior's hand. "I promise I'm not contemplating suicide. Just a little tired, I guess."

He smiled. "Below you, my dear, lies the Valley of the Shadow of Death. And you do not want to become a permanent addition."

Leah nodded, as a shot of humility flooded her soul. "I thought they were just words on a page."

Offering the smile of a loving father, Gregory shook his head. "No child. You and I are standing in the place where Jesus spent forty days and forty nights fasting and meditating, fighting Satan's temptations to bring Him down."

"Mount of Temptation," Leah whispered. "I was supposed to come here."

Gregory suddenly clapped his hands. "I can't wait for you to tell me all about it. But . . . breakfast first. You look even older than I do and we can't have that."

Leah laughed heartily as Gregory led her up the rocky steps and through the doors of the stunning monastery.

Inside, she was overwhelmed by the delicate work of true artisans. The stone walls were thick and solid, so that every visitor would have no fear that the building would slide down the treacherous mountain. The benches were polished, and gleamed in the sunlight filtering through the etched panes of glass. There was a quiet humming that met Leah's ears, like the invisible bodies of believers were scattered throughout the grand structure, offering their songs and prayers to the Son who'd stood on this very ground.

"Where is everyone?" She looked around at the empty rooms.

Gregory smiled. "Keeping to themselves, I suppose. Perhaps meditating; praying for the people who walk through these doors that when they step off this mountain, they'll be inspired to live a better life."

Leah nodded her understanding; but inside, her soul chastised her for being a hypocrite, walking through this place like she had *any* clue whatsoever about the power it held.

Gregory took her hand and led her into the dining hall. The bread was warm from the oven and the oatmeal was spiced with cinnamon, and Leah's body immediately began to unwind with every bite she took.

"To temptation," Gregory spoke softly inside the penitent palace. "That's what Robert told me; that a young, beautiful woman was being led *to* temptation. That's how I knew you'd come here . . . eventually."

"Your grapevine is extremely intelligent," Leah remarked. "Quick, too. I just met Robert two days ago."

Gregory nodded. "He took you to the tomb."

"Yes."

"And you found something there?"

Leah put her fork down. "Do you . . . do your people know what's going on?"

The monk shook his full head of bright, white hair, making it look like a huge cloud of snow was hovering above him. "I only know that you're on a journey that's built on fear."

Leah sighed. "I began in Athens, which is where this pendant comes from."

As she removed the stone from inside her shirt, Gregory's face grew as white as his hair. "What?" she asked.

"Nothing. Go on, child," he said, recovering quickly.

Hearing the strange tone in his voice, she continued slowly, "I followed Plato's words to Athena." She paused, trying to detect any sign of recognition in the monk's eyes.

"I actually know very little about the mythological goddesses." Gregory smiled. "She was a warrior, was she not?"

"Yes. Athens was named after her because of a gift she gave to its people . . . the gift of an olive."

A small light flickered in his eyes. "And when it's planted in the ground a tree will grow?"

Leah nodded.

"And then you appear in Gethsemane, searching the olive trees where the Savior once prayed while waiting for his betrayers to arrive and put Him to death. Then . . . here?"

Leah shook her head. "No. I traveled to Qumran, through a tunnel that's hidden inside a cave once used to crush olives into sacred oil. On the other side of the tunnel, we found Herodium. That's when I came here."

"Odd stops along the way. Tell me, is that pendant all you carry with you?"

Confusion welled in her soul. "Yes. Why?"

"It's nothing," he replied. "You must be looking for something very different this time out?"

Leah's frustration once again embraced her. "I honestly don't know what I'm searching for this time out. There are men . . . people who have taken my father and I have seven days to find a bunch of seeds, plant them in the ground . . . somewhere, and then . . . who knows what? The only clues I have to go on are pictures that my father left behind."

"What grows from these seeds?"

Leah sighed deeply. "I don't know that either. Some kind of magical tree with a staircase in the middle of it? Or, at least that's what the pictures show. There was also a notation that might refer to the location of the Silver Scroll from Qumran."

"The exact map to a treasure trove of gold and silver?" Gregory smiled wide.

Leah shook her head. "I know . . . I know . . . it sounds ridiculous. I mean, the Copper Scroll was just someone's idea of a joke."

Gregory held up his hand. "Now, there are many who feel that document is real, and that it shows the cache that was hidden when the Second Temple fell."

"Not you, too," Leah groaned. "Look, Gregory, no one has ever come close to finding anything that proves any of that existed."

Gregory shook his head. "Just because you can't see something doesn't mean it doesn't exist."

Leah stood up quickly, pacing the long, polished floor. "I can't believe all this is simply for . . . money. I mean, can't the bad guys of the world think about anything else? Not very creative, are they?"

Gregory stood up and took Leah gently by the elbow, leading her out the back doors and into a small, colorful garden set into the stone.

Leah admired the magnificent blossoms that seemed to grow from the absolutely barren rock. "This is beautiful."

"Yes. The brothers do not even cultivate it. The flowers just simply bloom. Perhaps it's He, thanking this deserted place for being with Him during His time of great need."

Leah turned to him. "You think these grow here because of Jesus?"

Gregory shrugged. "It's certainly a lovely thought. Have you seen our friend lately?"

Leah closed her eyes and thought back to the small, warm tomb. "Umm . . . He came and talked to me again. I saw Joseph there, too."

Gregory nodded, showing no surprise at the strange confession that Leah knew would get her locked up if she voiced it anywhere else in the world.

Comfort overwhelmed her soul. That was the strange thing about faith, Leah thought. Everyone says they believe, but if you tell them that you actually saw the Son—let alone spoke to Him—they'd mark you as some kind of crazed zealot.

The monk kept her hand and led her up the rocky slope "What was Joseph doing there?"

"He was holding the Grail in his hands."

"Was he?" Gregory asked. "So I suppose those other rumors were wrong?"

Leah grinned at the teasing tone. "It was bright green, by the way, like an emerald."

"Like your pendant," he observed. Gregory took a deep breath. "Some say the Grail was carved from his crown."

"I thought Jesus wore a crown of thorns?"

Gregory pointed out over the landscape to a small, dirt road in the distance. "That's the road from Jerusalem to Jericho. It winds through the Valley and up to this mountain and is where Jesus often traveled. He stood up on this mountain for forty days and forty nights staring down at Jericho, which was a lush paradise at that time. It was filled with the food and water that sustained life. It was even the site of the very first olive tree, which you're obviously quite familiar with now.

"The Son never went down this mountain, though. He fasted for all that time up here and didn't allow Himself to partake of the food and water that Jericho provided. Below the monastery is the cave where He sat . . . where Satan came to visit."

"The Devil was up here, too?" Her body shook. She wondered if the one who stalked the earth was standing inside one of the dark caves staring out at her right now.

"Yes . . . he came," Gregory continued, walking slowly up the hill. "He offered Jesus all that you see; if Jesus would simply kneel down and worship him."

"Jesus declined." Leah smiled.

A robust laugh burst from Gregory's mouth. "That He did. Supposedly He told the Devil that, *it was written that Thou shalt worship the Lord thy God, and Him only.*"

"Good speaker."

"Always was," Gregory agreed, with a wink. "But, of course, Satan wasn't done. He told Jesus to turn the rocks to bread and feed Himself. It was a dare. Lucifer said that He could do it if He was truly the Son of God. But Jesus told him that, *man shall not live by bread alone, but by every word that proceeded out of the mouth of God.*

"The Devil even went so far as to tell Jesus to kill Himself—to cast Himself down—because if Jesus was indeed the Son, then the angels would come to save Him. But Jesus simply said, *thou shalt not tempt the Lord,*" Gregory said with a wink. "That's the one I like the most."

Leah grinned. "So did the bad guy give up?"

"On Him, yes." Gregory nodded. "For a time, anyway. You see, Lucifer couldn't trick, beat, or tempt the Son, so he went on to—how do you say . . . Fry other fish?"

"Close enough," Leah said with a grin. "And the fish he chose?"

"Man."

"Ah, yes . . . the big fish," Leah snorted. "They certainly didn't give old Lucifer much of a fight. The Great White would've at least challenged the guy."

His voice grew soft, "Actually, there are humans who cannot be tempted."

"There's nothing money can't buy, Gregory," she sighed. "Most people have a price."

"Really . . . what's yours?"

"My father," Leah said, quickly. "Why else would I be here?"

Gregory nodded. "So give people what they desire most and everyone will sell their souls?"

"Pious, humble believers are in rare supply these days," she muttered.

"For a woman who has met the Son and read His words, you're still very cynical about life."

"The Son, I believe. Man lies." Her heart began to burn when the image of Gareth holding Anippe flooded her brain. She shook her head, banishing the thought, and pointed out at the building hovering over the landscape. "There's a perfect example right in front of you. Think about it . . . a casino in the middle of all this? I mean, what do you call that Gregory . . . progress?"

"Irony?" He laughed.

Leah turned to stare at the cheerful face; his eyes twinkled with humor.

"Don't look so upset, child. God loves irony."

She leaned back against the stone. "Temptation."

"Temptation," he nodded. "What you say is true, Leah. Everyone in the world is tempted. They come upon a hillside much like this one and are met with someone who's offering them the world . . . it's their choice to make. Of course, if someone offers you your dream and asks that you do nothing in return, then you kind of have it coming, so to speak.

"No one thinks of the consequences. If their families are starving, some have to steal food to put in their loved ones' mouths. Is this a criminal? Is this a faithless man? Or, is this simply someone who has worked and prayed all his life and has just become frustrated. He doesn't understand why prayers are answered for people who are far less deserving than he and his family. What this poor man doesn't know however, is that the ones who had their so-called prayers granted to them most likely had to give up something much greater in return."

Leah crossed her arms. "That's all well and good, Gregory. And it's a lovely story—to believe that there's something better waiting for you somewhere. But that idea . . . that belief . . . doesn't stop the man's family from dying of starvation. That thought doesn't stop wars. In some cases, it even creates them. 'God will provide' may mean a great deal to some, but when it's your loved ones being beaten, starved, or worse, by people who would rather spit on them than offer them a slice of bread, then they just become words, Gregory. . .nothing more."

He scratched his small beard, as if trying to understand the odd concept she spoke. "You're a librarian. You believe in words."

"I believe what I see."

"Lucifer still walks the earth, Leah. That's the truth. You know it is. He's here and he preys on people's weaknesses. He was cast out of Paradise and into our world."

Leah added, "And keeps right on plowing through it—unchallenged—gathering people on his side for the final showdown. I've heard the stories, Gregory. I even stood in front of the Gates and watched him try to slither on through."

"Ah." Gregory lifted his hand in the air. "There, you see? He was challenged. He was stopped . . . by Mr. Lowery; a believer who was extremely tempted to open that Gate for himself and see what was on the other side. Yet, he didn't. Instead, he listened to you."

"Gareth Lowery is not exactly a starving man feeding his family. It's a little different," Leah remarked.

"No," he replied. "It's exactly the same. The devil couldn't tempt Gareth with *money* to get him to open that Gate, and Gareth didn't need food or crave power, but he was tempted by his own beliefs. He'd spent his entire life searching for it and wanted nothing more than to see inside—reach the goal that his loving, deceased parents had tried so hard to reach." Reaching out, he took her hand. "Unfortunately, for the bad guy, Gareth wanted one thing more than that. Something Lucifer didn't know about."

Leah remained silent.

"You." He smiled. "What you'd found in each other was something the Devil hadn't counted on and couldn't break. Of course," Gregory continued, tilting his head and staring at Leah's newly-formed tears. "Now that he knows Mr. Lowery's weakness, he can certainly come back and prey on that."

"What are you talking about?"

"You were face-to-face with the Devil, Leah. Much like the Son was face-to-face with him here, on this mountain. The Devil found His weakness too, finally . . . if you really think about it."

"Jesus had no weakness."

"No." Gregory shook his head. "He did. The Son believed in the loyalty of the people. He was betrayed by the definition of a friend, and He was killed—cruelly and violently. Of course, He rose into Paradise and has since been acknowledged. Well . . . by most," Gregory continued with a grin, "To bring Gareth Lowery to the Devil's side he would've had to break the strongest belief Gareth has; and although his belief in God is great, his belief in you is far stronger."

Leah placed her head in her hands and began to cry, letting loose the torrent of emotions that rattled inside her soul.

Gregory rushed to her side and put her head on his shoulder. "Everything's going to be fine, child, I promise you. You're tired, is all. You haven't slept in days."

"I have to find my father," Leah muttered, sobbing into the monk's warm, brown robe.

"You will. There's a power in you, Leah. The faith you have in yourself is what keeps you standing. For a self-proclaimed critic, you can see through the shadows of the world to see the absolute truth. You hunt for it and you'll not be deterred . . . you will not fail. But your body isn't Divine, Leah."

"Gee, thanks a lot—nothing like kicking me when I'm down."

Rising, Gregory took her hand in his. "You need to rest, or you won't be able to get back up when the time comes, let alone find what you seek."

Nodding, Leah let the kind man lead her back through the beautiful garden and into the small bedchamber.

Even with the despair, confusion and anger that flowed through her, Leah's eyes soon closed to the world and she let her soul be enveloped by the Savior on the Mount.

CHAPTER 30

The church was covered in white satin and Leah's heart was, for the first time in her life, actually giddy with joy.

Walking down the red-carpeted aisle, she stared at the happy-faced monk who stood up at the altar waiting for her arrival. His eyes were twinkling and his smile was wide, as Leah continued her journey on the arm of her beloved father.

Taking in his handsome profile, Leah smiled as her father turned and one bright sapphire eye gave her a wink. Kissing him on the cheek, Leah then spotted the strange walls that abutted the carpet. Whatever church she was in had no pews. Instead, it was filled with aisle after aisle of bookcases.

Reaching out, Leah touched the floor-to-ceiling cabinets and stared at the well-known space that her brain recognized in seconds. Beginning with the spine that announced, *Atlantis*, Leah moved her fingers over row after row of her favorite dusty novels. She was beyond happy. . . . She was home.

"The library," Leah whispered, "Getting married in my library. All is right with the world."

Lifting the bouquet of colorful flowers, Leah took in a long, deep breath and let the beguiling scent of jasmine and lavender cloud her mind. Bringing her gaze back to Gregory, she kissed her father one last time. The bright sun beamed through the stained-glass window behind the altar and Leah could almost feel the Son looking down on their union; offering a smile.

Taking a deep breath, Gregory began to read from his favorite book. Bells rang out somewhere above their heads as the handsome groom dressed smartly in an elegant tuxedo, turned to greet his bride.

Gareth's green eyes were lit with warmth and love as he stared at her. Leah's heart thumped wildly against her ribcage when the man she loved with all her heart took her breath away with his perfect smile.

The bells grew louder as a new soft ticking sound entered the room. Building quickly around her, Leah thought that a thousand crickets had suddenly materialized behind the grand bookcases. She looked down at the fragrant bouquet and noticed the bright green olive that was now centered among the silvery leaves.

Gregory's voice filled the room, "Who comes to give this woman in holy matrimony?"

A deep voice echoed behind her, "Her mother and I do."

Leah turned to her father. The sun had set behind the large glass window, and shadows fell across her father's face, turning his sapphire eyes black as steel.

Her mother, the elegant Mary Tallent, stood at the end of the carpet at the back of the church. Her golden-blonde hair was dirty and hung limply down her back, like worms that'd dried in the sun. Her face was gaunt, and the silk robe she wore was covered with dirt. She screamed out inside the church, "I deserved better than this!"

The dark shadows around Leah's father moved like storm clouds above his head, suffocating his cries for help. He fell to the floor, writhing in pain, as Leah turned her gaze back to Gareth to beg for his help.

But the emerald eyes were gone. Standing in his place was the owner of the soothing accent and deep, brown eyes that promised a world of quiet splendor—a world where everything would be placed at her feet for the rest of her life, and she would never have to leave this wonderful safety of her library.

As she watched in total confusion, Daniel Bauer swept a curl of soft brown hair off his forehead and pointed to the back of the church.

Leah followed his movements, and her basement suddenly appeared. The old chairs, the smell of the rich, dark roasted coffee coming from the ancient pot, and the clanging of the old pipes made her heart swim with happiness.

Staring back into Daniel Bauer's face, he took her hand. Leah waited breathlessly to feel the small gold band embrace her ring finger. But, instead, he turned her hand upside down and placed the strange object in her palm. Confusion took over her soul as Leah stared at the bright red gift. She wondered why he would do such a strange thing during a wedding ceremony.

Raising her head, she looked over at Gregory's now saddened face, and asked, "What do I do with this?"

"Cast him out!" the monk replied loudly. "See through the shadows to the truth. Temptation is great . . . fight it. You're the only one who can." Tears rolled down his cheeks, and Leah felt the heat of Daniel's hand creep around her neck. She looked over at him and saw the fire gleam in his eyes as he lifted the heavy pendant away from her flesh.

He leaned in closer. "Just say, 'I do.'" His hot, sweet breath caressed her cheek as he gripped her hand hard in his own. "We're not through."

His touch burned her flesh and Leah stared down at the sapphire eye on the back of her hand. It seemed to be twisting and turning in pain—transforming its shape into a terrifying image.

Leah took a step back from the eerie man and let the red object fall to the ground.

Gregory let out a cry of despair. The ticking of the clock grew louder and her father continued his painful cry. A wall of black now surrounded him, pushing him to the ground and stealing the breath from his body. Only her mother seemed to be happy. She smiled at Leah as she threw open the church doors, and vanished into the night.

The bells grew louder, smothering her father's screams and Gregory's tears. A loud clang reverberated inside the room, causing the bookshelves to shudder from the impact of the harsh echo. The books fell to the floor as if an earthquake was suddenly shaking the foundation. And Daniel Bauer simply leaned against the altar as a shadow appeared above his head. There, Leah watched in silence as a bright blue and white image took shape—the shape of a woman.

Athena came to life—her sword in one hand, her shield in the other. She stared at Leah, as Daniel let out a hideous screech below the Goddess. "Be aware of your enemies, Leah. Be careful of the power they wield."

"What?" Leah whispered to the Hero's Companion.

"Go through Temptation now to the other side. There's no time left."

Leah reached out and tried to grab the rapidly disappearing vision. "Wait! I don't understand."

"Go . . . now. But . . . please," Athena begged. "Whatever you do, don't leave me with him. It would be a disaster."

Leah stared down at Daniel Bauer's head coming to a rolling stop at her feet. The blank eyes looked up at her from underneath an emerald crown. Reminding her of the mythical medusa, Daniel's hair had become a nest of bright green snakes—squirming and twisting—trying to get away from the diadem of death. The serpents arched their backs toward the sky and reached for one last gasp of air before falling to the floor—dead.

The last bell grew silent and Leah opened her eyes and screamed.

———

The door to the small bedchamber burst open and Gregory ran into the room.

"My God, what's the matter? Are you okay, child?" His eyes scanned the area and his white hair stood on end, as if he, too, had been scared to death by the power of Leah's nightmare.

Wiping the sweat from her lip, Leah tried to calm her breathing. It felt like the Lord of the Dance, himself, was jumping up and down on her heart—giving a stellar performance. She gasped for air, suddenly remembering where she was. "What?" She came back to herself slowly, leaving the horrible dream behind. "What time is it?"

Gregory smiled. "It is noon, child. I was going to wake you, but you really needed to sleep."

Leah bolted out of bed and raced to the window. The sun was indeed climbing high in the sky and she shook her head. "I wasted a whole day"

"Finding the truth takes time. Remember? Jesus sat here for forty days and nights."

Leah shouted rudely, "I don't have that kind of time!"

"But, Leah—"

She raced for the door. "Look, Gregory. I'm working on a pretty tight schedule here. Did Gareth come?"

The man stared at the floor and shook his head. "No one has come for you."

Marching down the long hallway, Leah tried with all her might to bury the pain and disappointment that was now swimming in her soul.

She almost cried as she tore out of the building and stared down at Jericho. Shielding her eyes, searching the long, winding road for the big, black limo that should be heading her way by now, she witnessed absolutely nothing. It was as if her . . . love, had simply forgotten she existed.

Gregory came up behind her. "Where are you going?"

"I have to go back to Herod's palace. Gareth and I have never been apart during something like . . . this. He's not here. Something's not right."

"Yes . . . safest way." Gregory nodded. "The hero needs his companion." He placed his hand on her shoulder. "I'm sure Gareth's fine, Leah. He'll be here soon. He probably just got caught up in the journey."

"Yeah," Leah sneered. "He's searching for the ever-elusive Silver Scroll."

Gregory remained silent at her angry words.

"No." Leah shook her head. "That's not it. Something's wrong. I have to get back there."

"I'm sure he's on his way to you."

Leah wrenched her elbow from Gregory's grip. "I have to find my father now. I only have seven days. Which means," she said, looking down at her watch. "I have . . . oh, about thirty-six hours left before he's lost forever. Or," she concluded, "until we all die."

"Just like Joshua," Gregory commented.

"Who?" Leah turned at the strange remark.

"Joshua . . . when he took over from Moses and led his people around the base of Jericho . . . trumpets blazing."

Leah sighed. "Please, Gregory. I can't take another Bible story right now . . . okay?"

"On the seventh day the trumpets blew," Gregory recited quietly, like he was reading off a prepared script, "And the walls came tumbling down."

Leah's body froze in the noonday sun, as she stared into the monk's innocent eyes. "What did you just say?"

"It was their first victory. Later, Joseph said that Jericho was cursed from that day forward, making it impossible for the city to ever be built again. That's why some believe Jericho remains a mound of dirt smack dab in the middle of what was once known as the Cradle of Civilization."

The words inscribed in the stone that sat in Plato's garden slammed her in the head. "Cradle of Civilization . . . seven days . . . walls tumbling down," Leah whispered.

Taking Gregory by the hand, she led him to a stone bench on top of the monstrous cliff. Staring down at Jericho, Leah once again knew she was back at the very beginning—an ancient beginning that would hopefully lead to her beloved father.

"Okay," she said softly. "Tell me about it."

CHAPTER 31

"Many believe that because of Jericho's mild climate, healthy vegetation, citrus groves and abundant water supply, that it was the actual 'Garden of Eden' during that time."

Leah squeezed his hand and smiled. "I hope this doesn't sound extremely rude or ungrateful, but we're on a time crunch here."

He raised a bright white eyebrow up his tanned forehead. "Just the facts . . . Ma'am?"

"Exactly," Leah laughed.

"Okay." Gregory sat quietly for a moment, probably sifting through the wealth of information he had locked in his brain about the ancient city. Taking a deep breath, he began, "Jericho kind of 'grew up' around a spring, which is still down there by the way, called Elisha's Fountain. It was a very strategic city because it not only offered an oasis in the hot, arid desert, but it also provided access to the heartland of Canaan—which is why the Israelites fought for Jericho on their way to conquering Palestine.

"They were led by Joshua who'd succeeded Moses as their leader. Now, 'spies,' I suppose is the right word, were sent out by Joshua to check Jericho and see if there was a way to conquer the fortified city."

Turning to her, he stared at Leah as if she was a pupil sitting before her wise professor. "You have to understand that Jericho had walls built around it during this time, barring anyone from getting inside. This posed rather a large problem for Joshua."

"Thank goodness he was a believer." Leah smiled.

Gregory shook his finger at her. "Don't be cheeky, child, or I'll stop telling this story right now."

Leah hung her head, feeling like a five-year-old who'd just stepped on the man's well-educated shoes. "Sorry."

He nodded. "A woman by the name of Rahab hid Joshua's spies inside her house, letting them see what they would be up against if and when they could figure out how to topple the walls. The spies told Rahab that she and her family would be spared because of her help.

"When Joshua arrived with his army they walked around Jericho, following seven priests that blew on ram's horn trumpets. Up in front of this legion was the Ark of the Covenant."

Leah grinned. "Yes, that one I know all about."

He grinned. "Good. The legion walked around Jericho one time every day for six days. Then, on the seventh day, the group marched seven times around the city. When they were done, the priests blew their mighty trumpets and Joshua ordered the believers to raise their voices. When they shouted, the walls of Jericho fell flat and the Israelites walked into the city. They burned it to the ground, sparing only Rahab and her family, as they'd promised."

"Why would they burn it to the ground?"

Gregory grinned. "In order to answer your question, we would have to have a conversation on the ins-and-outs of all the wars between these two countries and their people. And I definitely don't think you have time for a discussion about why men fight in the name of God."

Leah shook her head. "Gotcha. Okay . . . Jericho. What was in there? What could Jericho possibly have to do with my father . . . or, whatever it is I'm supposed to be looking for?"

Gregory simply shrugged. "That I don't know. Like I said before, Jericho was mainly an oasis—a fertile crescent, if you will—plunked down in the hot barren desert. It was called the 'moon city' by the locals and, to this day, they still believe it's a place of magic; a place that God put down on Earth to test out the idea of Paradise."

Leah looked out at the empty pile of excavated dirt and stone. "Looks like paradise didn't take."

Gregory nodded. "It's been proven that settlement after settlement, over centuries, came to Jericho to live. There were thriving communities that produced citrus fruit, grain and pottery—wonderful things that kept the area alive. The very *first* civilization ever has been dated back to Jericho, even though some believe Mesopotamia was settled first. There is much debate."

Leah waved her hand in the air. "Isn't there always?"

He smiled. "The first olive tree was said to have been planted in Jericho, like I told you. That's really the only thing I can think of that relates to anything you've done on your journey."

Confusion muddled Leah's mind. "What about the Silver Scroll? Was it ever written that the locations for all this supposed wealth from the Second Temple could have been buried in Jericho?"

Gregory shook his head. "No. I would think, considering how many locations speak of water, channels and cisterns that it's more likely the treasure was buried in Herod's palace. Herodium was the most complex building at the time. There was no palace on the Tel es-sultan—mostly farmers and laborers lived there in normal dwellings. The only real battlement, per se, was an old tower that sat in the center of the city. Perhaps it was used as a fortress to see their enemies coming."

"Didn't work."

"No, it didn't," Gregory agreed.

Leah touched the big emerald disc around her neck. "What about Jesus? Maybe He did something here that corresponds with all this?" Leah asked, her brain grasping for anything she could understand.

But the monk just shook his head. "Jesus came through Jericho, of course, many times on His way to or from Jerusalem. However, the New Testament does say that Jericho was the place where Jesus healed two blind men."

"Blind men?"

Gregory nodded. "Believers—He probably wanted to give them the opportunity to step into the light."

Leah mumbled, remembering Plato's point of "The Allegory of the Cave." She whispered, ". . . Venture out of the shadows and saw the truth before them."

"Well said," Gregory responded.

She sighed. "And I suppose . . . again . . . all of these stories are true."

"Always the cynic," Gregory chuckled. "Yes. I, of course, would believe them to be true because I . . . believe. But with Jericho, there have been many—like your Mr. Lowery, in fact—who have come here and uncovered enough evidence to support the story of Joshua causing the walls to fall down. A large revetment wall was excavated which once supported the mound in the Middle Bronze Age, which is about the time it would've happened. It was made of stone, brick, mud and, most importantly, there was a spot in the wall that'd cracked and practically disintegrated—a break that would have allowed people to walk inside.

"They also found huge store-jars of grain that were intact. They dated back to the last Canaanite city in Jericho, and were from a time of the last harvest, when the city would've burned."

Leah nodded. "Okay. But couldn't seismic activity be a factor? I mean, this land is over nine-hundred-feet below sea level. Something could've made it fall besides trumpeting priests."

Gregory leaned over; his voice came out like a whisper of a butterfly's wings, "Faith is believing in something bigger than yourself, Leah."

"I do," she said. "I believe in the beginning. I believe in Noah and Moses . . . how could I not?" she snorted. "But the middle gets kind of fuzzy, and as for the end, who really knows? There have been many 'truths' that have been proven incorrect. You know that."

"But were they proven wrong, Leah? Or, were they just not the 'truth' to begin with? You know that the New Testament had an editor. You know that certain things were added by a king who wanted to bring his people together. But the truth," he said, pointing at her heart, "is in there. Whatever it is that *you* believe."

"Yeah, I know." Lifting her hand, she wiped the sweat and grit from her forehead.

"No, no," he continued. "Don't roll your eyes at me. I'm not giving you . . . what is it you say? A Hallmark card answer?" He smiled. "You're a literal person, Leah. You're following a journey that was begun by a philosopher who believed in the lost city of

Atlantis, if I remember correctly. Yet this philosopher, this genius who believed in coming out of the shadows and seeing the truth, truly thought that this mythical city existed. Much in the same way that Mr. Lowery believes that the Silver Scroll exists."

Sitting back against the bench, Gregory gazed at the sun dipping lower in the sky. "Your time is nearly up, Leah. What I ask of you is to go down to Jericho and clear your mind. Get rid of the shadows of doubt that surround you. Throw them away for just a little bit of time. Below you resides a place of beliefs . . . of miracles. If you at least trust in the Son," he continued, with a grin, "and Gareth . . . use that power. Talk to the Son and listen to your heart where Gareth is concerned. Maybe one of them has the power to deliver you to paradise and save your father."

Leah felt the tears choke her throat. "Gregory, I—"

Leaning over, he kissed her cheek. "Go get your father. I will be very pleased to meet him."

Standing, Gregory walked toward the monastery doors and called back over his shoulder, "And don't worry about Gareth. The hero will always be with his companion. As it was in the beginning," he winked, closing the door behind him, "And all that other stuff."

CHAPTER 32

Leah wanted nothing more than to release her frustration as the cable car trudged back down the mountain, like a donkey that simply had no interest in bringing some new idiot to the bottom of the Grand Canyon. "I should've walked," she grumbled.

Just as she was about to scream, the car finally came to a stop. The bright pink glow coming from the Oasis Casino lit the night sky, letting her know that her hours were indeed numbered. She was about to begin her seventh day—her last day; all alone, there was no Gareth in sight. Fighting to locate something she didn't even know what it was—to find a father who she'd no idea where he was.

Leah jumped from the creaking red car and marched quickly toward the mound. It'd looked so much smaller from the top of Temptation. Standing before it, with the large broken stones towering above her, Leah suddenly felt like she was in way over her head.

Putting her hands behind her back, she walked around the great, dark hill searching for the easiest way to begin her climb. Passing a trench dug into the side, she stopped only briefly, continuing her walk around the dirt. After all, it *was* her seventh day, thought Leah. Perhaps she should do what was done once before.

Clearing her mind of every ounce of doubt, she reached down and touched the 'seeds' that hung around her neck. Leah had the power, now all she had to do was use her brain to find where the olive tree had sprouted from the dirt. Maybe that was it, she thought. She'd find the right place to plant the seeds in Jericho and the tree would grow . . . again.

The Silver Scroll, number sixty-four on her father's map, would then fall from its branches straight into her hands. Then, she'd simply wait by the side of the road for the bad guys to appear, take the scroll from her hands, and release her father into her arms. *I suppose I should get Anippe's uncle back, too.* Leah grimaced.

No, she yelled at herself. *Don't blame the guy for what his slimy little niece did. It's not his fault!* Shaking the negative thoughts from her head, Leah clutched the olives of the warrior, the Son, and Hell's King in her hand. She tried not to wonder why three such different entities would combine forces to grow a tree. *Talk about the good, the bad and the ugly,* she thought, with a laugh. Of course, Athena hadn't been ugly. At least, that's what they'd said.

Who is they? Who are these people who 'say' so much? And how the heck did 'they' know anything?

Leah sighed deeply, coming full circle to rest beside the trench once again, completing her seventh circuit round the mound.

She looked up at the midnight sky. "I don't have a trumpet," she whispered. "I can yell though. Boy . . . how I could yell right now."

But Leah wondered if she really should. There had to be a guardhouse somewhere near the imposing structure. After all, in a twenty-first century tourist trap, there had to be someone in charge of keeping the vandals at bay.

Eerily, though, there were no lights; only the strange pink glow of the casino hovered around her. Taking a deep breath, Leah extracted the flashlight that she'd taken from Daniel Bauer at Herodium.

A shiver raced down her spine as his handsome face hovered before her. It felt as if her nightmare was pushing against the closed box inside her head, begging to be set free. It was as if the images had something to tell her, to help her decipher exactly what it was that Leah was walking directly into.

Without thinking, she let loose a scream of monumental proportions and climbed into the bowels of Jericho.

Another sharp stone cut into her hand and Leah tripped, landing face-first in a pile of dirt inside the trough's walls. She grunted, "So much for resting on the seventh day. I don't remember reading about marching through an old, smelly hill."

As the slope turned into a sharp incline, Leah's head came even with the top layer of Jericho and she stared out at the casino and hotel across the street. Looking up at the brightly-lit windows, she briefly wondered if Gareth was in one of those luxury rooms talking with Anippe right now. Perhaps he was sharing his heartbreak over losing the love of his life. Would Anippe pat him on the shoulder and offer words of encouragement . . . tell him to go out in the darkness and find Leah? Or, would she get him drunk like the rest of the red-blooded women out there and lead him to the bedroom. After all, thought Leah. She and Anippe did have the same sapphire eyes. And maybe if he was completely loaded, Gareth wouldn't even notice the difference. Temptation is a powerful thing.

Her heart and head shouted at her simultaneously, reprimanding Leah for skewering the one man she knew she could count on—no matter what the picture was inside her head. Leah knew, deep down, that she had simply walked in at the wrong time. Gareth's hands hadn't been pressing against Anippe's back pulling her closer—they had been firmly planted on her shoulders, pushing her away.

Leah sighed. "I know," she said to the heavens above. "I'm an idiot. What would Moses say, I wonder?" She giggled, thinking about the brilliant man who'd led his people into Paradise. She wondered how the big guy would feel about his descendant—who barely believed in anything—being such a complete and utter moron. "Boy," Leah whispered. "I bet he never thought his family tree would fork this badly."

She practically went over backwards as she slipped on a small stair that'd come out of nowhere. Moving her flashlight, she illuminated the large stone base. Looking like a humungous tower had cracked and fallen over—Leah knew this must be the 'proof' of the fortress that Gregory had talked about. Looking inside the crevice of broken stone, her heart leapt as she stared at an old staircase leading deep into the darkness below.

Leah knew she was looking at the location that'd been drawn

on her father's map—the staircase painted into the belly of a tree. Lifting her leg over the cracked stone, she pressed her foot against the step. The staircase seemed solid; no creaking or splitting sounds came from the rock under her feet. She pulled her other leg inside the large, broken tower and set both feet on the small step. Clinging to the side of the wall, Leah waited for the staircase of rock to give underneath her weight.

Holding, Leah slowly moved her foot down to the next step, and so on, waiting for the bottom to arrive. Step after step Leah descended, keeping her flashlight aimed at her feet, wondering if there was simply a dark pit down below—a staircase that literally led to nothing.

But remembering Gregory's words, Leah pushed the panic and fear from her heart. She could feel the warmth of the pendant against her skin, as the ground finally leveled out beneath her. The tower base was large inside the hill, like a grand rotunda beneath the dirt. Gregory was right. At one time, the tower must've been tall enough to look out across the desert and spy anyone who was coming to take their city away.

Sitting on the bottom step, Leah looked around. The air smelled like a bottle of citrus spray had been used to clean the smooth walls of the round room—but there was literally nothing there. The tower walls were void of any decoration; no marking had been left behind that would lead Leah to bury the seeds in the right place. Other than the staircase that led up and out into the great, wide world, there was only a pile of grain in the center of the floor . . . and nothing else.

Leah sent the flashlight's beam around the walls one more time, hoping that it would shine brightly on a Silver Scroll tucked into a broken crevice. "Too easy," she laughed.

"Okay." She closed her eyes. "What now?" She thought back on Gregory's story. If Jesus had healed two blind men, then perhaps the Son would appear in the tower and literally lead her eyes to the answer.

Suddenly, a faint click echoed in the tower and Leah felt the big pendant move against her flesh.

Her heart beat faster when she reached up and took the olives from inside the emerald case. Leah aimed the flashlight at the large disc and watched it close by itself. The blue line where it'd cracked in the French cathedral so long ago, disappeared. The pendant was once again a solid emerald. But the size didn't change. The lovely gem didn't transform back into the small teardrop Gareth had given her once upon a time. Instead, the bright green disc remained large and flat, like a small Frisbee hanging from a chain around her neck.

Leah shrugged. At least it wasn't heavy anymore. But it was freezing cold. Gone was the warmth the jewel had given off. Instead, it felt like someone had thrown a hard-packed snowball directly at her chest; Leah could feel the pinpricks of ice coming from the stone. Pulling the necklace away from her body, she placed it on the outside of her shirt, protecting her flesh from the strange, chilling sensation.

Staring down at the palm of her hand, she looked at the colorful olives sitting side by side. The seed of the warrior was as black as the midnight sky. The seed of the Son was silvery-green, like the mystical wand of Merlin. And the thin green olive casing of Hell's King let the dark red interior shine through, like the flames of Satan's lair were trapped inside the flimsy shell.

Placing them on the hard-packed floor, Leah sat back to look at them. She wondered if she should pray, or channel Athena's warrior cry and let it echo through the tower walls—back up to Mount Olympus in order to call on the Goddess for help.

Warrior cry aside, Leah did let out a yelp when something fell into her hair. All she could think about was that the big, black scorpion had somehow come back to life and marched across the desert sands to kill her once and for all.

Raising her hand, she slapped at whatever it was, but the small, soft thing hopped from her head and flew to the floor.

Leah snorted when she recognized the tiny, pure white owl with the glowing blue eyes. "Welcome back," she whispered. "Thank you for playing."

Its eyes grew wide and it opened its small beak, releasing a shrill cry that pierced Leah's ears.

"*What?* What do you want me to do?" she yelled back.

If she didn't know better, Leah would've said that the small owl rolled its big blue eyes in disgust.

She sat straight and tall on the stone step and stared down at the little creature. "Okay," she said, softly, "Show me what I have to do."

The owl began to hop from one foot to the other as it moved forward and picked up the first olive in its beak.

"Like you're so damn smart," Leah mumbled.

Setting the olive on top of the pile of grain in the center of the floor, the glowing blue eyes snapped open and shut continuously.

Leah wondered if the small bird was telling her off in some kind of ancient owl Morse code, but she remained silent, watching the owl daintily pick up each individual seed and deposit them onto the grain. When it was finished, it hopped off the little mound and stared up at Leah, unmoving.

"*So?* I could've done that."

The bird tilted its head and sent out the most horrific squeal Leah had ever heard. She covered her ears, trying with all her might to stop the hideous noise from penetrating her brain. When it ended, she felt some sort of liquid plop down on top of her head and roll down her face. She kept her eyes shut tight. "Ewww . . . what is this now?"

Raising her head, she stared out through the hole of the mighty tower and was greeted with a face full of water; a dark cloud had centered right above her head and the water suddenly burst from the sky. She wiped the water from her eyes and glared at the small owl sitting very haughtily on the floor. Its head was raised to the sky and its small chest was puffed out, as if he was declaring himself king of the tower.

"What? You made it rain, too? That's nuts!" Leah issued a burst of laughter. "*That's* nuts? I'm the one who's talking to a bird."

The tower floor began to fill with water and soak the mound of grain. Leah reached down quickly, trying to save the olives from being flattened under the big, heavy raindrops. But as she leaned forward, the olives sank directly into the grain.

"Lovely," Leah remarked, as she began digging through the pile to retrieve the seeds she'd risked her life for. Her hand wrapped around something and she tried to hoist it from the ground.

Standing up quickly, Leah threw herself back up the staircase as the huge, gnarled root burst from the center of the floor and began climbing up the walls of the tower.

She scrambled on her hands and knees up the staircase, trying to reach the top of Jericho, but more and more roots slithered around her ankles like snakes, pulling her into the quickly-rising water. She tried to keep her head up; she tried to breathe in the air that was rapidly disappearing. The cold water enveloped her in its arms, as the roots clung to her legs and pulled her under again and again.

As she struggled to lift her head from the water, she watched the owl disappear, flying off into the night. With all her strength, Leah lunged for one more breath. As the root tightened around her skin, the scream died on her lips, and Leah was immediately sucked into the depths of Jericho.

CHAPTER 33

"Time to go!" The door flew open sending Aaron Cain and David Tallent tumbling off their couches to the floor.

David glanced out at the pitch-black night. "What?" he said, looking up at the evil faces of Max and his two goons, standing on either side, with guns pointed directly at his head.

"Time's almost up, gentlemen." Max grinned. "So it's time to go!"

Aaron raised himself off the floor, shifting his eyes from side-to-side as if looking for a way out, or a weapon he could somehow use to stop his death from becoming a reality.

The large men walked forward and tied the captives' hands behind their backs.

Max offered an evil chuckle. His bald head shimmered in the soft, pink glow coming from outside. "It's no use, Mr. Cain, you and Mr. Tallent are coming with us. But you will be very pleased to know," he continued, turning to David's ashen face, "that your little girl is an absolute genius. She has found, in one week, what we've been searching for since the 1940's."

Taking a deep breath, Max sighed through his yellowed teeth. "I am so happy she's still alive. It would be quite a coup to bring her over to our side."

"What have you done to her?" David struggled against the tight ropes that were cutting into his flesh.

Max's hand fluttered to his chest. "Me? Why, I haven't touched the woman, Mr. Tallent. Not that I wouldn't like to. But, alas, she's already been spoken for."

"Let her go!"

"You misunderstand me. I can't let go of what I do not have."

David gasped for breath; his heart begged for his daughter to be safe.

"Now, be a good man and come with me. We're on our way right this second to join your lovely Leah so you can see for yourself that she's just fine."

"What about Anippe?" Aaron shouted, as the gun-carrying captor pushed him across the room.

Max smiled "Oh, you'll see *her* much sooner than you think."

Silence hung in the air as David and Aaron were marched from the elegant room.

The leader leaned in close to David's ear. "I hope you were right, Mr. Tallent. I pray, after all this, that what you thought was at the end of this magical rainbow is actually there."

"The devil doesn't pray." David spit in his face.

A paper-thin eyebrow crept up the shiny flesh of Max's forehead. "Oh, believe me, Mr. Tallent. If there's one person who truly believes in God, it's the Devil. And he prays all the time. He winked. "You'll meet him soon, too. He's a great guy . . . I'm sure you two will get along famously."

———

Being led through the dark, abandoned hotel, David and Aaron were thrown into an empty elevator surrounded by the horrible men. David could smell the new paint on the walls, as the machine slowly descended. When it reached the ground floor, a quiet 'hush' of hydraulics came from beneath his feet. A bright and cheery chime announced their arrival, and the shiny platinum doors opened.

As a whoosh of air came into the elevator, David felt the last bit of hope empty from his soul. There, standing directly in front of him, was a bloody and battered Gareth Lowery.

CHAPTER 34

I can't believe this is the way I'm going to die, Leah thought.

Struggling against the gnarled, twisted roots that were now locked around her ankles like handcuffs, Leah could feel the burning sensation in her throat. She had no idea how long a human being could hold their breath, but she knew that she had no chance of even coming close to the World Record.

Her eyes peered through the cold, brown water. She could see the faint outline of the steps beside her—the staircase that would lead her out of the flooded tower if she could just get free. She reached out and tried to grab onto something . . . anything she could use to wrench herself free and climb out of the hole, but there was nothing.

Well, said Leah's mind. *Not nothing.* What was once smooth stone walls had now become cracked and scratchy. When she pressed her hand against the new blockade, she felt actual splinters pierce her skin. She groped further, her lungs burning, and felt large knots brush against the palm of her hand.

Leah reached down and tried to tear the unyielding ropes from around her ankles, but she couldn't. With each movement she made, the roots seemed to tighten their death-grip. Her chest was burning, her head begged for oxygen and, finally, Gareth's handsome face swam into her mind. Leah let her body go limp, as his green eyes sparkled and he offered her a smile of true love that filled her heart with . . . peace.

The brilliant librarian knew her limitations and came to the conclusion that her life, in fact, was over. She wondered briefly if the disbelief she still had in the Divine would stop the Son from letting her into Heaven. But it didn't really matter. Time was up. It was too late to correct any sins now.

With the image of Gareth before her eyes, and the bright silver light that seemed to envelope her body, Leah opened her mouth and floated toward the Gates of Heaven.

———

Her eyes felt like they were going to literally pop right out of their sockets. She bent over, coughing violently; her brain forced her lungs to breathe in and out, taking gulp after gulp of new air that seemed to have come from nowhere.

Tears welled in her eyes as she sat down and put her head between her knees. Confusion, pain, the burning sensation in her chest—all combined to make her body feel alive.

Putting her hands out, she touched the strange walls and a familiar scent entered her nostrils. Then . . . an image of her and her three sisters flashed into Leah's mind.

She could feel the cold air pummel her tiny, ten-year-old cheeks as she sat on the long, yellow sled with her sisters giggling behind her. Their tall, wind-blown father pulled them down the icy winter slope in their backyard, laughing all the way. Leah heard the wind whistle in their ears. She was so happy. Taking a deep breath as the sled came to a stop, her father rushed over. Bending down, he lifted Leah in his arms, spinning her in a circle as the fragrant pine trees danced around them. She could smell the wet bark and—

That's it! Leah opened her eyes and stared at her surroundings. The tower was gone; the water had disappeared down some kind of magical drain that must have appeared at the bottom of the staircase. She still sat on the bottom step, but the floor was covered with a layer of damp roots. Although they still looked like a pile of snakes twisted together, they were no longer moving.

She raised her eyes to the sky. Above her rested a canopy of silvery-green leaves and Leah's happy heart felt like it was about to explode inside her chest. The staircase in the tree . . . she'd made it. She was literally sitting inside a large olive tree that'd grown up around her.

In the trunk of the tree that'd sprung from the ancient dirt of Jericho, there was a small door carved into one side. Leah could see the square outline of sunlight beaming through the bark, and she could feel the warmth of a new day whistling through the leaves above her head.

Her emotions were crashing inside her like the waves of an ocean after a hurricane has left it far behind. She was alive. Leah was so grateful to be alive.

And now, excitement set in. Leah longed to see what lay on the other side of the door. Was it simply a silver treasure map that some man wanted for his own? Did someone really go to all this trouble to kidnap her father just for money?

The ticking of the clock grew louder inside her mind, and she took a deep breath. "Well . . . guess it's time to find out."

Leah kicked her foot against the door and crawled out. She cursed the librarian inside her for not reading more children's literature. Perhaps, if she had, she'd at least have some idea of the ogres, witches, or wizards who might just be waiting for her in the sunlight.

But when she exited the tree, all Leah saw was beauty as far as the eye could see. It was as if all the great artists throughout history had gotten together to paint this one magnificent scene. The field that stretched out in front of her was rich and green. The wonderful heady scent of freshly-mown grass filled the air. The trees towered above her into the bright blue sky, and the light of the sun made the leaves glimmer, as if little sprites were sprinkling gold dust in the breeze.

Leah walked away from the huge olive tree. She knew she should hurry, especially considering the fact that she had no idea when it would be dusk again, and when or where she'd have to meet these losers for the exchange. But Leah cleared her mind and kept her focus, knowing that there must be something she'd have to battle to get what she wanted.

Leaving the safety of the forest, she found herself standing in front of a small circle of houses. Leah walked toward the cluster of buildings, wishing with all her might she had Athena's sword. "Hello?"

No answer came from the strange yellow and black dwellings. She shuffled closer and peeked into one of the small windows. It certainly had been lived in at one time. There was a wooden bed covered with a fur pelt that'd come from a very large animal, and there were pieces of pottery set out on a counter that was probably once used as a kitchen—with a small wooden table and chairs in the center of the room.

There were place settings laid out for a family of two, as if waiting for them to arrive home from a hard day's work to sit and talk about their dreams for the future. Ashes decorated the hearth, as if someone recently sat by this particular fire and enjoyed an evening of peace.

Backing away from the abandoned dwelling, Leah continued around the circle of houses, attempting to find anyone who could tell her where she was. She ran her hand over the colorful facades. Each one was made from a mixture of bright canary yellow and black stones, blended together with a white and gray paste. The houses looked like unique caves sitting side-by-side—each with a lush green backyard surrounded by a white stone fence.

Giving up on finding a human being, Leah walked over the small green hill to discover yet another larger grouping that covered even more acreage. Looking into each window, the results were the same. Maybe everyone had gone off to work and were, right this very minute, stuck in some kind of horrific commute.

Leah stared up at the next hill and walked toward it, feeling a slight twinge of fear twisting in her stomach. Where was everyone? What had happened to the owners of the small houses? It felt like something or someone had simply walked into this place and kidnapped every human they'd seen. "What is this? Roswell, the sequel?" she wondered out loud.

Leah swallowed hard as she thought about how a theory of 'aliens' might not be far off, considering that no army had made these people disappear. Not a drop of blood, piece of flesh, broken bone, or carnage of any kind was visible. No part of the lovely landscape had been destroyed. Only the intense quiet alerted Leah that something was very, very wrong.

Her long legs carried her up hill after hill, passing clumps of abandoned houses, with each grouping larger than the first. As she sped up, running past each and every circle, her breath came in gasps. When Leah finally reached the tallest hill, her legs finally gave out beneath her.

Reminding herself to breathe, Leah stared out across the amazing landscape in front of her, trying to calm her heartbeat. The trusty card catalogue immediately opened inside her head and sent out a picture that almost perfectly matched the location Leah found herself staring at.

And . . . suddenly, a burst of laughter came from Leah's throat as she looked out at the beautiful, crystal-clear canals beaming under the sun. Her tear-filled eyes gazed at the three concentric circles of land bordered by vibrant waterways. It looked almost like a green and blue target had been carved in the earth, with a bulls-eye in the center circle that looked like a giant silver dome.

"You have *got* to be kidding!"

Shaking her head, she could barely believe it. In fact, she would never have believed this in a million years. Sitting on the grass, she looked up at the heavens wondering why she suddenly felt like the butt of some cosmic joke.

"Okay. I'm here," she announced, shaking her head at the ridiculousness of it all. "Freakin' Atlantis."

CHAPTER 35

David Tallent never knew he could be so happy and so unbelievably frightened all at the same time. He stared over at the young woman standing beside Lowery—slightly bruised, but alive. She was as lovely as Aaron had described. Her long, black hair was a glistening sheen of velvet, and her eyes . . . those sapphire eyes . . . David's throat closed when he remembered his still-missing daughter.

Moving his gaze away from the young woman whose hands were tied behind her back, David held his breath. He so wanted to talk to her—ask her questions, but the large gun of one of his captors pressed into his side, and he decided it wasn't the best time for making a new acquaintance.

Gareth Lowery sat across from him. All David wanted to do was grab him by the throat and toss him out of the limo. True, the man had been beaten to a pulp, but David didn't care. "Why would you just leave her? Why would you allow yourself to be separated from her?"

Gareth glared back at him. "No one tells Leah what to do. You should know that by now. And, as far as being separated, thank God we were. Or she would have been tortured and beaten, too."

"Maybe she got even worse treatment!" David screamed, as the gun poked him hard in the ribs.

Gareth looked out the window of the grand car. Turning back, he growled at the bald-headed man named Max who was sitting in the corner of the large leather seat. "Where are we going? I told you that the Silver Scroll has to be somewhere in Herodium."

Max smiled. "In this case, Mr. Lowery—as well as others I've heard—Ms. Tallent knew much more than you did."

"Where is she?" Gareth yelled. His voice was loud and frightening, and the look in his eyes was beyond enraged. It was as if the Devil, himself, had taken him over.

"Now, Now, Mr. Lowery—she's just fine. In fact, we are on our way to see her right now."

"If you hurt her . . ."

Max raised an amused eyebrow. "Yes?"

"I will fucking kill you."

Max issued a hearty laugh as he glanced at David. "Did you hear that emotion? I believe this useless man may be in love with your daughter."

David grunted, "He should have stayed by her side then."

"What kind of people are you?" Aaron yelled. He glanced across the small aisle at his beloved niece. "Why should I ask? You're the type of scum who beats up defenseless women."

Max's eyes grew wide. "I never touched this woman, Mr. Cain. In fact, this is only the second time I've met your niece. The first was back in the museum in Cairo, and you know personally that I never laid a hand on her there."

A sob broke through Anippe's lips.

Gareth whispered, "It'll be all right, Anippe. We'll get out of this."

Aaron immediately turned on Gareth, matching David's anger step-for-step. "Why didn't you protect her? You let Leah go off in the middle of the night all alone and then you let someone lay a hand on my niece?! What the hell is wrong with you? I thought you were some kind of hero?"

Gareth shook his head. "I did *not* let Leah go, and as far as Anippe is concerned, we were separated. By the time I found her again . . . they'd already gotten to her."

"Who?!" David and Aaron shouted in unison, wanting with all their hearts to face the man who would dare do such a thing to a woman.

"I don't know!" Gareth shouted back. "We'd met up with a man named Daniel Bauer." His voice grew deep as the emotions built up in his throat. He looked like the weight of his guilt was literally going to break his heart in two. "He was at Herodium. He said he was an archaeologist working the site. Bastard seemed benign . . . a loser, nothing more than a sad playboy. He started talking about the Silver Scroll and the treasure from the Second Temple. I started walking around after . . . Leah left to go back to the hotel."

"Definition," David seethed. "You chose to look for silver and gold instead of taking care of my daughter!"

Gareth sighed. "Leah needed . . . time. I thought I could find what these scum were after, and get you both back so she wouldn't have to put herself in any more danger."

Max's voice filled the backseat; his smile was firmly set in place. "But Ms. Tallent had the olives with her."

"How do you know about that?" Gareth yelled. He sat back against the seat and sighed. "Of course. You've been following us the whole time."

"Just taking care of my investment, Lowery. I've heard great things about what you and Ms. Tallent have accomplished together, and I certainly knew about David Tallent and the information he had already put together. All he needed was a place to begin, and Anippe had the answer to that buried in her museum." He smiled, as he pieced the puzzle together for Gareth. "Of course, I'm not nearly intelligent enough to know why Plato would be involved in all this, but by now Ms. Tallent has most likely figured it all out. That's why we're going to join her. Apparently, she's the only one in your little gang with a brain. I think my boss is right about Ms. Tallent. If we can bring her with us, she may just prove to be irreplaceable."

Gareth launched his sore body at the man but the barrel of the gun immediately came up and pressed against his forehead, forcing him back into the seat. "Daniel Bauer's your boss? Where is he?"

Aaron looked over at him. "I thought he was the one who did this to you," he said, staring at the cuts and bruises on Gareth's face.

"No," Gareth answered back angrily. "That chicken shit disappeared after Leah left. When he reappeared, he was adamant about looking for the treasure again. But we got separated. I was jumped from behind and beat by someone who has a hell of a lot more strength than that pretty boy has. There had to have been at least three of them." Gareth stared at Max's bodyguards.

Aaron shook his head. "They haven't left the hotel. Someone has to be working with Bauer."

Anippe nodded. "It wasn't Daniel who hit me either. I know that. I was in a chamber below the pool and a much larger man came up and knocked me out. Daniel wouldn't do such a thing, anyway. I'm sure of it. They probably got him, too. I'm sure he wasn't involved in this . . . situation." Seeing the mystified looks being shot at her, Anippe continued quickly, "The next thing I remember, Gareth and I were in this limo, handcuffed, being taken to your hotel. We pulled into some type of underground garage, and you just...stepped off the elevator."

David Tallent sat back against the seat. He wondered if Anippe was simply too upset to recognize what was going on, because he was amazed to hear a note of sadness come from her lips. It sounded as if she actually liked this Bauer person, and was trying to give him the benefit of the doubt.

"Well!" Max shouted happily, clapping his hands together. "Here we are. Now we'll get the answers we've all been waiting for."

———

Gareth shuddered. As the doors swung open and the sunlight poured into the vehicle, the large hand of the bodyguard pushed him from behind. It was so bright, and his eye was so swollen, that it took Gareth a long time to focus on the incredible sight.

As he stared up at the humongous tree, Gareth felt a wave of relief. He could feel Leah's presence, and the pride in his companion flooded his soul. New tears fell from his eyes; the salt burned the open cuts on his face.

He looked over at Max and rattled his handcuffs behind his back. "Get these goddamn things off me!" His voice was loud and confident; his determination to be with Leah was as strong as the mighty trumpets that'd once toppled the walls of Jericho. Gareth felt a lump form in his throat as that thought raced through his head. "The walls came tumbling down," he whispered.

Jesus, Gareth screamed at himself. *I should've known this was it.*

He turned back to the silent, but ever-smiling, Max. "I said . . . get these things off me!"

Max nodded at the huge bodyguard. "Why, of course, Mr. Lowery. But remember . . . any deviation up that hill and he'll shoot you in the back. We don't really need you anymore; I'd remember that if I were you. Ms. Tallent has already found the way in and will lead us to what we need."

Gareth's eyes turned to slits. "Then why am I still alive?"

"To go first, of course," he said. "We have no idea what may be inside this ancient hill. If Ms. Tallent met with some demise, her hero should go first so that the rest of us can live to fight another day."

Revulsion rose in Gareth's throat at the thought of anything happening to Leah. He wanted nothing more than to climb the large tree and find the woman he so loved. If he died by her side, so be it. In fact, he'd decided long ago that death in Leah's arms was the only way he wanted to exit his life.

Abandoning the cuffs, Gareth kept his mouth shut and climbed up the slope of Jericho. The adventurer that sat inside of him—like the librarian resting inside his Leah—didn't appear. He didn't give a damn about the ancient ruins of anything right now. Joshua, himself, could rise up out of the dirt with his army and Gareth would slam right past him. All he wanted was Leah . . . alive and well.

The dirt was wet, as if a giant thunderstorm had struck over Jericho in the middle of the night and turned the entire sight to mud. Gareth tripped and sank into the mound; he used his hands to claw his way up the side of the slippery mountain. And when he reached the olive tree in the center, he walked around the huge trunk.

The tree absolutely sparkled. Tiny drops of water clung to the silvery-green leaves, making the monument to nature glitter like a gemstone in the middle of the desert.

He couldn't believe that they'd been in the hotel right across the street. They'd stared out the huge window of the restaurant just a few short nights ago at the dark mound, and the answer still had not come to him. He'd completely messed this up and, God help him,

Gareth was going to save Leah. There was no way she'd be harmed because of his stupid mistake.

The trunk of the tree was buried deep inside the mud. Reaching up, Gareth began climbing the branches, searching for a way in. Hand over hand, his bruised body begged him to stop, but Gareth made his way to the top. He could hear one of the bodyguards traveling behind him and wanted to kick his foot out and let the man fall to his death, but Gareth knew if he did then Anippe, her uncle and Leah's supposedly beloved father would be killed by the remaining gunman. Heroism would have to wait for a later time.

Finally reaching the top of the gnarled trunk, his heart soared. Inside the hollow tree was a narrow stone staircase leading into the depths of Jericho. He couldn't see the bottom, but Gareth pleaded for Leah's body not to be lying twisted and broken in the darkness below. He heaved his body over the side of the tree and stepped as fast as he could down the almost vertical stairwell. Holding onto the sides of the tree, Garth grasped the knots with his fingers to stop himself from tumbling down and breaking his neck.

The man screamed out above him, "Stop right there! We'll wait for everybody else."

Gareth continued to step down, ignoring the threat. He could see a square of sunlight bursting through the gnarled bark and he raced toward it, hoping and praying that Leah would be there.

"I said, stop!" Gareth heard the bullet enter the chamber. "If you go any further, I will shoot the hostages."

Gareth shouted back, "Do that and Leah Tallent won't give you a damn thing."

He could hear the man yell out over Jericho. "He's making a run for it!"

Anippe's sudden shout flooded Gareth with fear. Stopping, he stared back up the staircase. The familiar tone that met his ears made him freeze in place, as confusion and sudden rage welled up inside his soul.

"Don't worry, he's not going anywhere. Not if he wants Ms. Tallent to come out of this alive."

CHAPTER 36

Leah walked across the large, stone bridge that spanned the canal, leading her to the next ring of dark green grass. The city was absolutely beautiful. The houses were every shape and size—from small pyramids to large square buildings—made from the same cheery yellow and shiny black stones.

Her senses remained alert, even though the amazement of her find was so great Leah could barely breathe. Plato had been right. All this time and people were still fighting over whether or not his play had been true. Everyone who'd ever 'discovered' a strange stone buried in the ocean had announced that they'd found the famous city. They wanted to be part of the legendary locale that'd been buried by a supposedly angry god who'd watched the beloved Atlanteans turn from a perfect civilization into the rest of the world . . . greedy humans.

And everyone, like Plato had said, was truly gone. But then why was the city still here? It was still standing. The buildings had not been destroyed, which they certainly would have been. There was no way any structure could remain standing under the horrendous pressure of molten lava spewing from a volcano, or a flood of absolute mythical proportions. Yet, here she was, walking between the fully-intact structures of the perfect land. The only thing that announced something horrible had even happened here was the complete lack of human life.

There was a part of Leah that wanted to slow down—enjoy the amazing place that she'd always believed was nothing more than a grand, epic tale. There were so many incredible buildings to explore; it was literally the find of a lifetime. But the center circle, shining its beam of silver across the irrigated fields was like a beacon, beckoning Leah forward—reminding her that she still had a job to do and a father to save.

Crossing the last canal, Leah walked up the hill in the center circle to the large temple that sat on top like a monument to some mysterious god. *Probably Poseidon*, she thought. The one who'd supposedly caused their ultimate destruction.

An archway of copper, silver and gold beamed above Leah's head. The entrance was open, and there was no barrier of rock or wire to stop her progress.

Walking under the arch, Leah peered inside. Unlike Athena's temple, there were no stone tiles or friezes telling a story of ancient peoples who brought gifts and bowed to a god or goddess. In fact, the room was almost completely empty. Every wall was made of a different precious metal; silver for one, gold for another, copper made up the third. Even the floor was made of highly polished metal. Leah stared down at her own image mirrored in the floor. She looked distorted and twisted, which perfectly matched the way she felt.

Wishing Gareth was beside her, Leah walked toward the small table in the center of the room. On it was a brown box. Lifting the lid, Leah stared down at the Silver Scroll. Her laughter echoed off the huge metal walls and slammed back into her ears, making them ring as if she was at a rock concert in the Alps.

Leah shook her head in disbelief. "Atlantis . . . the Silver Scroll . . . if I stay long enough I'll probably come face-to-face with the Easer Bunny."

Lifting the thin piece of silver out of the box, Leah saw that it did, indeed, offer locations of various treasures, starting from the exact spot where she stood. Reading over the Hebrew quickly, the top line of the document alerted her to the fact that she was standing in the center of the 'cistern' of Poseidon—an entrance that went straight down to the sea floor. In theory, Poseidon could use this to enter his temple when he wanted to wander the dry land.

Leah moved back to the archway as she deciphered the directions. She read aloud, craving some companionship in the lonely world. " 'The cistern's entrance is located under the large pacing stone threshold, joining the past and the future together as one. Six silver bars are located under that stone.' "

Looking, Leah saw the strange stone and reached her fingernails into the earth until she met up with a hard surface. Leah couldn't keep the smile off her face when she caught a glimpse of the shiny silver bars. "Gareth was right . . . again."

More surprising, however, was how a monk from the Dead Sea Sect would've known where this place had been. Then…the answer appeared. Atlantis was once above ground before it was pummeled by a natural disaster and sent to the bottom of the ocean floor. So, maybe the monk had once lived here and escaped the traumatic event after burying the silver. But his directions were so spot on that Leah knew he had to have buried the priceless treasure after the catastrophic event, so that he'd know exactly how many buildings were still in place in order to write his 'silver scroll' correctly. But how would he have known that Atlantis was hidden beneath the mound that became Jericho?

Leah's head was filled with questions. Her hands continued to excavate the bars of silver. Staring down at her work, she removed the treasure which caused her heart to tremble inside her chest. Two large, flat stones were under the lovely silver, etched with names. Slowly, Leah rubbed off the dirt in order to read the names that'd been carved into the two stones.

Immediately, Leah fell over backwards. Her hands were trembling. Clutching the freezing cold pendant in her hand, the icy sensation numbed her flesh in an instant.

Plato's words filtered through her head as the card catalogue of data opened and sent the facts racing through her skull.

'A city of gold and silver,' the philosopher had written in his play, referring to the precious land Leah now sat on. 'Blooming meadows and pastures feed herds of huge and mighty beasts. Humans lived as if Divine. As long as they were obedient to the laws and held affection for their god—whose seed they were from . . .'

The seed of the Son, Leah thought, Affectionate toward their god . . . lived in Divine nature until human nature had saddled them with a curse and greed had gotten the upper hand. They were then taken away from the land they so loved and cast out of paradise.

"No," Leah whispered. "Paradise had been emptied out until a race of humans could prove themselves worthy of returning."

She shook her head. Her voice came out as a whisper, "It's all about shadows. Atlantis was just a title—a 'shadow covering the truth.'" She stared down at the gravestones, knowing beyond a shadow of a doubt that she was at the beginning . . . the *very* beginning.

No monk had known about this location. Only the One who'd created this world—the One who experimented with putting Heaven on Earth—knew where to hide the wealth of the Temple. He'd stored the treasure far away from greedy humans who would never again be welcomed into this world.

This fertile land was like the Garden of Eden to the travelers coming across the desert. Gregory's words flowed through her brain, as the realization of what she'd been after for the last seven days slammed into her chest. Sweat broke out on the back of her neck and the landscape began to quiver around her.

As the blackness took over, the last thing Leah saw was the pair of stones . . . the long hidden graves . . . of Adam and Eve.

CHAPTER 37

"My God!" Gareth let out a gasp of surprise when he stared over the top of the green hill and rested his eyes on a literal dream.

"It's Atlantis," David Tallent whispered beside him.

"I don't believe this," Gareth added his own amazement.

David simply stuttered, "I just thought there would be a house . . . or, something . . . that held the scroll. I didn't know the entire . . . all this . . . would still be here."

Max spoke up behind them, as his gun-toting duo tried to keep their eyes from wandering across the landscape. "Well, Mr. Tallent, you certainly did give us more than we bargained for now didn't you? Hopefully, for your sake, the gem we seek is in here as well. Then *all* of our business will be concluded."

David turned and glared at the small, detestable man. "I told you, you have it all wrong. You always did. I have no idea where that gemstone is today."

"You stole it from the mine a long, long time ago!"

He shook his head violently. "No! When I left there, it was still in its rightful place. I have no idea what happened to it after that."

"No more of this!" Max screamed, pointing the gun at David's forehead. "Do you really want to die? Now? Before getting to say goodbye to your lovely daughter?"

Gareth half-listened to the confusing conversation and tried instead to locate Leah's figure weaving through the yellow and black houses. But the sudden crack that blasted through his ears made his blood run cold. Turning quickly, he stared at the small, bald man as he fell forward onto the grass.

Staring in silence, Gareth looked around and immediately saw the figure of Daniel Bauer calmly walk across the field. The smile never left his face as a small puff of smoke issued from the barrel of his shotgun. Looking down at the body, he shook his head. "Never could stand that man. Yap, yap, yap—all he ever wanted to do was hear himself speak. Too bad he didn't listen."

"You . . . you killed him," Anippe pointed out the obvious in a surprised voice. Her sapphire eyes, once filled with the excitement of a new romantic prospect, turned cold and dead as she stared at the handsome man who was now officially her enemy.

Gareth felt bad for her when he saw a flicker of hope suddenly dance in her eyes.

"Are you . . . saving us?" She swallowed, staring at the other two men holding guns. Although they both looked confused at the new turn of events, they took their places at the Australian's side.

Bauer offered his crooked, movie star grin. "Why would I want to do that?" He leaned closer to Anippe. "The only one I really want to survive all this is Leah. I thought you knew that."

Gareth launched his body at the cocky man but he wasn't fast enough; the guard lifted the butt of his gun and slammed it into Gareth's stomach.

Daniel Bauer chuckled. "Really?" he bent over Gareth, and his calm voice turned cold and sinister, "You betrayed her, Lowery. Then you let her run off in the middle of the night across the desert . . . all alone. Some hero. When we find her you should prepare yourself to let go of her for good." He grinned. "You know, there's a part of me that actually wants you to live through this all, too. Just so you can know that she is *my* companion when you die."

"Never gonna happen, asshole." Gareth said. "Leah had your number the minute she looked in your eyes."

"You mean the minute she fell into my arms and the color rose in her cheeks? That minute?"

"You're not as desirable as you think, Bauer," Anippe spat in his face. The look of hope was gone; in its place was a steely determination to destroy the Australian playboy.

Daniel smiled at her. "Yes, actually, I am."

"If you lay one hand on my daughter," David interrupted, "You won't have to worry about Lowery. He'll have to get in line."

"*Your* daughter? When she finds out the truth about her beloved daddy, Leah will walk hand-in-hand with the Devil, just to get away from you. Your betrayal was far greater than Gareth's."

David's eyes grew wide. "You don't know anything about me. You're no more than, what? Thirty-five?"

"I beg to differ." Daniel smiled. "I had a front row seat to hear all about the lies that one, David Tallent from America, told to a lady who did nothing more than love him."

"What?" David's voice turned to a whisper as an image of the beautiful Egyptian came into his mind. "How . . .?"

Aaron Cain sighed deeply and stared at the ground, avoiding his niece's gaze.

"What the hell is this moron talking about?" Gareth stared at the two men who'd suddenly become silent, before returning his gaze to Bauer's smiling face. "Who the fuck *are* you?" He stared down at the gold objects on the ground at Bauer's feet. "And what are you carrying those around with you for?"

"All in good time." He waved his shotgun back and forth, ordering the others to move. "Shall we proceed? At this very moment Leah may be needing company."

"I hope she buries that scroll so deep you never get your hands on it," Gareth seethed.

Daniel shook his head and sighed. "Do you really think this whole thing is just about gold? Money's nice and all, but there are other things I crave far more than wealth." His smile faded fast. "Now, move!"

CHAPTER 38

The sound of a gunshot ricocheted inside Leah's brain and brought her back to the real world.

She blinked her eyes rapidly and tried to focus on the graves that her mind said could not possibly be there. But they were. The names of the first human beings on Earth stared up at her.

Leah was unsteady on her feet as she stood and stepped over the trench she'd dug at the threshold of Poseidon's temple. The icy cold pendant around her neck made her skin tremble as her brain commanded her legs to run. All her body wanted to do was go back over the canals and get back to the tree; take the silly scroll to the kidnappers, get her father and be done with all this nonsense once and for all. But something . . . something in her soul just wouldn't follow the clear and concise directions of the realistic librarian's mind.

Walking slowly around the outside of the temple, Leah felt as if something was calling her—telling her that the silver and gold buried in the ground was not the treasure to be found.

As she came to the eastern side of the building, the sun seemed to cascade across the land, like a large spotlight showing her the way. In the near distance was a small grouping of the familiar olive trees. The numerous limbs seemed to connect to one another, forming an impregnable barrier for anyone wishing to see inside the grove.

Leah walked forward. Her head was literally reeling as she

tried to extract any information she could from her life of constant studying. Everyone knew the story, of course. Even non-believers such as she knew everything about Eve offering the apple from the Tree of Knowledge and then being cast out of Paradise with Adam because of their betrayal to God.

Now . . . Leah wondered. The yellow and black buildings once had housed the people who were reaching for Heaven? Maybe the families who'd once dwelled here were the descendants of the sinful couple who'd been given another chance; given a place where they could live harmoniously but work hard, loving their god and choosing to redeem themselves in order to one day be welcomed back Home? Was this Paradise? Until, of course, mankind screwed it up as they always do, and sinners were cast out of their gilded cage back into the world of death, war and destruction?

That's it. These people had been real, and Leah couldn't believe it. Creation, no matter what the scientists said, had begun with a couple named Adam and Eve. Leah didn't understand the pictures that popped up inside her head. Her father hadn't said much about religion, except for the story of Mary, but the words of Moses suddenly flooded Leah's brain.

The Lord came to Paradise to bury Adam when Eve was asleep . . . and when it was Eve's turn, she begged the Lord to be buried by his side—her hero—the man she loved. *Eve was the first Hero's Companion,* Leah thought to herself. Whether or not Athena was right, whether or not the serpent was the being of enlightenment or the bringer of death, Eve had been in love with Adam and had chosen to live her life . . . and afterlife . . . by his side. The proof was written on the graves.

Moving closer to the grove of trees, Leah took a deep breath. She poked her head under one of the low branches and stared ahead.

Walking into the small garden, she kept her eyes firmly fastened on the grand centerpiece. Unlike Gethsemane, there was no tomb for the fallen; no rock or stone slabs had been excavated here, revealing ancient figures. Here, there was simply a lone tree, with no olives or silvery-green leaves decorating the branches.

Taking a deep breath, Leah stared up at the small apple tree in wonder. Visible in the tree's trunk was the small outline of a door, and a bright light spilled through the edges like the one back in Jericho's mound of dirt. But this one, with the light beaming from the inside, seemed to promise a path into a place even more perfect than the paradise where Leah now stood. And, then . . . she finally understood everything that was laid out before her.

Unlike the door that'd been used to cast out humans from the perfect world, this tree held a ladder of steps that climbed much higher than the mound of Jericho. This one led to the real Paradise—a door for the true believers to use.

Staring up at the tree, Leah took in the sight of the gold apples. Plato had it right again all those years ago, yet he covered up the story with tales of gods and goddesses that his people believed in. Although the philosopher had referred to it as the Garden of Hesperides, on an island in the sea where the sun never set, Leah knew that this is what he'd actually meant—the Tree of Knowledge in the Garden of Eden.

On one branch, and one branch only, hung a bright red apple. On all the rest, there were apples of pure gold offering wealth beyond anyone's imagination. Leah felt her mouth water, staring at the seductive red fruit that hung in the garden like a beacon, calling out to her to take a bite.

As she took a step toward the beautiful tree, the sound of the familiar voice suddenly hit her like a brick.

Turning to face the golden-brown eyes, Leah sucked in her breath. Paradise was about to become dark . . . yet again.

CHAPTER 39

The full force of the horrible scene hit Leah squarely in the chest. Her father was finally standing in front of her, which made Leah want to shout out with joy at the top of her lungs. Unfortunately, the man with the gun standing behind him made Leah freeze in place.

Anippe stood beside her father and Leah felt sympathy choke her soul as she stared at the face that was covered in bruises and cuts. But the sapphire eyes remained alert and angry, like she was biding her time just waiting to make her move.

Leah moved her gaze to Aaron Cain. She remembered the last time she'd seen his face—waving goodbye at Emmanuel and Kathryn's wedding as he followed his niece's quick footsteps out of the party.

Leah willed her legs to stay still when her eyes landed on Gareth's face. Like Anippe, his flesh had been bruised. There was a cut above his eye that oozed a small river of blood down his cheek. His shirt was shredded, like a whip had sliced through the fabric and beat him within an inch of his life. But his jaw was clenched tight and the emerald eyes were filled with relieved tears. His smile was faithfully tugging at the corners of his mouth, and his face registered the heartfelt love that Leah understood was meant for her and her alone. She wanted to cry. She wanted to run into his arms and beg his forgiveness for being such an idiot when he'd needed her the most.

But something about Daniel Bauer's smug face made Leah remain perfectly still. The peace she'd felt the last time she'd stood next to him in the moonlight was now gone. Instead, she felt overwhelmingly sick. It was like she could feel the mortal peril descend around her shoulders, as Daniel aimed his unwavering stare into her soul.

He lifted his arms in the air, a gun held tightly in his grip, like a ringmaster announcing to the crowd that the show was about to begin. "The Tree of Life . . . the Tree of Knowledge . . . perfect!" he yelled.

Leah noticed that the leaves of the olive trees surrounding them had literally stopped moving; they were no longer 'clapping' for their Creator. It was as if the sweet, cool air had disappeared at the sound of Bauer's voice disturbing the peaceful grove.

"It was said," he continued, staring at Leah, "that after Adam and Eve's expulsion from the garden, guardians with flaming swords that flashed back and forth in the air, stood in front of the gates making sure that only the worthy would get anywhere near the Tree of Life ever again."

He walked toward Leah, circling her like a predator as he stared up into the green leaves of the apple tree. "I never heard of golden apples before, though. That is interesting."

Leah heard him come up close behind her and felt the whisper of his breath on her neck, "Now . . . where is that Silver Scroll, my dear?"

"In the temple over there sitting in a box." She pointed.

Daniel nodded to one of the guards, sending him over to the silver domed building. "Did you search for any for yourself, dear?"

Leah shook her head.

"That's too bad," he replied. "You could have, you know. I have no problem sharing with you. After all . . . we are far from through, you and I."

Her body trembled as the image of her nightmarish wedding flooded her thoughts. She shuddered to think how long their relationship was supposed to last if they were still 'not through.'

"In fact," he raised his voice, circling around her yet again. "I have even more to share with you."

"Who *are* you?" she suddenly demanded.

Daniel tilted his head to the side. "I am a man with a dream."

She rolled her eyes immediately. "Give me a break."

The cocky smile returned to his handsome face. "I'm a young man who was raised on lies, Leah—stories that adults handed to me on a silver platter and swore to me were the truth. Just like you were."

"Get over yourself," Leah snorted.

He smiled wider. "Strength is such a remarkable gift. I am thrilled that you have it in spades, because it will make what's coming at you a whole lot easier to bear."

The gun-wielding man ran out of the temple in the center of the circle and rejoined them in the Garden. He carried the scroll gently, handing it to his boss with care.

Daniel snorted, "Geez, the Copper Scroll was huge compared to this. It must have taken forever to etch these directions so daintily into a piece of silver. Almost impossible."

"A miracle even," Leah grunted, knowing that only the Divine would have had the ability to hide the treasure inside this earthbound paradise.

Daniel grinned. "Maybe you're right."

"Uh, huh. So you have your gold and silver," Leah said. "Can I go home now? I can't even begin to tell you how sick I am of the sound of your voice."

"This is the Garden of Eden, Leah," he replied. "Do you have any idea the significance of this?"

"Yeah . . . it's bigger than Santa Claus," Leah snapped. She didn't want to be sacrilegious in this place of worship, but she needed Daniel Bauer to believe that she simply didn't care—that none of them gave a damn about his glorious treasure. Perhaps then he'd let them go and get on with excavating the find of a lifetime.

She stared at Gareth's battered face, watching the pride literally beam from his eyes.

Daniel took a step back. "You don't care? Not even a little about this? You don't even want to know how long this has been here? Who may have lived here?"

She pointed to her love. "That's his job."

"And I don't give a . . . fig," Gareth laughed.

"I know your thirst for knowledge, Leah," Daniel continued, ignoring the pair. "Don't you understand that the apple behind you is an object that holds a wealth of absolute knowledge? You could become the smartest person in the world with just one bite."

Leah ignored his smug expression and shot back one of her own. "I already am. You want to test me? Go right ahead."

He grinned.

Leah continued on, "You know, speaking of smart, you of all people should know that biting into that thing causes punishment. It will cast you out of this Paradise you've wanted to get into, moron boy. Considering how smart you think you are about all this stuff, you should certainly know that."

"I don't believe in ancient magic, Leah," he replied.

"Magic?" Leah's father interrupted. "If you believe that this is the Garden of Eden, shouldn't you also believe the story?"

Daniel immediately turned on him. "I might have, actually, if it wasn't for your daughter."

"What?" David Tallent was a ball of confusion.

"You see, on Leah's most recent adventure she stumbled over the fact that a British gent had been hired to edit the Bible, the one you so believe in, for King James. He was simply supposed to take stories and rework them for the masses."

"The story of Adam and Eve was out there way before the sixteen hundreds," Gareth reminded him.

Daniel waved his hand dismissively. "If one can be a fake, they all can." His eyes grew distant as he stared up at the bright red fruit. "There are many in my family who believed everything without question . . . to their own detriment."

Bauer shook his head, as if blocking out a strange vision, and turned to Leah. "It's hard for people like you and I. We may be cynical, but that's better in the long run, isn't it? Follow your heart and have faith, unconditionally, and you get screwed every single time."

"I don't believe that anymore," Leah whispered. She felt a shot of panic rising in her chest.

Daniel moved closer to her. "You should. You've been lied to by almost every single person you've ever met."

Aaron Cain's voice broke though the conversation, "Look! If you're going to kill us just get it over with. You have your treasure, so get on with it!"

Leah stared warily at the older man. He didn't seem to care that his beloved niece was standing beside him as he rattled off his demand for death. Even more surprising was her own father; David stood quietly, his eyes aimed at the ground.

Where was the master of the business world who stood strong and tall at all times? Leah wondered. Had he truly been beaten into submission in just seven days? She inched forward. "Dad?"

The sapphire eyes that matched her own rose to meet her question. Leah took a deep breath. There was no anger or fear beaming in her father's eyes—only guilt . . . remorse . . . a face that needed forgiveness was all that met her gaze.

"What's going on?" she whispered.

David's lips parted but Daniel spoke faster, "Maybe you should really eat that apple, Leah. Then you would have the knowledge to understand good and evil immediately; then your poor father wouldn't have to go through this moment of pure hell."

He turned to Leah's father. "You're standing in the very spot where God walked with Adam . . . if you really believe this crap, Tallent. This is Divine ground in your eyes. You can't continue to lie in this place, so tell your daughter the truth."

Leah turned on him. "What do you know about my family? I only met you two freakin days ago."

Bauer's smile grew wider until she couldn't bear it any longer. "Someone better tell me what the hell is going on . . . *now*!"

Aaron Cain cleared his throat. "Leah . . . your father is my brother."

Confusion addled her brain as she stared at Gareth's surprised face. "Okay," she said, not understanding why his words would be such a travesty of justice. "My dad has a brother. So?"

Aaron tried to offer a smile, but his attempt failed. "Anippe is my niece, and I don't have any other siblings."

"Okay," Leah continued to nod, starring over at Anippe's suddenly wide sapphire eyes.

The truth of his words suddenly hit Leah like a sledgehammer. In less than a second, Gareth raced forward, ignoring the guard in order to reach Leah's side.

She felt his large hand curve around her waist, and watched Bauer lift his hand to stop the guard from firing.

"It's okay," Gareth whispered.

Leah looked over at Anippe and then back to her father's still bowed head. "So . . . I have a stepsister. You were married before?"

David shook his head.

"She's my *real* sister?" Leah choked.

Her father finally stood up straight and faced her. "Leah . . . you have to let me explain."

"Explain," she shot back quickly. The image of her blonde-haired mother appeared in her mind. This woman had cried the tears of a wife who was scared beyond belief for her husband's safety. Of course, she'd also known all her life that Leah was not her own. *That explains why she's been so cold over the years*, Leah thought. Even through she'd raised her and kept quiet, Leah had always known that she didn't belong. And yet she was suddenly enraged . . . but not at Mary Tallent. Mary had given what she could and expected much more from the man who'd swept her off her feet so long ago. She'd known about this other woman which must have been the reason she'd said to Leah that she deserved so much more.

Leah felt the tears choke her throat. She *did* deserve more. So did Leah. So did Anippe.

Leah glared at the man she thought she knew as he literally lost strength and height right in front of her. The man she believed was a true icon lost every ounce of his glitter before her eyes. David Tallent owed three women—and owed them big!

Her father stood stoic, with his hands folded in front of him. "Your grandfather was part of the 1945 dig; he was an archaeologist who absolutely loved Egypt. He married your grandmother and they had me. A couple of years later my . . . brother, Aaron, was born."

Leah's voice was cold. "Spare me the trip down memory lane and get to the point where you decided to lie to me for the rest of my life."

David winced. "My parents broke up. My mother took Aaron and went to America. I stayed in Egypt with my father." Tears cascaded down his cheeks. "Leah . . . I met your mother here. I was young and I fell head over heels in love with her. We married right away and then . . . you were born. Then . . . Anippe came along."

Leah moved her gaze to Anippe. Anger flew from the woman's sapphire eyes, directed between the uncle who lied to her and the father who'd abandoned her.

David hung his head to the ground. "Your mother was an up and coming scientist; she was truly a remarkable woman and her ability to study and understand ancient ruins was . . ."

"Stop!" Leah screamed. "If you loved her so damn much, why am I hearing about her now?"

"Your mother was taken in the middle of the night. I searched for her for a year. I couldn't understand . . . I didn't want to imagine that she'd just . . . left us. But then a note came in the mail . . . on a New Year's Eve long ago, with her handwriting on it. She told me we were in danger. She said I had to get out of the country and to split up you girls to make sure we could all survive. I called Aaron in America and we agreed to switch places, so to speak. He would come back to Egypt and take care of Anippe because no one knew him, and I would bring you to America. If I hadn't, they would've found me . . . us . . . and killed the whole family."

"Who?"

"I didn't know, Leah. I swear I didn't know then."

"There had to be a reason for you to . . . destroy our family?" Anippe yelled.

Bauer joined the conversation; his smile was wide and happy like the Cheshire Cat. "Your father was excavating something at the time, Anippe. I believe the people who took your mother took her for leverage. They wanted your father to turn over something he'd come across."

Leah stared at him. "How is it that *you* know about this?"

Every muscle in Bauer's face froze into an angry mask. "My father was one of the men who took her."

Gareth pounced, trying with all his might to get his hands around Bauer's neck. But just as before, his injuries had taken away his quickness and Gareth was slammed in the jaw, sending the large man to his knees.

Daniel ignored the scene completely. "All my father wanted was one small artifact that David Tallent had uncovered out there in the desert. Your mother knew what it was; she knew what was out there, and refused to tell my father."

"So he killed her?" Leah concluded with disgust.

"*Killed* her?" Bauer took a step away. "God, no. That would be like killing . . . well, *you*, Leah. No one could destroy something so beautiful and intelligent."

"My mother is still alive?" Anippe sent a sudden shout through her tears; a yell so loud that it seemed like a tornado had just touched down beside her.

Daniel stared at Anippe. "Of course. My father was rather fond of her, in fact. He didn't come after you or Leah because of that fondness. He simply waited for your father to make another mistake, and . . . he did."

"Unfortunately," he continued. "My father has passed away now. So it has fallen upon me to hunt you all down and finally get what is rightfully mine."

Walking away from Leah's side, he took Anippe's hand. "I heard about you first. My friend in England had the sheer good luck of knowing you and then running into your sister when she came over there on her quest. He told me all about you. He even sent me a picture when I was in Germany, which I showed to your mother. Her face went absolutely white, and I knew right then and there that you were most definitely her child."

"William Knight," Anippe choked on the name of the wretched man who'd tried to kill her; the man who'd made her pick up the Sapphire Staff, believing that she was the one descendant of Moses who could. He had played on her heart and her feelings in order to steal the ridiculous power that the Staff could wield—caring nothing about her.

Daniel's voice came out with a tone of sympathy in the silent garden. "I know he hurt you, my dear. But Knight was simply a hard-working man who thought that my way was the way the world should be. He scoured the country, had a fake tattoo put on his hand so that the 'group' in England would believe he was one of them, and found out the information I needed to have in order to build a brand new paradise on earth . . . my kind. Then Leah, your *sister*, literally fell into my lap when she went looking for Gareth's soon-to-be brother-in-law."

"The staff is gone. You'll never get it back," Leah spoke loudly, forcing the man to turn back in her direction and leave Anippe alone.

"Oh, I know." he smiled. "You and Mr. Lowery made sure of that. You even somehow hid the Ark—both of them are, oddly enough, not able to be had by me anymore. I wanted to kill you for that. But there are other things, Leah—far more powerful things out there that will help make my father's and his father's dreams come true." Bauer pointed to the sword and shield of Athena leaning against an olive tree.

Athena's voice rushed back into Leah's mind, as the nightmare from the monastery once again reared its ugly head. The Goddess had begged Leah not to leave her alone with this horrible man. And yet here he was, possessing the mystical artifacts that could protect and serve any army that Bauer led from here on out. Panic rose in Leah's throat, trying with all her might to find a way to make the horrible situation right.

"Athena is just one of the three, Leah," Daniel said, with a smile. He took her hands in his harsh, unyielding grip. 'We needed the seeds to begin, but you really should have left the weapons in Athens. With them . . . I'll be unstoppable."

"What else?"

"Excuse me?"

Leah ripped her hands from his grip. "What else? What are the other two you need? You said there are three and you're going to kill us all anyway, so why don't you clue me in on my other two screw-ups? What else did I bring into Paradise that you'll use to destroy the world? I'd like to at least know the sins I'll be paying for when I'm sent to Hell."

"The seed of the warrior," Bauer began, "gave me protection. The seed of the Son brought me to this garden in order to gain the knowledge that only the Divine truly knows. And the seed of Hell's

King . . ." His eyes dropped to the pendant around Leah's neck. "Well, that brought me to the stone that my father had been looking for his whole life. The lovely pendant you wear around your neck is something I need, Leah."

She took a step back. "What? Why?"

"The wealth that the scroll will provide me is an excellent way to fund my new career, but that pendant will make sure that no one—Divine or human—will ever be able to stop me."

"Stop you from doing what?" Gareth screamed.

Leah's heart raced underneath the icy-cold pendant as she watched Daniel Bauer reach into his pocket and pull out a pair of dark sunglasses. Her breath caught in her throat. He was their limo driver—the man who'd retrieved her from the base of Herodium. She'd left Daniel Bauer at the top of the monstrosity—a man who'd already spent a great deal of time exploring the site—and he'd apparently taken a short-cut to get back into his costume and pull the car out from wherever he had hidden it. She remembered the small puff of dust that'd risen from his coat when she'd patted him on the shoulder—the way he always hung his head to the ground, offering only the top of his hat to stare at. God . . . she felt so dumb. All he'd needed was a mustache and he'd been able to follow along with them every step of their journey, listening to every word they said. "Our driver," she whispered.

"Our pilot."

Leah turned to Gareth. "What?"

"He was the pilot on my plane. Dark glasses, blond wig . . . didn't even notice."

Daniel laughed. "Rich men don't really take notice of the people who serve them. I was simply another one of your slaves, Lowery."

Gareth shook his head.

Leah could see the disgust in Gareth's eyes as he, too, realized that he bore some of the blame for what was happening around them.

Leah sighed. "So I led the devil right back into Paradise, after all. Even after Gareth banished the real one from the gates, I brought a scum like you straight through the damn door!"

CHAPTER 40

The wind began to blow again, caressing Leah's overheated flesh. She heard the rustling above her head; it reminded her of the relaxing sound that came from walking through a pile of autumn leaves in Central Park back home. Staring up into the bright blue sky, she spied the small owl perched on the branch above her head.

Its wide eyes stared back at her; the slightly haughty expression still firmly affixed to its face. Its tiny chest went up and down, slowly breathing in the Divine air around it, and as the bright blue eyes of the bird closed, Leah could swear that the owl was sending up a prayer, thanking its mistress for allowing it to come back home.

Noticing Gareth's profile out of the corner of her eyes, Leah watched him raise his head and stare at the small bird. Leah turned to him. She couldn't find it in her to meet her father's anxious gaze, but she knew it was filled with regret and remorse . . . and she just didn't care. He'd lied to her all her life. He'd forsaken her mother, or who she thought was her mother, to map out this ridiculous journey that'd led them all straight to death's door. And, for what? To regain some pride? To relive the glory days of being an adventurer in Egypt? Why would he have abandoned her real mother so long ago, leaving poor Anippe to live a life without her parents while he became a filthy rich American with a blonde goddess by his side? Leah couldn't even fathom the monumental sadness that slithered through her body like a serpent waiting to strike, and knowing that inside Anippe's soul it must be even more venomous than in her own.

Aaron Cain was the same type of villain in Leah's opinion. An uncle she'd never know, living his life in a foreign country, keeping her own sister from her like she'd been the bearer of a plague that would bring down her father's carefully built 'fake' house.

Anippe . . . she was the one Leah kept going back to. Not only had she been denied her rightful place in the world and her real last name, but she'd also been told that her parents were both dead and she was to live the rest of her life as an orphan. She'd been given the love of her uncle. Although theirs was an honest relationship, DNA-wise, he was still part of the biggest lie of her entire life. It was because of these adult's sins that Anippe had been thrust into the path of William Knight, the vindictive bastard who only cared about using her to get what he wanted . . . what his boss wanted. And for that reason alone, Leah knew it would take her forever to forgive any of them.

She felt so sick. She tried to pray for help, but she knew that the Son *should* abandon her. She was a far greater sinner than Eve ever thought to be in this Garden. Leah had brought the evil in with her . . .

The cooing of a small, white dove joined in with the soft breathing of the owl, as it came to rest beside the blue-eyed bird on the branch above.

Gareth's voice, a whisper on the wind, suddenly floated through her mind like a message that'd been sent from above. "Cast out," Gareth said.

She felt the heat of Gareth's hand on her own as it squeezed tightly. With no more of a warning, he suddenly broke from her and barreled into the surprised guard, knocking him to the ground. Racing back to the olive tree, he picked up Athena's shield and placed it in front of his body. Gripping the spear, he turned around and ran back to the hostages.

Bullets bounced off the magic metal; not one made even the slightest nick or dent in the daunting image of writhing snakes slithering around the head of Athena's sister.

Anippe yelled in fear and Gareth immediately stopped, staring at the scene before him. He picked up the spear like a javelin and threw it through the air; Anippe remained stunned, watching the man who'd turned his gun on her receive the ancient golden weapon right through his neck.

The actions and reactions took only seconds, but Leah felt as if she was watching everything in slow motion. She saw the other gunman stand up and turn slowly toward Gareth. He fired. Leah tried to call out, to warn her love, but she was too late. The bullet missed the safety of the ancient shield and plowed directly into Gareth's thigh. Uttering nothing more than a grunt, the shield wobbled in his hands and fell to the ground at Leah's feet.

David Tallent threw himself forward and picked up the mighty object. Turning it in the air like an athlete readying for his chance at the shot-put, Leah's father brought the shield crashing down on the other guard's skull—rendering him useless.

Leah turned her head and stared into the golden-brown gaze of Daniel Bauer. He, like her, had not moved at all. He simply stood, shaking his head as he reached out for her. But Leah was too fast. Turning on her heel, barely twisting away from his grip, she watched Gareth's large fist appear over her shoulder and connect with Daniel's jaw, sending him sprawling out on the lush, green grass.

Leah lunged up the trunk of the famous tree, scrambling to reach the bright red object that she'd seen in her nightmare. She now knew why Gregory, the sweet-faced monk, had been crying when she'd tossed it onto the floor of the church. He was telling her to use it. She had to . . . it was the only way they'd survive.

Racing to Gareth's side, Leah took his arm and reached out for Anippe. Gareth grabbed her father and ordered Aaron to take his brother's hand. Confusion reigned in the faces surrounding Leah, but she lifted the forbidden fruit to her lips and took a bite.

The world seemed to spin out of control, as God once again kept the promise and cast all the sinners out of Paradise. As the apple fell from Leah's hand and she gripped her loved ones tight, she locked her limbs, making sure that everyone she wanted with her would join her for the ride.

Her head felt like it was going to explode as she watched the ground disappear from under her feet. She heard Anippe shriek beside her and Leah tightened her grip—using every ounce of strength she had left to save the fragile woman. The black and yellow houses zoomed by, followed by the quick images of the crystal-clear water in the sparkling canals. The branches of the olive trees scratched the flesh from Leah's face and Gareth bowed his head in front of her, protecting her from any more pain.

The sound was like a sonic boom, as they were thrown into the trunk of the tree. Painful groans could be heard as their bodies slammed against the narrow stone staircase that would lead them back into the imperfect world they called home.

Leah saw, through Gareth's crumpled body, the door closing behind them—shutting her out of Paradise for good. Suddenly, fear hit her mind and Leah reached her hand through the opening, trying to crawl back inside.

Gareth held her body tight. "Where are you going?" he shouted.

"Athena's sword . . . the shield . . . the apple . . .!" she gasped, trying to work her way out of the trunk. "The gold and silver . . . Gareth, he'll have it all!" She knew the apple was in there, meaning Daniel Bauer had plenty of time to collect his wealth and transport himself out whenever he decided to resurface. "We have to go back, Gareth. He can't have it! He'll be unbeatable!"

"Not without this," Bauer's voice suddenly echoed inside the great tree of Jericho.

Leah saw his hand enter through the door and she pulled hers back inside. His fingers gripped the pendant around her neck and began to pull. The heavy chain cut through her skin and she felt the blood seep from the deep gash being made . . . but she held on.

Closing her hand over his, Leah pressed Daniel's flesh against the ice-cold stone. She listened to him howl in pain as his skin immediately turned gray from the frostbite that was eating away his hand. She scratched her fingernails across the skin and watched as his tattoo began to flake away.

The anchor that stood for men who watched over Noah's home disintegrated before her eyes, revealing a twisted black insignia that was the one truly burned into Daniel Bauer's hand.

"We're not through," he screamed.

Gareth kicked out his leg and slammed his boot into the man's face. Blood shot from Daniel's nose like a popped balloon releasing its warm air.

Gareth yelled, "You're wrong, asshole. Where Leah's concerned you're more than done!"

Daniel tore his blackened hand from the pendant and Gareth threw one final kick.

As the door was pulled closed, the bloody sight of Bauer's mangled face was all Leah could see. As his promises of revenge were silenced, all became quiet. Leah could only hear God's creatures now, as the small owl screeched its goodbye and the dove cooed its final call.

Leah hoped they were telling her that no matter what she'd done—no matter what would come—she *would* be given the time to fix all that she'd ruined in order to one day be welcomed back into Paradise . . . by her hero's side.

CHAPTER 41

The climb up the staircase was a long one. Limbs were broken, ribs were bruised, and blood was flowing from the cuts that'd almost destroyed them all. But Leah knew that the deepest cuts—the ones that would take the longest to heal—were buried far under the skin that was torn.

She wondered what the motorists and pedestrians thought as their strange-looking group walked across the street and into the hotel. But if their wide eyes and barely moving vehicles were any indication, she knew they must look like a train wreck.

The five wounded people walked slowly across the marble-inlaid floor, passing the well-dressed guests of the hotel. Leah saw a drunken man rub his eyes, probably wondering where his current hallucination had come from. Perhaps he was rethinking spending all his nights at the casino tables waiting for 'lady luck' to pay him a visit.

The elevator emptied out and Leah stepped into the smooth-moving, creak-free box that carried them effortlessly back to their rooms. They walked inside in utter silence, each keeping their gazes aimed at the floor.

Leah walked directly to the window and stared out at the mound of dirt that was Jericho. The tree had disappeared, but she knew that Daniel Bauer would not be stuck for long. The forbidden fruit that still lay on the ground where she'd dropped it would provide him his exit. He would use it to be cast from the place once he'd gotten all he needed. Leah knew that it was only a matter of time before she would come face-to-face with Daniel Bauer again.

Unhooking the emerald pendant from around her blood-soaked neck, Leah dropped it in the pocket of her jeans. She could feel the cold spot against her leg immediately, warning her that if she made contact with the strange stone, her bare skin would turn black as night.

"We're not through," Leah whispered. She thought back on Herod and the innocents who were buried beneath his palace of power and greed. She knew that's what Daniel was all about. He would grow to be the next 'king' to defile the world, causing the loss of innocence and peace wherever he went.

Her heart felt sick, remembering Plato's words at the beginning of their adventure. With wisdom that came from eating the fruit off the Tree of Knowledge, Daniel Bauer could just become the first philosopher-king. "He'll be back."

"Not soon," Gareth spoke behind her.

Leah nodded. She knew her love was right. Daniel would spend weeks enjoying the comforts of Paradise while collecting every scrap of treasure he could possibly find with the help of the Silver Scroll.

Wrapping his arms around her shoulders, Leah could see by the way Gareth moved and stood that there were definite broken bones inside his muscular frame. She knew he should be at the hospital right now tending to his wounds. But he held on tight, and Leah reveled in his strength.

"We beat him twice, angel. We got the orbs first, we got the Staff which led to the Son's words . . . we beat him twice."

"I guess it was time he won one, huh?"

"No," Gareth said, softly. "This time it was a draw."

"I'm so sorry."

Lean turned when she heard Anippe's quiet apology. The anger, jealousy—all those stupid emotions were gone now, as she stared into the sapphire eyes filled with pain. "You're not the one in this room who needs to be sorry."

"Leah." David Tallent walked toward his daughter.

She immediately held up her hand. "Don't!" Her voice was unforgiving, "Not now."

"What are you going to do?" he asked carefully

The image of her own paradise leapt to mind, calling out to her. "I'm going home." Leah looked up into the emerald eyes that still held every ounce of the future she craved "I want to go home . . . back to work."

"Home's good for me." Gareth smiled, pulling her into his arms.

After a few seconds of pure bliss in the arms of the man she loved, Leah raised her head from his chest and stared at her father. "And you're going with us."

"But . . ." he stuttered. "I can't."

"Excuse me?"

"She's alive, Leah." His eyes grew wide.

"I don't care," Leah replied heartlessly, not wanting to think about a mother she didn't even know who'd left her long ago. The loyalty in her soul reached across the ocean to the mother who she'd made a promise to. "She deserves better than this. Mary, *your wife*, deserves better . . . and so do I."

David hung his head and nodded his acceptance.

Turning to Anippe, Leah continued, "You deserve better, too."

Anippe straightened her spine. "I need to stay here. I need to . . . see."

Leah nodded, knowing that Anippe didn't have the moral battle raging in her soul. She just wanted to find a mother who'd supposedly died over thirty years ago; any war she felt like waging would be put off until the entire truth was known.

Gareth walked to Anippe and gave her a hug. Leah felt the emotion of love settle around her, knowing that he was offering her *sister* solace. "If you need us, you call us, okay?" he said. "Immediately. Do you understand that? You're not alone in any of this."

Anippe smiled up at him through her tears, as if she was beyond thrilled that she finally had a big brother who was looking out for her somewhere in the world.

Leah held out her arms and they hugged; the sapphire-eyed women made a promise to each other as each went forward on the separate paths they needed to walk . . . for now.

David stared at the two females and tears rolled down his cheeks. Leah noticed the pride that beamed from her father's face as Anippe walked toward him and stuck out her hand. He took it and smiled. Leah knew that the woman was nowhere near ready for anything more, and her father would just have to take whatever peace offering he could get for now—because as far as Leah was concerned, he didn't deserve any at all.

"Goodbye, Leah," Aaron Cain said, stepping forward and offering his hand.

Leah took it slowly, wondering if she was ready to offer an olive branch to either one of the deceiving brothers. "You knew all this back in Petra and didn't say a thing."

Aaron winced at her cold, steady tone. "It was not my place."

Glaring at him, Leah dropped his hand.

"I made a mistake," he added quickly.

"That's an understatement."

Turning, Aaron shook Gareth's hand and patted him on the shoulder. "Take care of her."

"For the rest of my life," Gareth replied.

Aaron followed Anippe to the door and Leah smiled, knowing that the determined young woman was about to run her uncle across hot coals and demand the entire truth. She wanted answers, and Leah knew she wouldn't rest until she got them all. "You go, sis," Leah whispered.

As the door shut behind them, Leah tried not to glare at her father who was now sitting in the chair at the foot of the luxurious bed. Instead, she cleared her throat. "Get a room. Get sleep. And don't even think about disappearing in the middle of the night . . . *Dad*. You already tried that trick once and look how it turned out, so I wouldn't recommend doing it again."

He sighed deeply.

Leah waited for a comeback, a fiery retort of some kind that a father always used to put his child in her place and reprimand her for her rudeness. But there was none. She wasn't worried though, even with the lies Leah knew him too well. The light in his sapphire eyes had dimmed, but the fire remained in his soul; fire that would lead him to find a woman he'd obviously never gotten over. She thought about the blonde-headed family who awaited him back in Connecticut. "At the very least, they deserve an explanation."

Cupping his hands together in his lap, as if he was praying for the words he needed in order to make amends, David sighed. "I'll go home. But you know that Bauer's right. We're not through with him, Leah." He pointed to her pocket where the mysterious stone was sending a chill through her bones. "He's certainly not through with you."

"Do I even want to know what this thing actually is?"

"Where did you find it?" His voice was distant, searching for a plausible explanation of how his beloved daughter had come up with the one stone he'd been searching for, thirty years after the fact.

"Gareth purchased it in a store in Whitechapel."

"Jack the Ripper world?" His face was confused.

"Yes. Apparently the woman who owned the store had bought it while she was on a shopping spree in Athens." Leah's voice was matter-of-fact, reciting details so calmly that it sounded as if she was a politician delivering a memorized speech. "It opened an item that released a parchment that'd once belonged to Plato."

"*The Allegory of the Cave?*" her father whispered.

"How did you know that?" she demanded.

"Shadows, Leah," her father said, stealing a glance at her face. "This whole thing . . . my whole life, has been a world of shadows."

"I think the word that better represents your life is lies, Dad."

He shook his head at her bitter tone. Taking a deep breath into his lungs, David raised his head and sent a gaze burning through her. "What do you know about the Nazi's?"

The left-field question slapped Leah like an iron mallet upside her head. She literally burst into laughter. "I'd say we just took a wrong turn. Paradise, remember? Athens? Egypt? Jericho? Now you want to talk about *Nazi's*?"

"We're going home," Gareth announced, ending the conversation immediately. His voice was loud, his back was absolutely rigid, and it looked as if he was begging for David Tallent to fight with him so he could bury his body in the fertile Jericho dirt.

Leah closed her eyes. Gareth was right—she wasn't ready for the truth. She wasn't ready to exit her peaceful cave, the life she'd always known, and have all the shadows lift at once to expose secrets she had no desire to hear. The only thing Leah truly believed in with every fiber of her being was Gareth, as he sent love and support straight into her weary heart.

Erasing the odd need to hear more of her father's secrets, knowing that anything he said would be detrimental to her health, Leah took a moment to thank the Creator for Gareth.

At least, for one more day, she could live the blessed life of being her hero's companion.

EPILOGUE

After burying the secret for thirty years, the truth was now rising to the surface . . . and there was no way to stop it.

Neith had assumed her life was over the night they'd taken her away from her family, blackmailing her to reveal the information that her beloved husband had uncovered. But she'd held strong. She'd kept quiet, hiding the emerald herself.

A tear rolled down her cheek, remembering the face of the man she'd loved so much. David Tallent had been all she'd ever thought of . . . and her precious baby girls. She would have done anything to save them, and she had. But now the secret was out. The son of the bastard who'd kept her all these years with his evil threats now knew the truth. Bauer knew the object existed, and even more terrifying was the fact that he knew what other objects were needed in order for his plan to succeed.

God help the world if he's already laid his hands on Athena's shield and sword, Neith thought. With those, any army created by him and for him would be victorious anywhere they went. And . . . the garden. God, how she hoped the Garden hadn't really existed. If it did, and Bauer became privy to the knowledge of the Divine, only someone with the same dose of power would be able to out-think and out-maneuver him. She *had* to speak to her daughter . . .

Neith had received Khait's message. Her friend who'd worked on the Acropolis every day all these years just waiting for the emerald to reappear in Greece, had delivered the news that Leah now possessed the sought-after stone. Around her neck, she was carrying the last piece of the powerful gem that'd once fallen from the sky, and Neith was scared to death.

She couldn't believe her own daughter had it . . . and poor Leah didn't even know what it was for; that if it was placed into the crown it could bring about absolute destruction. All Neith could hope for was that the crown would never be found by Bauer or any of his minions.

Her skin crawled as yet another scream echoed inside the castle walls. The music of Wagner was turned up to the highest decibel and it blasted through her ears like a runaway train. She closed her eyes. Neith knew what was going on inside the fortress of pain, not to mention the outside. Out there in the world, the new banners were being prepared, and the rings were being dug up from the graves to pass out to the new men who wanted to pick up where the other bastards had left off.

She hung her head. After all she'd given up—her freedom, her family—and *still* the sinister plot had risen from the ashes like a mystical, diabolical phoenix.

Neith was torn. There was such a large part of her heart that prayed for Leah's safety and wanted to keep her as far away from this horror as she could. But the nightmare was coming. The troops were assembling. And Neith knew Leah was perhaps the only one on Earth who could possibly stop history from repeating itself.

At least she wasn't alone. With all the information Khait had gotten to her over the years, Neith was well aware that the team of 'Tallent and Lowery' was making quite a name for themselves among the grapevine of followers and believers. All she could do was pray that they would be able to take on one last adventure and walk in the footsteps of the infamous 'angel of death.'

The innocents demanded to be heard from their graves before millions more came to a fiery end at the hands of Daniel Bauer . . . and his new, far deadlier, Reich.

ABOUT THE AUTHOR

As the daughter of a career librarian Amy grew up loving books; 'Patience & Fortitude' at the NYPL are still her heroes. Beginning in the genre of historical romance with, "The Heart of a Legend," Amy moved into the YA world where her first team from *The Angel Chronicles* became a beloved hit. Moving into the action/adventure world with *Tallent & Lowery*, Amy has created a new, incredibly suspenseful, team that has once again exploded with readers everywhere. Born in Connecticut, Amy is now living in the bright sunshine of Roswell, NM, delving into her next adventure.

To learn more about Amy Lignor, check out her website at http://tallentandlowery.blogspot.com.

www.ingramcontent.com/pod-product-compliance
Lightning Source LLC
Chambersburg PA
CBHW070812180626
46818CB00001B/231